Hollyleaf let out a yowl of terror. Greedy scarlet tongues licked toward her and her littermates, blocking their path away from the edge of the cliff. Smoke billowed up as rain fell on the bushes; Hollyleaf choked on it and began to cough, but the downpour was easing off and the remaining flurries weren't enough to put the fire out.

A wave of heat rolled over Hollyleaf; instinctively she moved back and felt the rock begin to crumble beneath her paws. Scrambling away, she glanced down to see the clearing patched with flame and darkness. There was no escape that way, even if they could manage to climb down safely amid the fire and rain.

"What's happening?" Jayfeather was cowering under the searing heat. "Which way should we go?"

"We can't go anywhere. We're trapped."

WARRIORS

Book One: Into the Wild

Book Two: Fire and Ice

Book Three: Forest of Secrets

Book Four: Rising Storm

Book Five: A Dangerous Path

Book Six: The Darkest Hour

THE NEW PROPHECY

Book One: Midnight

Book Two: Moonrise

Book Three: Dawn

Book Four: Starlight

Book Five: Twilight

Book Six: Sunset

POWER OF THREE

Book One: The Sight

Book Two: Dark River

Book Three: Outcast

Book Four: Eclipse

Book Five: Long Shadows

Book Six: Sunrise

OMEN OF THE STARS

Book One: The Fourth Apprentice

EXPLORE THE WARRIORS WORLD

Warriors Super Edition: Firestar's Quest

Warriors Super Edition: Bluestar's Prophecy

Warriors Field Guide: Secrets of the Clans

Warriors: Cats of the Clans

Warriors: Code of the Clans

MANGA

The Lost Warrior

Warrior's Refuge

Warrior's Return

The Rise of Scourge

Tigerstar and Sasha #1: Into the Woods

Tigerstar and Sasha #2: Escape from the Forest

Tigerstar and Sasha #3: Return to the Clans

Ravenpaw's Path #1: Shattered Peace

Also by Erin Hunter

SEEKERS

Book One: The Quest Begins

Book Two: Great Bear Lake

Book Three: Smoke Mountain

Book Four: The Last Wilderness

ERIN
HUNTER

HARPER
AN IMPRINT OF HARPERCOLLINS*PUBLISHERS*

Long Shadows

Series created by Working Partners Limited

 For information address HarperCollins Children's Books, a division of HarperCollins Publishers, 10 East 53rd Street, New York, NY 10022.
www.harpercollinschildrens.com

Library of Congress Cataloging-in-Publication Data
Hunter, Erin.
Long Shadows / Erin Hunter.— 1st ed.
p. cm. — (Warriors, power of three ; [bk. 5])
Summary: Firestar's three grandchildren, Hollyleaf, Lionblaze, and Jaypaw, struggle to restore faith in StarClan as Sol works to tear apart the bonds between Clans and turn them away from their warrior ancestors.
ISBN 978-0-06-089216-6
[1. Cats—Fiction. 2. Brothers and sisters—Fiction. 3. Adventure and adventurers—Fiction. 4. Fantasy.] I. Title.
PZ7.H916625 Lon 2009 2008032097
[Fic]—dc22 CIP
AC

Typography by Hilary Zarycky
10 11 12 13 14 LP/CW 10 9 8 7 6 5 4 3 2 1
❖
First paperback edition, 2010

Dedicated to the memory of
Jimmy, Dana, and Emmy Grace Cherry

Special thanks to Cherith Baldry

ALLEGIANCES

THUNDERCLAN

LEADER **FIRESTAR**—ginger tom with a flame-colored pelt

DEPUTY **BRAMBLECLAW**—dark brown tabby tom with amber eyes

MEDICINE CAT **LEAFPOOL**—light brown tabby she-cat with amber eyes
APPRENTICE, JAYPAW

WARRIORS (toms, and she-cats without kits)

SQUIRRELFLIGHT—dark ginger she-cat with green eyes
APPRENTICE, FOXPAW

DUSTPELT—dark brown tabby tom

SANDSTORM—pale ginger she-cat with green eyes

CLOUDTAIL—long-haired white tom with blue eyes

BRACKENFUR—golden brown tabby tom

SORRELTAIL—tortoiseshell-and-white she-cat with amber eyes

THORNCLAW—golden brown tabby tom

BRIGHTHEART—white she-cat with ginger patches

ASHFUR—pale gray (with darker flecks) tom with dark blue eyes

SPIDERLEG—long-limbed black tom with brown underbelly and amber eyes

WHITEWING—white she-cat with green eyes
APPRENTICE, ICEPAW

BIRCHFALL—light brown tabby tom

GRAYSTRIPE—long-haired gray tom

BERRYNOSE—cream-colored tom

HAZELTAIL—small gray-and-white she-cat

MOUSEWHISKER—gray-and-white tom

LIONBLAZE—golden tabby tom with amber eyes

HOLLYLEAF—black she-cat with green eyes

CINDERHEART—gray tabby she-cat

POPPYFROST—tortoiseshell she-cat

HONEYFERN—light brown tabby she-cat

APPRENTICES

(more than six moons old, in training to become warriors)

JAYPAW—gray tabby tom

FOXPAW—reddish tabby tom

ICEPAW—white she-cat

QUEENS

(she-cats expecting or nursing kits)

FERNCLOUD—pale gray (with darker flecks) she-cat with green eyes

DAISY—cream long-furred cat from the horseplace, mother of Spiderleg's kits: Rosekit (dark cream she-cat) and Toadkit (black-and-white tom)

MILLIE—striped gray tabby she-cat, former kittypet, mother of Graystripe's kits: Briarkit (dark brown she-cat), Bumblekit (very pale gray tom with black stripes), and Blossomkit (pale brown she-cat with a dark stripe along her spine)

ELDERS	(former warriors and queens, now retired)
	LONGTAIL—pale tabby tom with dark black stripes, retired early due to failing sight
	MOUSEFUR—small dusky brown she-cat

SHADOWCLAN

LEADER	**BLACKSTAR**—large white tom with huge jet-black paws
DEPUTY	**RUSSETFUR**—dark ginger she-cat
MEDICINE CAT	**LITTLECLOUD**—very small tabby tom
WARRIORS	**OAKFUR**—small brown tom
	ROWANCLAW—ginger tom
	SMOKEFOOT—black tom **APPRENTICE, OWLPAW**
	IVYTAIL—black, white, and tortoiseshell she-cat
	TOADFOOT—dark brown tom
	CROWFROST—black-and-white tom **APPRENTICE, OLIVEPAW**
	KINKFUR—tabby she-cat, with long fur that sticks out at all angles
	RATSCAR—brown tom with long scar across his back **APPRENTICE, SHREWPAW**
	SNAKETAIL—dark brown tom with tabby-striped tail **APPRENTICE, SCORCHPAW**
	WHITEWATER—white she-cat with long fur, blind in one eye **APPRENTICE, REDPAW**

QUEENS	**TAWNYPELT**—tortoiseshell she-cat with green eyes (mother of Rowanclaw's kits, Tigerkit, Flamekit, and Dawnkit)
	SNOWBIRD—pure white she-cat
ELDERS	**CEDARHEART**—dark gray tom
	TALLPOPPY—long-legged light brown tabby she-cat

WINDCLAN

LEADER	**ONESTAR**—brown tabby tom
DEPUTY	**ASHFOOT**—gray she-cat
MEDICINE CAT	**BARKFACE**—short-tailed brown tom **APPRENTICE, KESTRELPAW**
WARRIORS	**TORNEAR**—tabby tom
	CROWFEATHER—dark gray tom **APPRENTICE, HEATHERPAW**
	OWLWHISKER—light brown tabby tom
	WHITETAIL—small white she-cat **APPRENTICE, BREEZEPAW**
	NIGHTCLOUD—black she-cat
	GORSETAIL—very pale gray-and-white she-cat with blue eyes.
	WEASELFUR—ginger tom with white paws
	HARESPRING—brown-and-white tom
	LEAFTAIL—dark tabby tom with amber eyes
	DEWSPOTS—spotted gray tabby she-cat
	WILLOWCLAW—gray she-cat **APPRENTICE, SWALLOWPAW**

ANTPELT—brown tom with one black ear

EMBERFOOT—gray tom with two dark paws
APPRENTICE, SUNPAW

ELDERS

MORNINGFLOWER—very old tortoiseshell queen

WEBFOOT—dark gray tabby tom

RIVERCLAN

LEADER

LEOPARDSTAR—unusually spotted golden tabby she-cat

DEPUTY

MISTYFOOT—gray she-cat with blue eyes

MEDICINE CAT

MOTHWING—dappled golden she-cat
APPRENTICE, WILLOWSHINE

WARRIORS

BLACKCLAW—smoky black tom

VOLETOOTH—small brown tabby tom
APPRENTICE, MINNOWPAW

REEDWHISKER—black tom

MOSSPELT—tortoiseshell she-cat with blue eyes
APPRENTICE, PEBBLEPAW

BEECHFUR—light brown tom

RIPPLETAIL—dark gray tabby tom
APPRENTICE, MALLOWPAW

GRAYMIST—pale gray tabby she-cat

DAWNFLOWER—pale gray she-cat

DAPPLENOSE—mottled gray she-cat

POUNCETAIL—ginger-and-white tom

MINTFUR—light gray tabby tom
APPRENTICE, NETTLEPAW

OTTERHEART—dark brown she-cat
APPRENTICE, SNEEZEPAW

PINEFUR—very short-haired tabby she-cat
APPRENTICE, ROBINPAW

RAINSTORM—mottled gray-blue tom

DUSKFUR—brown tabby she-cat
APPRENTICE, COPPERPAW

QUEENS

ICEWING—white cat with blue eyes, mother of Beetlekit, Pricklekit, Petalkit, and Grasskit

ELDERS

HEAVYSTEP—thickset tabby tom

SWALLOWTAIL—dark tabby she-cat

STONESTREAM—gray tom

THE ANCIENTS

LEADER

FURLED BRACKEN—dark ginger tabby tom with amber eyes

SHARPCLAWS

BROKEN SHADOW—slender orange she-cat with white paws and amber eyes

SHY FAWN—dusty brown she-cat with amber eyes

WHISPERING BREEZE—silver-gray she-cat with blue eyes

DAWN RIVER—tortoiseshell she-cat with amber eyes

STONE SONG—dark gray tabby tom with blue eyes

DARK WHISKERS—large black thick-furred tom

CHASING CLOUDS—gray-and-white tom with blue eyes

JAGGED LIGHTNING—black-and-white tom with amber eyes

CATS IN TRAINING TO BE SHARPCLAWS

JAY'S WING—gray tabby tom with blue eyes

DOVE'S WING—pale gray she-cat with blue eyes

HALF MOON—white she-cat with green eyes

FISH LEAP—brown tabby tom with amber eyes

QUEENS

RISING MOON—gray-and-white she-cat with blue eyes

OWL FEATHER—wiry brown she-cat with yellow eyes

ELDERS

CLOUDY SUN—pale ginger she-cat with green eyes

RUNNING HORSE—dark brown tom with yellow eyes

CATS OUTSIDE CLANS

SOL—long-haired white-and-brown tabby tom with pale yellow eyes

OTHER ANIMALS

MIDNIGHT—a stargazing badger who lives by the sea

GREENLEAF TWOLEGPLACE
TWOLEG NEST
TWOLEG PATH
CLEARING
TWOLEG PATH
SHADOWCLAN CAMP
HALFBRIDGE
SMALL THUNDERPATH
GREENLEAF TWOLEGPLACE
HALFBRIDGE
STREAM
ISLAND
RIVERCLAN CAMP

ABANDONED TWOLEG NEST
MOONPOOL
OLD THUNDERPATH
THUNDERCLAN CAMP
ANCIENT OAK
LAKE
WINDCLAN CAMP
BROKEN HALFBRIDGE
TWOLEGPLACE
HORSEPLACE
THUNDERPATH
THUNDERCLAN
RIVERCLAN
SHADOWCLAN
WINDCLAN
STARCLAN

Hareview Campsite
Sanctuary
Cottage
Sadler Woods
Littlepine Road
Littlepine
Sailing
Center
Littlepine
Island
River Alba
Whitchurch Road

Abandoned Workman's House
Quarry Road [disused]
Crystal Pool
Quarry
Hare Hill Woods
Hare Hill
Sanctuary Lake
Hare Hill Riding Stables
Hare Hill Road
Knight's Copse
Deciduous Woodland
Pine Forest
Marsh
Lake
Footpaths
NORTH

Prologue

Wind swept across bleak moorland, carrying with it flurries of rain. The tough grass was sodden and water had burst the banks of a stream, spreading out in a wide pool; its surface bubbled as raindrops splashed into it.

At the edge of the pool a badger crouched, apparently oblivious to the icy wind and rain. For a long time she gazed into the water as if she could see something there, beyond the broken reflection of gray cloud; then she raised her head and looked around.

"I have come," she announced.

A black she-cat emerged from behind an outcrop of rocks. She was barely more than a shadow; starlight flickered at her paws. She was followed by a silvery gray tom whose green eyes stretched wide as he approached the badger. The starlight that shone around him made him seem a cat formed out of rain.

"Why are we here?" The silver tom's voice was hoarse, as if he hadn't used it for a long time. "On a day like this we should be curled up in a warm den."

"True, River," the black she-cat meowed. "Whose idea was it to drag us out here in weather not even fit for foxes?"

"Mine." A third cat appeared from behind a gorse bush, a broad-shouldered ginger tom with white paws. Starlight gleamed in his amber eyes, yet he seemed as insubstantial as a flame. "As you know very well, Shadow. We have to meet."

Shadow snorted. "I don't *have* to do anything you tell me, Thunder."

Thunder dipped his head. "Of course not. But we have been summoned by the danger to our Clans. They are on the brink of being lost forever—and it's your fault, Midnight." His voice sharpened.

Before Midnight could reply, River spoke. "Where is Wind? We can't discuss this without her."

"I'm here." The voice came from farther up the stream. The wiry brown she-cat was barely visible against the drenched moorland grass; only the shimmer of silvery light around her revealed her outline. She sprang down the slope toward the pool, her paws scarcely touching the ground. "Why are you all huddling here like lost kits?" she asked, a hint of mockery in her tone. "It's only a bit of rain and wind."

Shadow opened her jaws, but Thunder interrupted her. "We're not all used to living in the open, Wind. But that doesn't matter now. We need to know why Midnight has revealed the secrets of the Clans."

"But why us?" River complained, shivering. "There are younger cats than us in StarClan. Why call us back from the very beginning?"

Wind nodded. "Haven't we done enough? We formed the Clans and guided them through their first seasons. They have owed us a debt in all the moons since we walked the forest."

"We must still watch over our Clans," Thunder murmured. "This is a danger like none they have ever faced before." He turned to the badger. "Midnight, why did you tell our secrets?"

"Yes, and tell them to that mange-ridden, crow-food-eating loner?" Shadow spat, tearing at the grass with her claws. "My Clan have abandoned their warrior ancestors since he forced his way among them."

"On sandy cliffs I met Sol," Midnight began calmly. "First time of meeting, that was."

"And do you give away secrets to every stranger who happens to pad by?" Wind growled.

"Can't you see that you gave him power over the Clans when you told him so much about us?" Thunder pressed.

"Knowledge not always power," Midnight replied. "Clans not need secrecy to protect themselves. Rogues and loners stay away; they know Clan life is not for them."

"This loner didn't stay away," River pointed out.

"Clans not need to hide," Midnight insisted. "If did, not strong enough to meet challenges from outside."

"My warriors can meet *any* challenge," Wind snapped.

"Challenges not always from teeth and sharpened claws," the badger commented.

Wind let out a hiss. Her neck fur bristled as she unsheathed her claws. "Don't talk to me as if I'm stupid! You're only trying to avoid admitting that you made a huge mistake. The warriors of StarClan revealed their secrets to you, and you told them to a stranger! There wouldn't be any trouble in ShadowClan right now if it wasn't for you."

Midnight rose to her paws. "Sheathe your claws, small warrior." Her voice was a rumbling growl. "Stupid is to pick a fight with someone not your enemy."

For a few heartbeats, Wind stood her ground, only stepping back and sheathing her claws when Thunder rested his tail on her shoulder.

"Quarreling won't help," the first-ever ThunderClan leader meowed. "The secrets are out. We have to decide what we can do now to help our Clans."

River shook his head. "Well, I don't know."

"Nor do I." Shadow lashed her tail in frustration. "I'd like to rip the throat out of this ungrateful badger, but it's too late to change anything."

"We don't understand," Thunder meowed, meeting Midnight's gaze. "We shared our secrets with you, and you have done so much for our Clans. Why would you want to destroy them like this?"

Before he had finished speaking, the wind picked up and the starry cats began to fade, blown away like mist. Midnight watched them with berry-bright eyes until their frail forms were gone and the glimmer of starlight had died away.

A cat emerged from behind a windblown bush a few taillengths away: a hairless cat with bulging, sightless eyes.

"You heard, Rock?" Midnight asked.

Rock nodded. "I knew the Clan leaders would be unhappy that you confided in Sol," he rasped. "But you had no choice. The power of three is coming, and the Clans *must* be ready."

Chapter 1

The moon was huge, a golden circle resting on a dark ridge of hills. Stars blazed above Hollyleaf's head, reminding her that the spirits of her ancestors were watching over her. Her fur prickled as something stirred on the ridge. A cat had appeared there, outlined against the moon. She recognized the broad head and tufted ears, and the tail with its bushy tip; even though the shape was black against the light, she knew the colors of its pelt: white with brown, black, and ginger blotches.

"Sol!" she hissed.

The outlined shape arched its back, then reared up on its hind paws, its forepaws stretched out as if it was about to rake its claws across the sky. It leaped upward, and as it leaped it swelled until it was so huge that it blotted out the moon and the blazing stars. Hollyleaf crouched, shivering, in darkness thicker than the deepest places of the forest.

Screeches of alarm rose up around her, a whole Clan of hidden cats wailing their fear of the shadow cutting them off from the protective gaze of StarClan. Above the noise, a single voice rang out: "Hollyleaf! Hollyleaf! Come out!"

Hollyleaf thrashed in terror and found her paws tangled in

soft moss and bracken. Pale gray light was filtering through the branches of the warriors' den. A couple of foxlengths away, Hazeltail was scrambling out of her nest, shaking scraps of moss from her pelt.

"Hollyleaf!" The call came again, and this time Hollyleaf recognized Birchfall's voice, meowing irritably outside the den. "Are you going to sleep all day? We're supposed to be hunting."

"Coming." Groggy with sleep, every hair on her pelt still quivering from her nightmare, Hollyleaf headed toward the nearest gap between the branches. Before she reached it, her paws stumbled over the haunches of a sleeping cat, half hidden under the bracken.

Cloudtail's head popped up. "Great StarClan!" he grumbled. "Can't a cat get any sleep around here?"

"S-sorry," Hollyleaf stammered, remembering that Cloudtail had been out on a late patrol the night before; she had seen him return to camp with Dustpelt and Sorreltail while she was keeping her warrior's vigil.

Just my luck. My first day, and I manage to annoy one of the senior warriors!

Cloudtail snorted and curled up again, his blue eyes closing as he buried his nose in his fur.

"It's okay," Hazeltail murmured, brushing her muzzle against Hollyleaf's shoulder. "Cloudtail's mew is worse than his scratch. And don't let Birchfall ruffle your fur. He's bossy with the new warriors, but you'll soon get used to it."

Hollyleaf nodded gratefully, though she didn't tell Hazeltail the real reason she was thrown off balance. Birchfall didn't bother her; it was the memory of the dream that throbbed through her from ears to tail-tip, making her paws clumsy and her thoughts troubled.

Her gaze drifted to the nest where her brother Lionpaw—no, Lion*blaze* now—had curled up at the end of his vigil. She wanted to talk to him more than anything. But the nest was empty; Lionblaze must have gone out on the dawn patrol.

Careful where she put her paws, Hollyleaf pushed her way out of the den behind Hazeltail. Outside, Birchfall was scraping the ground impatiently.

"At last!" he snapped. "What kept you?"

"Take it easy, Birchfall." Brambleclaw, the ThunderClan deputy and Hollyleaf's father, was sitting a tail-length away with his tail wrapped neatly around his paws. His amber eyes were calm. "The prey won't run away."

"Not till they see us, anyway," Sandstorm added as she bounded across from the fresh-kill pile.

"If there is any prey." Birchfall lashed his tail. "Ever since the battle, fresh-kill's been much harder to find."

Hollyleaf's grumbling belly told her that Birchfall was right. Several sunrises ago all four Clans had battled in ThunderClan territory; their screeching and trampling had frightened off all the prey, or driven them deep underground.

"Maybe the prey will start to come back now," she suggested.

"Maybe," Brambleclaw agreed. "We'll head toward the ShadowClan border. There wasn't as much fighting over there."

Hollyleaf stiffened at the mention of ShadowClan. *Will I see Sol again?* she wondered.

"I wonder if we'll see any ShadowClan cats," Birchfall meowed, echoing her thought. "I'd like to know if they're all going to turn their back on StarClan, and follow that weirdo loner instead."

Hollyleaf felt as if stones were dragging in her belly, weighing her down. ShadowClan had not appeared at the last Gathering, two nights before. Instead, their leader Blackstar had come alone except for Sol, the loner who had recently arrived by the lake, and explained that his cats no longer believed in the power of their warrior ancestors.

But that can't be right! How can a Clan survive without StarClan? Without the warrior code?

"Sol's not such a weirdo," Hazeltail pointed out to Birchfall with a flick of her ears. "He predicted that the sun would vanish, and it did. None of the medicine cats knew that was going to happen."

Birchfall shrugged. "The sun came back, didn't it? It's not that big a deal."

"In any case," Brambleclaw interrupted, rising to his paws, "this is a hunting patrol. We're not going to pay a friendly visit to ShadowClan."

"But they fought beside us," Birchfall objected. "WindClan and RiverClan would have turned us into crow-food without the ShadowClan warriors. We can't be enemies again so soon, can we?"

"Not enemies," Sandstorm corrected. "But they're still a

different Clan. Besides, I'm not sure we can be friends with cats who reject StarClan."

What about our own cats, then? Hollyleaf didn't dare to ask the question out loud. *Cloudtail has never believed in StarClan.* But she knew without question Cloudtail was a loyal warrior who would die for any of his Clanmates.

Brambleclaw said nothing, just gave his pelt a shake and kinked his tail to beckon the rest of the patrol. As they headed toward the thorn tunnel they met Brackenfur pushing his way into the hollow with Sorreltail and Lionblaze behind him. The dawn patrol had returned. As all three cats headed for the fresh-kill pile, Hollyleaf darted across and intercepted her brother.

"How did it go? Is there anything to report?"

Lionblaze's jaws parted in a huge yawn. *He must be exhausted,* Hollyleaf thought, *after keeping his warrior vigil and then being chosen for the dawn patrol.*

"Not a thing," he mewed, shaking his head. "All's quiet on the WindClan border."

"We're going over toward ShadowClan territory." Alone with her brother, Hollyleaf could confess how worried she was. "I'm scared we'll meet Sol. What if he tells the other cats about the prophecy?"

Lionblaze pressed his muzzle into her shoulder. "Come on! Is it likely that Sol will be doing border patrols? He'll be lying around the ShadowClan camp, stuffing himself with fresh-kill."

Hollyleaf shook her head. "I don't know. . . . I just wish we'd never told him anything."

"So do I." Lionblaze's eyes narrowed and his tone was bitter as he went on. "But it's not like Sol is bothered about us. He decided to stay with Blackstar, didn't he? He promised to help us after we told him about the prophecy, but he soon changed his mind."

"We're better off without him." Hollyleaf swiped her tongue over her brother's ear.

"Hollyleaf!"

She spun around to see Brambleclaw waiting beside the entrance to the thorn tunnel, the tip of his tail twitching impatiently.

"I've got to go," she meowed to Lionblaze, and raced across the clearing to join Brambleclaw. "Sorry," she gasped, and plunged into the tunnel.

The morning had been raw and cold, but as Hollyleaf padded through the forest with her Clanmates the clouds began to clear away. Long claws of sunlight pierced the branches, tipping the leaves with fire where they had changed from green to red and gold. Leaf-fall was almost upon them.

Brambleclaw led his patrol away from the lake toward the ShadowClan border, keeping well clear of the old Twoleg path and the abandoned nest where the Clans had fought their battle.

Tasting the air in the hope of finding a squirrel or a plump mouse, Hollyleaf caught a stale trace of her own and her littermates' scents, lingering from their trek across the forest to find Sol. She hoped that none of the patrol would notice, especially not Brambleclaw or Sandstorm, because that would mean awkward questions she wasn't sure she could answer.

To her relief, the other cats seemed too intent on tracking prey to notice. Sandstorm raised her tail for silence, and Hollyleaf could hear the crisp sounds of a thrush knocking a snail shell against a stone. Peering over a clump of bracken, she spotted the bird: a fine fat one with its back turned to the group of cats, too intent on its own prey to realize that hunters were creeping up on it.

Sandstorm dropped into the hunter's crouch and glided over the forest floor, pausing to waggle her haunches before the final pounce. The movement alerted the thrush; dropping the snail, it let out a loud alarm call and launched itself into the air.

But Sandstorm was too fast for it. With an enormous leap she clawed it out of the air in a flurry of wings; it went limp as she bit down hard on its neck.

"Brilliant catch!" Hazeltail mewed.

"Not bad," Sandstorm purred, scratching earth over her prey until she could collect it later.

Hollyleaf picked up the scent of mouse and followed it along a bramble thicket until she spotted the little creature scuffling among the debris beneath the outer branches. A couple of heartbeats later she had her own prey to bury beside Sandstorm's.

Brambleclaw was clawing earth over a vole; he gave her an approving nod. "Well done, Hollyleaf. Carry on like this and the Clan will soon be full-fed." He stalked off into a hazel thicket, his jaws parted to pick up the faintest trace of prey.

For a few heartbeats Hollyleaf stood looking after her father, his praise warming her. Casting about for more prey, she picked up the trail of a squirrel, but as she rounded the trunk of a huge oak she spotted Hazeltail ahead of her, following the same scent. There was no sign of the squirrel, but the trail led straight toward the ShadowClan border. Hollyleaf could already make out the scent of the border markings, but Hazeltail seemed too preoccupied with her hunt to notice.

"Hey, Hazeltail, don't—"

Hollyleaf broke off as three cats emerged from a clump of bracken on the other side of the border. Hazeltail was only a couple of tail-lengths away; startled, she halted, her ears flicking up in surprise.

Relief surged through Hollyleaf as she recognized the newcomers: Ivytail, Snaketail, and his apprentice, Scorchpaw. All three of them had fought on ThunderClan's side in the battle; Hollyleaf could still see gashes along Ivytail's side, and Scorchpaw's ear was torn. They surely wouldn't be angry with Hazeltail for coming right up to the border.

"Hi," she meowed as she bounded up to stand beside Hazeltail. "How's the prey running in ShadowClan?"

"Keep back!" Ivytail spat. "You've no right to come into ShadowClan territory. Just because we helped you in the battle doesn't make us allies."

"Typical ThunderClan," Snaketail added, his voice a low snarl. "Thinking every Clan is their friend."

"And what's wrong with that?" Hollyleaf demanded, stung by their hostility.

No cat answered her question. Instead, Ivytail stalked up to the border until she was nose-to-nose with Hazeltail. "What do you think you're doing, this close to the border?"

"I was tracking a squirrel." Hazeltail sounded bewildered. "But—"

"Prey-stealing!" Snaketail interrupted, the fur on his shoulders fluffing up in anger and his striped tail lashing.

"We were not!" Hollyleaf mewed indignantly. "We're still on ThunderClan territory, in case you hadn't noticed. Hazeltail hasn't crossed your border."

"Only because we turned up in time to stop her," Snaketail growled.

Rustling sounded from the undergrowth behind Hollyleaf; she whipped around to see Brambleclaw and Sandstorm approaching, with Birchfall just behind. "Thank StarClan!" she murmured.

Brambleclaw padded forward until he stood beside Hollyleaf and Hazeltail. "Greetings," he mewed, dipping his head to the three ShadowClan cats. "What's going on here?"

"We had to stop these warriors of yours," the ShadowClan cat explained. "Another couple of heartbeats and they would have crossed our border."

"That's not true!" Hollyleaf exclaimed hotly.

"I was tracking a squirrel." Hazeltail faced the ThunderClan deputy with an apologetic look in her eyes. "I did forget where I was for a moment, but Hollyleaf warned me, and then the ShadowClan patrol appeared. I promise, I never set paw over the border."

Brambleclaw nodded. "You're as close to the border on your side as we are on ours," he pointed out to the ShadowClan cats. "But no cat is accusing you of trying to cross."

"We're a border patrol!" Snaketail flashed back at him. "And it's just as well we came along when we did."

"No cat can trust ThunderClan," Scorchpaw added, padding up beside his mentor.

Birchfall let out a hiss of fury; thrusting his way through the long grass he halted beside the ThunderClan deputy. "Brambleclaw, are you going to stand there and let an apprentice insult our Clan? When we haven't even done anything?"

Sandstorm flicked his shoulder with her tail. "That's enough, Birchfall. Let Brambleclaw handle this."

The younger warrior let out a snort of disgust; he said nothing more, but stood glaring at the ShadowClan patrol.

"Birchfall's right!" Hollyleaf protested. "These cats are just trying to make trouble. We haven't broken the warrior code."

"Oh, the precious warrior code!" Ivytail's voice was full of scorn. "You think it's the answer to everything, but you're wrong. The warrior code didn't stop the sun from vanishing, did it?"

"Right." Snaketail supported his Clanmate. "Maybe it's time the Clans stopped being so obsessed with dead cats, and started looking for other answers instead."

Hollyleaf stared at them in dismay. She knew that these thoughts came from Sol. Was this what the strange cat had wanted all along—to destroy the warrior code from inside the Clans?

He meant to start with us. Hollyleaf remembered how friendly and helpful Sol had seemed. But maybe ShadowClan had been an easier prospect; Hollyleaf couldn't imagine Firestar abandoning his beliefs as easily as Blackstar.

I have to save ShadowClan! In her desperation Hollyleaf was scarcely aware of the cats around her any longer. *They can't turn their backs on StarClan and the warrior code! There have to be four Clans!*

"Hollyleaf, calm down," Brambleclaw murmured beside her.

Hollyleaf realized that her pelt was fluffed out and her claws were digging into the damp earth. The three Shadow-Clan cats were staring at her, fur bristling as if they expected her to leap on them. Taking a deep breath she sheathed her claws and tried to make her fur lie flat again.

"I'm okay," she muttered to her father.

"This is Sol talking, isn't it?" Birchfall jeered, taking a pace forward so that he stood right on the border. "You're all cra-zier than a fox in a fit! It's mouse-brained to listen to a cat that no Clan cat has ever met before."

"We listen because Sol talks sense," Snaketail retorted, stepping forward until he faced Birchfall. "He knows what to do to give ShadowClan a better life for the future. Maybe if ThunderClan listened they would be able to fight their own battles. Maybe that's why the sun vanished, to tell us that the time of the Clans is over, and cats have to work out how to live on their own. If ThunderClan is too cowardly to face that—"

With a screech of fury, Birchfall leaped on Snaketail.

The two cats rolled over in a spitting knot of fur. Scorch-paw jumped on top of them, clawing at Birchfall's shoulder. Hazeltail launched himself onto the apprentice, trying to thrust him away from Birchfall.

"Birchfall, Hazeltail, get back here *now*." Sandstorm took a pace forward, only to find her way blocked by Ivytail.

"Can't your young warriors fight their own battles?" the ShadowClan warrior sneered. "A battle *they* started?" She unsheathed her claws and drew back her lips in a snarl.

Brambleclaw bounded forward to stand at Sandstorm's side. "No. This battle was provoked by ShadowClan."

Another yowl split the air from the fighting cats. Hollyleaf cringed at the sound of ripping fur, as if the claws were raking her own pelt. "Stop!" she screeched. "What are you doing?"

To her surprise, the battling cats fell apart, panting. At once Brambleclaw stepped forward and thrust Birchfall and Hazeltail back across the border onto their own territory.

"There's been enough fighting," he meowed. "Come on, ThunderClan." As they started to leave, he paused and looked back over his shoulder at the ShadowClan patrol. "You can believe what you want, so long as you stay on your own side of the border."

"We weren't the ones who crossed it in the first place," Ivy-tail hissed.

Brambleclaw turned his back on her and bounded ahead to lead the patrol away.

"Are you okay?" Hollyleaf murmured to Hazeltail; her

Clanmate was blundering through the woods, stumbling over branches and letting trailing brambles rake her pelt.

"I'm a little dizzy," Hazeltail confessed. "I hit my head on a branch when I was trying to pull Scorchpaw off Birchfall."

"Here, I'll guide you." Hollyleaf rested her tail on Hazeltail's shoulder. "We'll let Leafpool take a look at you when we get back to camp. Birchfall was lucky that you did help him," she added. "He would have got an even worse clawing without you."

The young ThunderClan warrior was limping along with blood oozing from a gash on his shoulder. When the patrol paused by the bramble thicket to collect Sandstorm's thrush and their other prey, he sat down and began to wash the wound with vigorous strokes of his tongue.

"Birchfall, you asked for that." Brambleclaw paused in digging up his vole. "ShadowClan shouldn't have accused us of trying to cross the border, but you put us in the wrong when you started the fight. Warriors should know how to control themselves."

"Sorry," Birchfall mumbled.

"So you should be."

When the patrol set off again, Brambleclaw and Sandstorm remained grimly silent. Birchfall padded after them with his head down.

Hazeltail was beginning to recover. "Thanks, Hollyleaf," she mewed, shaking off her friend's tail. "I can manage now. Don't you think Brambleclaw was hard on Birchfall?" she went on. "ShadowClan was asking for a fight."

"That doesn't mean we were right to give them one," Hollyleaf replied absently. She was finding it hard to pay attention to anything. Horror gripped her like an extra pelt, thick enough to choke her. ShadowClan believed that Sol held the answers to a better future, but they were wrong.

He'll destroy the Clans, she thought, terror freezing her limbs until she could barely set one paw in front of another. *Somehow, we have to find a way to stop him.*

CHAPTER 2

Jaypaw slid into the nursery with a bunch of catmint clamped in his jaws. The sharp scent of the herbs didn't disguise the warm, milky scent of the nursing queens, or the underlying sourness that made Jaypaw's fur prickle uneasily.

Daisy's sleepy voice greeted him. "Hi, Jaypaw."

"Hi, Daisy," Jaypaw mumbled around the mouthful of herbs. "Hey, Millie."

Millie's only reply was a cough. Jaypaw padded over to her, across the thick layer of moss and bracken that covered the nursery floor, and dropped the herbs beside her. "Leafpool sent you those."

"Thanks, Jaypaw." Millie's voice was hoarse. "Will you take a look at Briarkit? Her pelt feels really hot."

Jaypaw nuzzled among the kits, who were sleeping pressed up close to their mother's belly, until he identified Briarkit by her scent. The little kit was restless, letting out faint mews in her sleep and shifting about in the moss as if she couldn't get comfortable. Jaypaw sniffed her all over, catching a whiff of the same sour scent that came from Millie. Her pelt was hot, just as Millie said, and her nose was dry.

Briarkit might have caught her mother's cough! he thought worriedly. Aloud he said, "I'll get Leafpool to send her some borage leaves for the fever. I'm sure she'll be fine." *I hope I sound more confident than I feel,* he added to himself.

As he listened to Millie chewing up the catmint, Jaypaw wondered whether it would be better to move her and Briarkit out of the nursery, so that the infection wouldn't spread any further. It would be easier to look after them in Leafpool's den.

But then Millie wouldn't be able to feed Blossomkit and Bumblekit.

He could sense sharp pangs of anxiety coming from Daisy, the fear that Rosekit and Toadkit would start coughing, too. There was nothing Jaypaw could say to reassure her. His claws worked impatiently in the mossy bedding. *If I've got the power of the stars in my paws, why can't I cure a cough?*

The nursery felt hot and stifling, cramped with all five kits and the two mothers in there. Jaypaw was eager to be out in the open again, but he needed to wait and see if the catmint had helped Millie at all.

He heard a scuffling from Daisy's direction, and Toadkit's voice. "I'm a WindClan warrior, and I'm coming to get you!"

"I'll get you first!" Rosekit mewed back.

The two kits started to wrestle; one flailing paw hit Jaypaw on the shoulder.

"That's enough!" Daisy scolded. "If you want to play, go outside."

The two kits bundled past Jaypaw and he heard their excited mews dying away as they dashed out into the clearing.

The long-furred she-cat sighed. "Sometimes I can't wait for them to be apprenticed."

"It won't be long now," Jaypaw meowed. "They're strong kits."

Daisy sighed again; Jaypaw could still sense that she was worrying, but she didn't try to put her fears into words.

"My throat feels better now," Millie announced, swallowing the last of the herbs. "Thanks, Jaypaw."

Another loud bout of coughing interrupted her. Jaypaw flinched as a ball of sticky spit caught him on the ear. "I'll go and talk to Leafpool," he mewed hurriedly, backing toward the entrance to the den.

On his way out he clawed up a pawful of moss and rolled over on it to clean his ear. *I wonder what happens if a medicine cat gets sick. Who looks after the Clan then?* Shrugging, he headed across the clearing toward the den he shared with Leafpool.

As he brushed past the bramble screen, Jaypaw picked up the scents of other cats as well as Leafpool; sniffing, he distinguished Birchfall and Hazeltail. There was a tang of blood in the air.

"Who's hurt?" he demanded, his neck fur rising at the thought of another battle.

"Birchfall has a wounded shoulder," Leafpool explained. "Picking a fight with ShadowClan cats, by the sound of it."

"*They* picked a fight with *us*," Birchfall protested.

"And whose claws came out first?" the ThunderClan medicine cat retorted. "Brambleclaw told me all about it. You're lucky it's no worse. That cobweb should stop the bleeding," she went on, "but come back if it starts again. And I want to see you tomorrow in any case, to make sure the gash is healing well."

"Okay." Birchfall sounded disgruntled, then added, "Thanks, Leafpool."

"You too, Hazeltail," Leafpool continued. "If the dizziness comes back, I want you in here straightaway. Now both of you take these poppy seeds and go and have a good sleep in the warriors' den. No more duties until tomorrow."

Hazeltail and Birchfall brushed past Jaypaw on their way out of the den. As their scents faded, Leafpool asked, "How's Millie?"

"She says her throat feels better," Jaypaw replied, "but she's still coughing. And Briarkit is feverish. I think she might have caught the cough too."

"Oh, no!" Jaypaw picked up Leafpool's sudden spurt of anxiety. "I'll go over there and take a look," she meowed. "And then I'll have to go into the forest—we're low on borage leaves for fevers. Can you check the elders?"

Jaypaw stifled a groan. "Sure." He would much rather go out into the forest; he could find borage by scent just as well as Leafpool could by sight.

"I'm worried Mousefur might still be stiff after scrambling up to the Highledge during the battle," Leafpool went on. "And they'll both need checking for ticks."

That's an apprentice job, Jaypaw thought resentfully as his mentor padded past him on her way to the nursery. He answered himself: *So? That's what you are, an apprentice. Get on with it.*

He had been proud of his littermates when Firestar had made them warriors, but Jaypaw had no idea when Leafpool would give him his name as a full medicine cat, and he would walk in her shadow until she died. He didn't want her to die, and yet . . . *Can't I have* anything *for myself? How long before the prophecy is fulfilled?*

Trying to banish the thoughts clawing at his belly, he found a twig and collected a ball of moss soaked in mouse bile from the cave where Leafpool kept her supplies. Wrinkling his nose against the acrid smell, he stalked across the clearing to the elders' den under the hazel bush.

"Hi, Jaypaw," Longtail meowed drowsily as he approached; Jaypaw was surprised that the blind elder could pick out his scent even with the tang of mouse bile in the air.

"It's good to see you," Mousefur added. "I've got a tick on my shoulder that feels as big as a blackberry."

"Let me look," Jaypaw mumbled around the twig. At least Mousefur sounded in a good mood today. If she was in a bad temper she could claw with her tongue almost as harshly as Yellowfang, the former ThunderClan medicine cat whom Jaypaw met in his dreams.

He soon found the tick—not as big as Mousefur said, but swollen enough to make her uncomfortable—and dabbed mouse bile on it until it dropped off.

Mousefur flexed her shoulder. "Thanks, Jaypaw. That's a whole lot better."

Jaypaw set the twig aside and began searching the skinny elder's fur to see if she had picked up any more ticks. "Leafpool wondered if you were stiff after climbing to the Highledge."

Mousefur snorted. "Tell young Leafpool that I may be an elder but I'm not completely helpless. Why would I be stiff after a little climb like that?"

"Good," Jaypaw muttered. "Now, do you want your ticks fixed? 'Cause if you do, keep still."

"Is that how you talk to an elder?" Mousefur's voice was tart, but Jaypaw could feel her amusement. She settled herself comfortably and went on, "You were at the Gathering, weren't you? What happened? I know there was trouble, but no cat tells us anything. Was it WindClan again?"

"No . . ." Jaypaw hesitated. He didn't want to discuss Sol with any cat.

"Well?" Mousefur snapped. "Badger got your tongue?"

"ShadowClan didn't come," Jaypaw began, choosing his words carefully. "Just Blackstar. He had Sol with him."

"Sol? That tricky lump of fur who told us the sun would disappear?"

"Yes." Jaypaw was surprised that Mousefur seemed so hostile. "You didn't like Sol, then?"

"I don't trust any cat who knows things that StarClan hasn't told our medicine cat," Mousefur replied. "There's something wrong there, or I'm a rabbit."

"Blackstar spoke to the Gathering," Jaypaw went on, relieved that Mousefur didn't know Sol had almost become his mentor for fulfilling the secret prophecy. "He said that Sol had persuaded him and ShadowClan not to listen to StarClan anymore."

"What?" Jaypaw felt Mousefur's pelt begin to bristle. "But every Clan cat listens to StarClan. What else are they supposed to do?"

Jaypaw shrugged. "Blackstar thinks living cats can look after themselves."

Mousefur snorted. "No more than I'd expect from that flea-brain. So what did StarClan have to say about it?"

"Nothing," Jaypaw admitted. "The moon kept on shining, bright and clear."

He felt Mousefur's muscles tense under his paws. "That doesn't make sense," she muttered.

Though Jaypaw agreed, he didn't reply, just retrieved the ball of mouse bile to deal with another tick near the old cat's tail. "There, you're done," he mewed when the tick plopped onto the floor.

Mousefur grunted her thanks, and Jaypaw turned to Longtail. The blind elder had remained silent as Jaypaw passed on the news of the Gathering; Jaypaw could pick up mingled feelings of guilt and confusion. He guessed that Longtail was still feeling bad that he hadn't been able to fight beside his Clan in the battle. There wasn't much Jaypaw could say to comfort him. He was blind, too, but at least he had been able to use his medicine cat skills to help.

"Keep still," he meowed, parting Longtail's fur gently and making sure his claws were sheathed. "I'll soon check you for ticks."

"Thanks, Jaypaw." Longtail relaxed a little. "Could you check my pad, too?" he added, holding out one forepaw. "I think it got scraped on the stones when I climbed up to the Highledge."

"Sure." Jaypaw didn't find any ticks, and set the mouse bile on one side to run his paws over Longtail's pad. There was no sign of blood, but he could feel grit embedded in the roughened skin.

Bending his head, Jaypaw rasped his tongue over Longtail's paw until it felt smooth again. "I don't think you need any yarrow, but I'll check it again tomorrow. Keep it clean, and give it a good lick now and again."

"I'll do that," Longtail meowed. "It feels better already."

Jaypaw picked up the twig and squeezed his way out of the elders' den. *I wish we could sort out Sol and ShadowClan as easily as I can sort out a scraped pad.*

He picked up Hollyleaf's scent close by. A blast of anxiety hit him, like walking into the teeth of a gale; he could almost feel his fur flattened by it.

"I thought you'd never finish!" his sister exclaimed.

"What's the matter?" Jaypaw asked her.

"We've got to talk." Hollyleaf's voice was low and tense. "There was a fight on the ShadowClan border this morning."

"I know," Jaypaw replied. "So what? There are border skirmishes all the time."

"This *wasn't* just a border skirmish," Hollyleaf hissed. "It's all about Sol. He's telling the ShadowClan cats to ignore the warrior code."

"We already knew that," Jaypaw pointed out.

Hollyleaf's anxiety crackled like lightning. "Look, we can't talk now. We need Lionblaze here. Sandstorm and Cloudtail are waiting for me to go on another hunting patrol, so we'll meet when I get back, okay?"

"Okay." Jaypaw knew that Hollyleaf wouldn't give up until he agreed.

"Hollyleaf!" Cloudtail's voice came from the other side of the camp.

"Coming!" Hollyleaf called back. "I'll catch you later," she mewed to Jaypaw, and bounded off.

Shaking his head, half irritated and half worried by his sister's distress, Jaypaw padded back to his own den.

Jaypaw was tidying the supply of yarrow when Leafpool returned from the forest with a huge bunch of borage leaves. "I was lucky to find these," she meowed, dropping the stems at Jaypaw's paws. "It's time we started stocking up getting ready for leaf-bare."

"I can go out and start collecting stuff," Jaypaw suggested hopefully. *Anything to get out of camp!*

"In a day or two, maybe," Leafpool replied. "We should go through the stores first, and check on what we need. Meanwhile, you can shred some of these leaves and chew them into pulp for Briarkit."

Boring! But Jaypaw knew better than to object. He pushed the yarrow to the back of the cleft where they stored herbs and began tearing the borage leaves apart with his claws. He'd gotten through less than half the pile when he heard paw steps outside the den and caught a whiff of fresh-kill. He picked up

Hollyleaf's scent, too; the hunting patrol had returned.

"Sorry," he mewed to Leafpool, springing to his paws. "There's something I've got to do."

He brushed past the bramble screen and tracked his sister by her scent. He bounded forward and felt her muzzle brush his shoulder as she ran to meet him.

"Come on," she urged breathlessly. "Lionblaze is waiting for us behind the warriors' den."

Jaypaw followed her, squeezing into the space where they used to play when they were kits. "It's a bit more squashed in here than I remember," he muttered as he edged between his two littermates.

"Because we're bigger, mouse-brain," Hollyleaf snapped.

"And they extended the warriors' den," Lionblaze added. "There's still not enough room in there, though. I kind of envy Foxpaw and Icepaw, now they've got the apprentices' den all to themselves."

"Not for long," Jaypaw replied. "Rosekit and Toadkit will be in there pretty soon." He winced as Hollyleaf stuck her paw into his side. "Hey, watch it!"

"There's a thorn stuck between my toes and I can't reach it," Hollyleaf explained.

"Okay." Jaypaw felt around his sister's paw until he located the thorn, digging in deep between the beds of her claws.

"Hollyleaf, tell us what's on your mind," Lionblaze suggested; Jaypaw could feel his impatience like a cloud of stinging flies. "We can't stay stuck behind here all day."

"I'm worried about what Sol is teaching the ShadowClan

cats," Hollyleaf began. "Ivytail said he told them not to listen to StarClan anymore."

Jaypaw drew back from Hollyleaf's paw with the thorn gripped between his teeth. He spat it out. "We heard that at the Gathering," he pointed out. "Is it such a bad thing?"

"What?" Hollyleaf sounded outraged.

"I don't mean about ignoring StarClan. But it's good for cats to question things instead of just accepting them."

"There are some things you just don't question." Hollyleaf spoke with utter certainty. "Sol doesn't think we should follow the warrior code. And without that, what are we? Just a band of rogues."

"This still isn't anything new," Lionblaze meowed. "Why are you getting so upset?"

"What's new is that now we know the whole of Shadow-Clan is agreeing with Sol, not just Blackstar. Honestly, are you both mouse-brained? Do you *want* a Clan on our borders who doesn't follow the warrior code? What's to stop them from crossing the border and stealing our prey? Or maybe even raiding our camp and stealing our kits?"

"I'd like to see them try," Lionblaze growled; squashed up against him, Jaypaw could feel his brother's muscles flex as he extended his claws and dug them into the ground.

"The Clans will be destroyed if we don't stick together and believe in the same things," Hollyleaf went on, her anger rising. "We have to *do* something."

"I'd like to tear that mange-ridden rogue apart." Lionblaze's irritation was deepening into anger as fierce as his sister's; Jaypaw struggled not to feel overwhelmed by the force of their fury surging over him from both sides. "Sol *promised* to help us with the prophecy, and then he left us and went to ShadowClan." After a heartbeat's pause Lionblaze added, "Do you think there's a prophecy about ShadowClan, too?"

"I'm sure there isn't," Jaypaw meowed. "*We* are the three. I know we are."

He hoped that neither of his littermates would ask him how he could be so sure. He couldn't imagine how he would tell them about his dreams in the mountains when he had visited the Tribe of Endless Hunting.

"I still think Sol knows more about the prophecy than he's telling us," he went on. "And if he won't come to us, then we'll have to cross the border and find him."

"Trespass in ShadowClan territory?" Hollyleaf's shock struck Jaypaw like a blow. "We can't do that! *We'd* be breaking the warrior code."

"That's just what I was saying," Jaypaw meowed. "Sure, we can't do without the warrior code. But there are times when it's right to break it. Great StarClan!" he went on, as he sensed that his sister was rejecting his idea. "When we were kits, didn't we hear stories about how Firestar sometimes broke the warrior code if he thought it was right? We can't do anything about the prophecy until we know whatever Sol knows. Whether he's right or not about StarClan, he knew the sun was going to disappear, and StarClan didn't. And we're not going to learn anything from him by staying here."

"I'm up for it," Lionblaze snarled. "I'll *make* Sol tell us the answers. Hollyleaf, you don't have to come if you don't want to."

Hollyleaf's shock was fading into uncertainty. "No, we're in this together. Besides," she went on, more determined, "maybe the prophecy means that we're the only cats who have the power to *save* ShadowClan."

Jaypaw didn't say anything. If the only way Hollyleaf could bring herself to trespass was by thinking she was doing it for ShadowClan's sake, he'd let her go on thinking that. But he and Lionblaze were doing this for the three of them, to find out what the prophecy really meant and how they could achieve the power they had been promised.

"Jaypaw? Are you there?"

Jaypaw's ears flicked at the sound of Lionblaze calling softly from the other side of the bramble screen. He listened a moment longer, until he picked up regular breathing that told him Leafpool was soundly asleep. Then he climbed out of his nest and slid out of his den into the clearing.

The scents of Lionblaze and Hollyleaf wreathed around him. "Follow closely," Lionblaze whispered. "The moon is shining and we have to keep to the shadows. Cloudtail is on guard at the entrance."

"We're going to sneak out through the dirtplace tunnel," Hollyleaf added.

"Oh, great." Jaypaw wrinkled his nose.

"You can crawl out underneath the brambles if you'd rather," Lionblaze muttered. "Come on."

Jaypaw's pelt prickled as he crept after his brother around

the edge of the stone hollow. But when he felt the tunnel walls closing around him, the thorns snagging his pelt, there had been no yowl from Cloudtail. He relaxed slightly when he emerged from the other end and picked his way across the dirtplace. As they headed into the forest he tried sniffing out clumps of herbs and brushing through them to get rid of the nasty smell.

The forest was silent except for the gentle rustling of leaves and the occasional scuttling of prey in the undergrowth.

"We need to keep together, and keep quiet," Lionblaze murmured. "There might be ThunderClan cats out for some night hunting, and we don't want any cat asking questions."

"Okay," Hollyleaf replied. Jaypaw could tell she was scared, not by the thought of a fight with ShadowClan warriors, but because she didn't want to be caught breaking the warrior code. *I wish she'd lighten up. If we've got the power of the stars in our paws, we're more powerful than the code, right?*

Lionblaze led them to the stream that marked part of the border. "Keep right behind me," he instructed Jaypaw. "It's not deep."

Jaypaw bristled. "I'm fine, thanks," he muttered. He didn't want any cat to know how scared he was of water, even after teaching Cinderheart to swim. His belly churned when he felt the water lapping around his paws, then rising up his legs as he waded deeper. But before the water lapped his belly fur he felt it sink again, and soon he was scrambling out onto the bank in ShadowClan territory, the reek of ShadowClan scent all around him.

"We should roll in their scent marks," Hollyleaf suggested. "That way we'll disguise our ThunderClan scent."

"Wonderful," Jaypaw grumbled, even though his sister's idea was a good one. "The dirtplace, and now ShadowClan. I won't be able to lick my fur for a moon."

Thoroughly covered in ShadowClan scent, the three cats headed deeper into the rival Clan's territory. Jaypaw's ears were pricked for the sound of approaching patrols, his jaws parted to pick up the stronger scent that would warn him of approaching warriors. But the forest was eerily silent.

"Where are they all?" Hollyleaf whispered. It was unusual for no cats to be out at night, not even a few hunters, especially when there was a bright moon.

No cat answered her. They went on until Jaypaw felt the fallen leaves under his pads give way to sharp pine needles. "We must be getting close to the camp," he whispered.

Lionblaze took the lead again, guiding Jaypaw in short dashes; Jaypaw understood that they were flitting from shadow to shadow. At last he could taste an overwhelming surge of ShadowClan scent from somewhere ahead. The ground underpaw began to rise, and became broken up, with rocks poking out of the pine-needle covering.

Soon Jaypaw felt Lionblaze's tail barring his way. "Keep down!" his brother hissed. "Then creep forward about a taillength."

Jaypaw did as he was told, feeling the prickle of thorns raking the fur on his back. Sniffing, he caught the scent of gorse, and realized they must be hiding under a bush. His littermates' pelts were pressed against his, one on either side.

"What can you see?" he demanded.

"We're looking down into the camp. Sol is there," Hollyleaf breathed into his ear. "Standing on top of a rock. The whole Clan is listening to him—even the kits! I can see Blackstar, and Russetfur, and . . . oh, there's Tawnypelt!"

"Shut up!" Lionblaze growled. "I want to hear what Sol's saying."

Jaypaw flicked his ears forward. He could already make out Sol's voice rising from the hollow, and as the others fell silent he heard what the loner was saying.

". . . no cat should just accept what has gone before," Sol meowed, his voice ringing above the faint sounds of the forest. "StarClan's time is over. These cats are *dead*, and their spirits have no power over you."

Jaypaw suppressed a shiver. No cat who had met with StarClan at the Moonpool would agree that StarClan had no power. *We will have* more *power*, he thought. *But we're the three in the prophecy. Ordinary cats should still look to StarClan.*

"I've shared tongues with StarClan." Jaypaw recognized the voice of Littlecloud, the ShadowClan medicine cat. He sounded worried. "I can't believe that our warrior ancestors are powerless. Or has everything I've experienced been a lie?"

"StarClan is good at deceiving," Sol replied smoothly. "Ask yourselves, did they warn you that the sun would vanish? No! That means either they didn't know about it, or they don't care about you enough to warn you. Why should any cat go on trusting them?"

Murmurs of agreement rose up to where the three Thunder-Clan cats were hiding. Littlecloud didn't protest again.

"When the sun vanished, everything you believe in changed," Sol continued. His voice was so powerful and persuasive that Jaypaw could understand how ordinary cats would be influenced by him. "What you must ask yourselves is what should you do about it? Where will you find your answers now?"

"In ourselves." Blackstar spoke, a deeper, rougher voice than Sol's. "What this cat says is true," he added, addressing his Clan. "StarClan led us to live beside this lake, and I've always had my doubts that it was the right decision. There are too many Twolegs, for a start."

"And too much has gone wrong," Cedarheart growled. "The two kittypets in the Twoleg nest—"

"Arguments about borders," Toadfoot put in.

"Hang on a moment." Jaypaw stiffened as he heard Tawny-pelt speak up. "Things went wrong in the old forest, too. You can't expect life to be all mice and moonlight."

"That just goes to prove what Sol is saying." Blackstar's voice was harsh. "StarClan couldn't help us there, either. They couldn't even stop the Twolegs from driving us out."

"What does Blackstar mean?" Lionblaze whispered, press-ing closer to Jaypaw. "Does he want to lead ShadowClan away from the lake? He must have bees in his brain! One Clan alone, and leaf-bare not far off?"

"He *can't*!" Hollyleaf's voice shook. "There *have* to be four Clans."

"Shhh!" Jaypaw hissed, trying to concentrate on what was happening in the hollow. But before he could hear any more, jagged lines of silver flashed across his vision. He seemed to be looking down a long forest path; moonlight silvered the forest floor, barred with black where the shadows of trees lay across it. Lumbering toward him was a badger, the white stripe down its face glowing like a silver flame. Jaypaw had barely caught his breath with shock when the creature was gone, and the familiar night of his blindness swallowed up his vision.

"What's the matter?" Lionblaze murmured.

Jaypaw realized that all the muscles in his body were tense; he was crouching with his claws dug into the earth and every hair on his pelt bristling.

"I saw a badger!" Jaypaw remembered just in time to keep his voice low.

"You *saw* . . . ?" Hollyleaf sounded bewildered.

"I had a vision." Jaypaw was too spooked to explain in detail. "We're in danger here."

He heard Lionblaze draw in a long breath, and pictured his brother with his jaws gaping, tasting the air.

"There's no badger here," Lionblaze reported. "Are you sure you saw it?"

Jaypaw lashed his tail. "No," he snapped. "I'm just making it up for fun. What do you think, mouse-brain?"

He paused to taste the air himself, and listened for the sound of the huge, clumsy creature trampling through the undergrowth. But the forest was still and silent, except for the sound of voices coming from the ShadowClan camp, and he couldn't pick up the slightest trace of badger scent.

"It's got to be a sign of *something*," he mewed. "I don't understand it yet, but I don't think we're safe here anymore. We should get back to the stone hollow as quickly as we can."

"But we haven't spoken to Sol yet," Lionblaze protested.

"And we won't, tonight," Hollyleaf pointed out. "Not with all ShadowClan listening to him. I think Jaypaw's right. We should go while we have the chance."

Jaypaw could feel that Lionblaze was unhappy with the decision, a sullen anger with Sol churning away inside him, but his brother didn't argue when Hollyleaf led the way down the slope away from the camp and back toward the border.

Jaypaw's pelt didn't lie flat again until they had waded back across the stream and were creeping through the tunnel into the ThunderClan camp. He slipped back into his den and flopped down beside the sleeping Leafpool.

Badgers, he thought as he slid into an exhausted sleep. *StarClan, what are you trying to tell me?*

Jaypaw woke with a paw prodding him sharply in the side. The sun warmed his fur, and Leafpool's scent swirled around him.

"Wake up, Jaypaw! What do you think you are, a dormouse?"

Jaypaw blinked drowsily. "Wha . . ."

"There's work to be done. I need you to check on Millie and Briarkit."

"Oh . . . okay." Jaypaw staggered to his paws, flinching at a scuffling sound outside the den until he realized it was only Icepaw and Foxpaw dashing past.

He didn't feel that he had slept at all after the previous night's expedition. It took an effort to pull his mind away from Sol and the ShadowClan cats, and the terrifying vision of the badger. "What do you want me to do?" he asked.

"I've been across to the nursery to check on Millie and Briar-kit. Millie needs more catmint. And I've made a leafwrap of borage for Briarkit. You can take them over there when—"

Jaypaw stopped listening and flattened himself to the ground at the sound of a throaty bark somewhere out in the forest.

"Jaypaw, what's the matter with you?" Concern replaced Leafpool's irritation. "Are you ill?" He heard her sniffing as her nose touched his fur. "You smell a bit funny."

Jaypaw cringed inside. He didn't want to discuss his scent, in case it led to more awkward questions. "I'm fine," he asserted. "That barking startled me, that's all."

"But you've heard a fox bark before. It was a long way off, and if it comes any closer the patrols will spot it."

"I know." Jaypaw scrambled into a sitting position, giving his chest fur an awkward lick. "It's just . . . I had this dream last night." *No need to say* where *I had it.* "I saw a badger. I . . . I wondered if it meant danger."

"One badger on its own?" Leafpool checked. "Not a whole horde of them?"

Jaypaw shook his head.

Leafpool sat down beside him. He could sense her

uncertainty, but she didn't seem to be afraid. "I think the badger you saw might have been Midnight," she told him.

"Who's Midnight?"

Leafpool settled herself more comfortably among the bracken stalks. "Back in the old forest, StarClan called four cats, one from each Clan, to make a long journey to the sun-drown-place to find a badger called Midnight."

Jaypaw's ears pricked. "Was that how they knew the Clans would have to leave the forest?"

"That's right," Leafpool meowed. "Brambleclaw was chosen from ThunderClan, and Squirrelflight went with him. Midnight warned them that the old forest would be destroyed, and then helped all the Clans to find this home beside the lake."

Jaypaw felt his neck fur beginning to rise. "StarClan gave a message to a *badger*? But badgers kill cats!"

"Not Midnight," Leafpool assured him. "She's no ordinary badger. Later, when we had settled here by the lake, a horde of hostile badgers invaded our camp and tried to kill us all and drive us out. And Midnight . . ."

She trailed off. Jaypaw felt a rush of mingled emotions surge through her, fear and regret and grief. He wondered why she should feel so strongly about a battle that had been over and done with before he was born, but he was too curious about Midnight to try to make sense of what she was feeling.

"What happened with the badgers?" he prompted.

"We tried to fight them off." Jaypaw realized that his mentor was making a great effort to keep her voice steady. "But there were too many. They would have destroyed ThunderClan if

Midnight hadn't brought WindClan to help."

"A *badger* helped *cats*, against her own kin?"

"Yes." Leafpool drew in a long breath and let it out again. "There is nothing to fear from her. But she may have been trying to warn us of some other danger. You will tell me if she comes to you again?"

"Of course." *Maybe*. Jaypaw knew that if this strange badger appeared again he would find out what she had to say before he decided whether to tell any cat.

"Why do we have to sit around waiting for her?" he asked. "Brambleclaw knows where she lives, so why can't we go and visit her?"

"It's too far," Leafpool replied firmly. She seemed calmer now that they had stopped talking about the badgers' invasion. "There's a lot of tension between the Clans right now, so Firestar would never spare warriors for that sort of journey. Especially not Brambleclaw. He's deputy now; he's needed here."

"What about—" Jaypaw stopped himself. He had been about to suggest Squirrelflight, but she had only just left Leafpool's den after being so badly wounded in the battle against WindClan. She wasn't even back on warrior duties yet; there was no way she could make a long journey. "I guess you're right," he muttered.

So, Midnight, if you want me, you'll have to come and find me.

CHAPTER 3

A scarlet leaf spiraled lazily down from a branch above Lionblaze's head. He sprang up, batting at it with his forepaws, then dropped to the ground again, his pelt hot with embarrassment. Had any cat seen him behaving like a kit?

The dawn patrol was heading back to the stone hollow. The sun had climbed above the trees, but in the shadows the leaves and grasses were still rimmed with frost. Leaf-fall was creeping over the forest, and the harsh days of leaf-bare were not far away.

Ashfur was leading the patrol; he had drawn a few fox-lengths ahead with Thornclaw and Brightheart. Lionblaze drew a breath of relief as he realized none of them had been watching him. He stood still for a couple of heartbeats, jaws parted and ears pricked for any sign of WindClan trespassers. But the faint traces of their scent all came from their own side of the border.

"Lionblaze!" Ashfur had halted, looking back over his shoulder. "Are you going to stand there until you take root?"

"Coming!" Lionblaze called back, bounding forward to

catch up with his former mentor. "I was just checking for WindClan."

Ashfur gave him an approving nod. "That's good, but I don't think we have anything to worry about."

"We can't be too careful," Lionblaze meowed, falling in beside the older warrior as they set off again.

Brightheart and Thornclaw had disappeared through the thick clumps of bracken; Lionblaze realized he had the chance he had been waiting for, to talk to Ashfur alone. Giving him a sidelong glance, he began, "Can I ask you something?"

Ashfur's whiskers twitched. "Sure."

"I feel like I need some extra battle training. Will you work with me?"

His former mentor stopped and faced him, his blue eyes stretched wide in surprise. "You're a warrior now, Lionblaze," he reminded him. "And one of the best fighters in the Clan. Do you really think you have any more to learn?"

Ashfur's praise warmed Lionblaze like a ray of sunlight; sometimes, when he was an apprentice, he had despaired of ever pleasing the gray warrior.

"There's *always* something more to learn," he declared. "I want to stay as strong and fit as I can, so I'll be ready for the next battle."

Ashfur blinked thoughtfully. "I'm not sure there'll be another battle. Not for a while, anyway."

"WindClan might cause more trouble. And anyway, I still need the practice," Lionblaze insisted. He flexed his claws, ready to tear frustratedly at the grass, then stopped himself.

He didn't want Ashfur to know how much this meant to him. "Please."

"Okay." Ashfur still looked unconvinced, but to Lionblaze's relief he didn't object anymore. "We could have a session now. I'll just catch up to Brightheart and tell her to report to Firestar. Meet you at the training hollow."

He bounded off, leaving Lionblaze to head to the training hollow by himself. The sunlight suddenly seemed brighter, and he relished the cool touch of the breeze in his fur and the dew on his pads. He knew that he had to keep training, to make the best use of his powers that he could, but he didn't want Tigerstar to act as his mentor anymore.

Lionblaze shivered, as if thinking of the dark warrior could summon him; he glanced around but there was no sign of the striped shadow and burning amber eyes.

At first he had felt special, honored to be chosen by Tigerstar for extra training, and delighted to be able to beat the other apprentices with a move the dark warrior had shown him. But in the last few moons Tigerstar had changed, showing a hostile side and trying to control Lionblaze.

Or maybe he hasn't changed. Maybe I'm just seeing what Tigerstar has been like all along.

He remembered Ferncloud scolding Foxkit and Icekit before they became apprentices: "If you don't behave, Tigerstar will come and get you!"

The two kits had squeaked in terror, and burrowed close to their mother's belly.

Was I completely mouse-brained? Lionblaze wondered. *Did I think he was helping me when all the time he was using me?*

If he practiced with Ashfur, he wouldn't need Tigerstar anymore. And if Tigerstar kept visiting him, he would be strong enough to fight him off.

Maybe he'll leave me alone if I can prove I'm a good enough warrior without him.

The training hollow was empty this early in the day, with a few wisps of mist still clinging to the grass. Lionblaze padded into the center and began practicing his battle moves, leaping and twisting in the air, imagining how he would land on Tigerstar's broad shoulders and dig his claws into the dark tabby pelt.

"Pretty good." Ashfur's voice came from the other side of the hollow.

"Thanks," Lionblaze panted.

He was turning to face his former mentor when Ashfur crashed into his side, knocking him off his paws. Furious that he hadn't been ready, Lionblaze let out a screech. He battered at Ashfur with his hind paws, while Ashfur tried to sink his teeth into his neck fur. The gray warrior's heavier weight pinned Lionblaze down, driving all the breath out of him.

"Still want to fight?" Ashfur taunted him.

With a tremendous effort, Lionblaze rolled over, thrusting Ashfur away. He scrambled to his paws, breathing heavily, and sprang on top of Ashfur before his opponent could recover. He gave the gray warrior two quick blows from his forepaws, then tried to leap away.

But Ashfur was too quick for him. Flashing out a paw, he

hooked Lionblaze's hind legs from under him, and the two cats wrestled together on the ground. Lionblaze's ear stung as Ashfur cuffed him. He pummeled his opponent with his forepaws, finding it hard to keep his claws sheathed as the red haze of battle threatened to engulf him.

"Stop!" Lionblaze hardly heard the yowl, but Ashfur rolled off him right away and sprang to his paws. Lionblaze was left scrabbling on the ground, shaking his head to clear it.

"What in StarClan's name are you doing?"

Now Lionblaze recognized Firestar's voice. He struggled to stand, blinking grit from his eyes, and spotted Firestar on the edge of the hollow with Whitewing, Icepaw, and Birchfall just behind him. The ThunderClan leader's eyes flashed green fire.

"Warriors fighting? Why?" he demanded.

Ashfur shook scraps of debris out of his fur. "It was just a practice bout, Firestar."

"But Lionblaze is a warrior now," Firestar pointed out. "Not your apprentice any longer."

"It was my idea, Firestar," Lionblaze meowed. "I asked Ashfur to practice with me. We were just trying to—"

"I don't want to listen to excuses." Firestar's voice was cold. "What I saw just now was far more vicious than a practice bout. At a time like this, with trouble on both sides of our territory, we can't afford to have warriors injured. And with leaf-bare coming on, Leafpool can't afford to waste her herbs on unnecessary wounds. Are you both mouse-brained?"

"I'm sorry, Firestar." Lionblaze hung his head. "It's my fault.

Don't blame Ashfur." *But how are we supposed to fight well if we aren't allowed to practice?*

"Ashfur is an experienced warrior. He should have more sense," Firestar retorted with a flick of his tail. Then he relaxed slightly. "I know you're keen, Lionblaze, and that's good, but try to think ahead, will you? This isn't a good time to be taking risks."

His pelt crackling with shame and frustration, Lionblaze muttered agreement.

"Whitewing, Birchfall, and Icepaw are going hunting," Firestar continued. "You had better go with them, Lionblaze. Work off some of that energy on prey instead of another warrior. Ashfur, come with me." With a flick of his tail, he padded out of the glade, followed by the gray warrior.

"We thought we'd try down by the lake," Whitewing mewed to Lionblaze.

"Whatever." Lionblaze let Birchfall and Whitewing take the lead; they padded close together through the undergrowth, with Icepaw bouncing excitedly at the back.

The heat of battle was still pulsing through Lionblaze's body. He wanted to sink his claws into *something*; he hoped a squirrel or a rabbit would cross his path soon.

He couldn't stifle the feeling that Firestar had been unfair. Surely this was the *right* time to practice fighting moves? There could be another battle any day with WindClan or ShadowClan. And how was he going to fulfill the prophecy if he never had the chance to work on his skills, to be the best warrior any Clan had ever seen?

* * *

Lionblaze pushed his way through the thorn tunnel, two mice and a vole dangling from his jaws, the scent of the prey flooding his senses. When he reached the clearing he spotted his brother and sister together outside the medicine cats' den. Hollyleaf signaled to him with her tail, so when he had dropped his fresh-kill on the pile, he bounded over to them.

"What's this I hear about you and Ashfur fighting?" Hollyleaf demanded.

"What?" Lionblaze gaped at her. "How did you know?"

Jaypaw twitched his ears. "News runs through this camp faster than a rabbit. Don't you know that yet?"

"Berrynose told me." Hollyleaf sounded defensive. "He heard you when he was out with a hunting patrol. He said you sounded really vicious."

"Berrynose!" Lionblaze spat with a single lash of his tail. "Hasn't he got anything better to do than gossip about other warriors?"

"Anyway, is it true?" Hollyleaf persisted. "What were you fighting about?"

Lionblaze felt his neck fur rising. His claws slid out and his muscles tensed; he wanted a real enemy to fight, not just gossip and unnecessary questions.

"We weren't *fighting*," he snapped. "We were *training*. Just leave it, will you? I've already had Firestar clawing my ears over it, and I think he's wrong! I *need* more practice. How can I defend my Clan if I forget what to do?"

By the time he had finished speaking he was spitting out

the words, his claws raking the ground in frustration.

After a heartbeat Hollyleaf took a pace toward him and gently laid the tip of her tail on his shoulder. Lionblaze shivered, trying to push down the surge of fury that had nearly spilled over.

"You won't lose your fighting skills," Hollyleaf mewed. "Don't you see? That's the special power the prophecy gave you, to fight better than any other warrior in the Clans."

"You don't understand," Lionblaze muttered. "It doesn't feel like that. It feels like I have to keep practicing."

"Well, you'd better not let Firestar catch you again. Cats are already starting to talk," Hollyleaf warned. "We can't let the rest of the Clan know about the prophecy, not until we're sure what it means."

"I'll do my best," Lionblaze promised, letting his shoulders sag. "I won't get into any fights with other warriors." *At least, not where Firestar can hear us.*

Thick darkness surrounded Lionblaze; the shrieks of battling cats echoed in his ears. He could taste the reek of blood and felt it clogging his paws and plastered in his pelt. His chest heaved as though he had been fighting all night. A gleam of moonlight pierced the clouds that churned across the sky; a single ray shed pale light on the ground at his paws. Lionblaze caught his breath in horror as he made out the body of Heatherpaw splayed out in the mud in front of him.

A gash ran down her body from her neck to her tail. Her

light tabby fur was soaked with blood, black in the silver light. Her lips were drawn back in a frozen snarl and her blue eyes stared sightlessly at the sky.

"No . . . no . . ." he whimpered.

He started at the touch of a tail on his shoulder and whirled around to face Tigerstar's intense amber gaze.

"Well done," the huge tabby purred. "That was a battle well fought."

"But this—this isn't what I wanted!" Lionblaze protested.

"Isn't it?" There was the hint of a growl in Tigerstar's voice, and his eyes blazed. "Remember how she betrayed you! She nearly destroyed your whole Clan by telling WindClan about the tunnels."

"But . . ." Lionblaze reached out a paw and laid it gently on Heatherpaw's flank. Her fur was cold. "She didn't deserve to die like this," he murmured.

"All traitors deserve to die!" The fire in Tigerstar's eyes flared up until Lionblaze was smothered in it; he let out a yowl of terror, expecting to feel his fur being scorched. His paws thrashed on the blood-soaked ground, but he couldn't move.

Another cat thrust a paw into his shoulder from behind. Lionblaze turned and unsheathed his claws, ready to spring on his enemy.

Dustpelt stood in front of him, his gaze glittering with annoyance. Sunlight was pouring through the branches of the warriors' den.

"Great StarClan, I thought WindClan was invading," he snapped. "Do you have to make such a racket?"

"Sorry," Lionblaze muttered. The moss and bracken from his nest was scattered from his thrashing around, and several other cats were looking up drowsily to see what the noise was about.

"I should think so." Dustpelt turned away and went to curl up beside Ferncloud again.

Lionblaze was still shaking from his dream, his blood pounding with the heat of battle. He rose to his paws and pushed his way out of the den. Sandstorm and Spiderleg, over by the fresh-kill pile, turned to look at him curiously.

The vision of Heatherpaw's broken body hovered in Lionblaze's mind, clearer than the clearing in front of him. *Is that what I'm becoming? A cat who slaughters? A cat like Tigerstar?*

He wished he had never heard of the prophecy, and could be just an ordinary warrior with the same fighting skills as all his Clanmates.

But the words of the prophecy had been spoken, and Lionblaze knew there was no escape from the destiny it would bring down upon him and his littermates.

Chapter 4

Jaypaw turned away from counting poppy heads when he heard Leafpool brushing past the bramble screen into the den. Briarkit's scent mingled with hers, and he heard a feeble cough from the young kit dangling from the medicine cat's jaws.

"Briarkit's worse?" he asked anxiously.

Leafpool set the kit down in a nest of bracken; Jaypaw heard the stems rustling as Briarkit tried to make herself comfortable.

"It's what I was afraid of," Leafpool meowed. "Briarkit has caught Millie's cough. And Millie's no better. I'd like to move her in here, too, but I don't think Daisy could cope with feeding Bumblekit and Blossomkit as well as her own. And we've no room for all of them in here."

Jaypaw felt steady waves of anxiety coming from his mentor like the surge of waves on the lakeshore. "Why are you so worried? It's only whitecough."

Leafpool sighed. "It could easily turn into greencough, especially with the cold weather coming." Lowering her voice in case Briarkit was listening, she went on, "There are several kits in the Clan, and Mousefur is very frail. We could end up losing cats."

She slid beside Jaypaw into the storage cave. "We're almost out of catmint," she murmured. "There's enough for Briarkit now, and another dose for Millie, and that's all."

"I'll go and fetch some more," Jaypaw offered instantly.

"That would be a big help," Leafpool mewed. "Take another cat with you—no, *not* because I think you can't manage on your own," she added as if she knew he would start bristling. "Two of you can carry twice as many stems."

"Okay. Shall I take the other catmint to Millie first?"

"No, I'll do that. The sooner you go, the sooner you'll be back with fresh supplies."

When Jaypaw emerged into the clearing, the first cat he located was Poppyfrost, crouched by the fresh-kill pile. He hurried over to her.

"Are you busy?"

Poppyfrost gulped down a mouthful of vole. "Not very," she replied. "Brightheart suggested I might help clear the bedding out of the warriors' den—there's so much of it now, and it's a hard job when there are only two apprentices. But to be honest, I wouldn't mind an excuse not to do it." She swallowed the last of the prey and rose to her paws. "What do you want me to do?"

Jaypaw explained about Briarkit and the need to fetch more catmint.

"Poor little scrap," Poppyfrost mewed sympathetically. "Of course I'll help. Let's go!"

She bounded across the clearing to the tunnel, leaving Jaypaw to follow. Once through the tunnel he caught up to her, and they headed for the abandoned Twoleg nest. Jaypaw felt his paws prickle at the memory of the battle; though the scents of blood and fear had faded, the screeches of fighting cats still echoed in his head. He steered Poppyfrost away from the tunnel where the WindClan cats had invaded ThunderClan territory; he didn't want to think about what it meant if there was another entrance into the underground caves where he had first met Rock.

He began sniffing for catmint as they approached the Twoleg nest, but instead of the sharp, clean scent of the herb all he could pick up was a musty smell.

"Oh, no!" Poppyfrost halted abruptly.

"What's the matter?"

"The catmint. Oh, Jaypaw, it's almost all gone!"

"Gone? It can't be!"

Poppyfrost bounded forward and Jaypaw followed. He felt soft, thick grass under his paws, then a strip of churned soil where the Twolegs had once grown plants. The musty smell was all around him now, mingled with the occasional hint of fresh leaves.

"What can you see?" he demanded.

"It's all squashed," Poppyfrost replied, her voice filled with distress. "The stems are broken down, all black and rotten."

Jaypaw felt a dark space of fear open up inside him. "That won't help the sick cats."

"I know. It must have happened in the battle."

Jaypaw lashed his tail. "I bet WindClan and RiverClan did this deliberately."

"Surely no cat would be that cruel?" Poppyfrost meowed.

Jaypaw worked his claws furiously into the earth and felt torn stems beneath his claws. "We'll have to tell Firestar. They can't get away with this!"

"No—wait." Jaypaw had been ready to dash back to camp, but Poppyfrost stopped him with her tail across his chest. "Cats were fighting all around here. The catmint probably just got trampled."

Jaypaw grunted; she might be right, but that didn't stop him from being suspicious. Still, it was more important to see if he could find any fresh catmint for Briarkit and Millie. Reporting to Firestar could wait.

Tasting the air carefully, he managed to identify a few new shoots of catmint poking through the ground, but they were very small, and there weren't many of them. He began to bite carefully through each stem.

Poppyfrost was moving around close by, rustling among the leaves. "I'm pulling all the broken stems away," she explained. "That way the new ones will have room to grow."

"Good idea," Jaypaw meowed. "I'll help you. Pick any of the new stems you come across, and put them with mine."

He began clawing away the dying stems and the fallen leaves that clogged up the new growth. He imagined the sun warming the battered plants, encouraging them to shoot up again. But soon it would be leaf-bare, when nothing grew. Could they wait until newleaf for fresh catmint?

At last there was nothing more they could do. Jaypaw and Poppyfrost divided their gleanings between them, though one cat could easily have carried all they had managed to find. Then they headed back to camp.

"What happened?" Leafpool's voice, sharp with worry, greeted Jaypaw as soon as he rounded the bramble screen. "What took so long? Why haven't you brought back more than that?"

Jaypaw dropped the herbs at her paws. "This is all there is."

"What?"

Poppyfrost padded up beside him and added her stems to the pile. Quietly she explained what they had found near the Twoleg nest.

"This is terrible!" Leafpool exclaimed. "That's the only catmint I know of in our territory."

"Then you've got to give it all to Briarkit." Jaypaw hardly recognized the cat who had spoken, the voice was so harsh. Then he detected Millie's scent, and guessed that she had come to be with her kit. "I'll be fine, Leafpool, honestly." She broke off in a bout of coughing.

Jaypaw didn't believe her. She sounded even sicker than the last time he had spoken to her, and he could sense Leafpool's fear for her.

"I'll go and report to Firestar," Poppyfrost murmured, slipping out of the den.

"You're *not* fine, Millie." Leafpool's worry made her sound sharp. "Look at all the stuff you've coughed up. You have greencough. You'll have to stay here, where Jaypaw and I can look after you."

"But what about Bumblekit and Blossomkit?" Millie's voice

rose to a wail that ended in another spasm of hacking coughs. "Daisy can't manage to feed them as well as her own."

"I'm not arguing with you," Leafpool retorted. "Daisy will have to manage. Besides, Briarkit is already ill. Do you want to give greencough to the other kits as well?"

Before Millie could reply, paw steps sounded at the mouth of the den, and Jaypaw recognized Graystripe's scent. "What's going on?" the gray warrior demanded. "Millie, I could hear you coughing from the other side of the camp."

"She has greencough," Leafpool told him. "No—stay where you are!" She brushed past Jaypaw, who pictured her blocking Graystripe from hurrying to his mate's side. "Do you want to catch it, and spread it to every cat in the camp?"

There was a pause in which Jaypaw picked up Graystripe's swirling anger and fear for Millie. "All right," the gray warrior meowed at last. "What can I do to help?"

"Go and talk to Daisy," Leafpool replied. "She'll have to feed all four kits in the nursery, because there's no way I'm letting Millie out of here. Rosekit and Toadkit are eating fresh-kill, so that should help."

"Okay." Graystripe sounded relieved that there was something he could do. "I'll make sure she gets enough prey—and I'll fetch some for all of you, too. Just tell me if there's anything else you want."

"Thanks, Graystripe," Leafpool mewed.

"I love you, Millie," Graystripe called out to his mate. "Don't worry about the kits. I'll visit them every day."

Millie's only reply was an exhausted murmur; she was worn

out by coughing. Jaypaw heard her draw Briarkit close to her belly. "Feed well, little one," she whispered. "Get strong, and you'll soon be better."

"I could take some borage to Daisy to help her milk to come," Jaypaw offered.

"Fine, but wait here first with Millie and Briarkit," Leafpool instructed him. "I have to tell Firestar that we have greencough in the camp." She whisked out of the den.

Jaypaw padded to the cleft to check the supply of borage leaves. They were running low, too, but he knew where he could find more. He set aside enough leaves to take to Daisy, and set to work chewing up their pitiful supply of catmint, ready for Millie and Briarkit.

We need more, but I don't know where to find it. And if these are the only two cats we have to treat before newleaf, then I'm a mouse.

By the time Leafpool returned, a cool dusk breeze stirred the brambles at the entrance to the den. A crisp half-moon floated above the hollow, its tip just clear of the tallest trees.

"It's time to go to the Moonpool," she mewed fretfully. "If only the sky would cloud over! I don't want to leave Millie and Briarkit."

"You don't have to go," Jaypaw pointed out. "You're right, you're needed here. I can go by myself."

"Oh, but . . ." Leafpool's protest died away.

Jaypaw made himself stay still and quiet as he listened to her silence. He wanted to add that she was too tired to go; she had exhausted herself taking care of the sick cats, and if she insisted on making the journey she would probably fall off the mountain. But Jaypaw knew better than to tell his mentor that; if he suggested she wasn't capable, Leafpool would be even more determined to prove she could do everything.

"Apprentices don't usually go without their mentor," Leafpool murmured, half to herself. "But I can't see it would matter for once. You know the way . . . and I *have* to stay with Millie and Briarkit."

Yes! Jaypaw stopped his paws from pushing him up into a triumphant leap.

"All right," Leafpool decided at last. "But be careful. And *don't* get into an argument with Willowshine."

Would I? Mothwing's apprentice wasn't Jaypaw's favorite cat, but he had enough sense not to brush her fur the wrong way when he was the only cat representing ThunderClan.

"I'll be off, then," he mewed.

"Right . . . and Jaypaw, if you happen to scent any catmint—"

"I'll bring it back with me," Jaypaw promised, though he knew how empty the promise was. There was nowhere else in ThunderClan territory where catmint grew. Perhaps they would need to travel farther from the lake if they were to find enough of the herb to save the sick cats.

Chapter 5

♣

Jaypaw slid out through the thorn tunnel and stalked into the forest. The night scents and noises seemed sharper than ever, just because he was on his own. There were no other cats to fuss over him, and if he tripped over a branch or put his paw into a hole, he could recover just fine by himself.

By now the territory was familiar, especially since he had taken part in the battle. Soon he had left ThunderClan territory behind and was climbing the rocky ridge. Ahead of him he scented other cats, and identified them as Willowshine from RiverClan and Barkface from WindClan with his apprentice, Kestrelpaw. Littlecloud wasn't with them.

The scents quickly grew stronger, and Jaypaw realized that the other medicine cats were waiting for him to catch up. He halted in front of them, dipping his head. "Greetings."

"Greetings, Jaypaw," Barkface meowed. "How's the prey running?" He sounded awkward, and Jaypaw picked up a strong sense of regret, as if the WindClan medicine cat wanted to apologize for the hostility between their Clans.

Jaypaw dipped his head in acknowledgment of what the older cat couldn't say out loud. "Fine, thanks."

"And where's Leafpool?" Willowshine added.

"She couldn't come," Jaypaw replied. "She had stuff to do." Even though medicine cats lived by different rules, he didn't want to tell the other Clans that ThunderClan had greencough in the camp. It made them sound weak.

Surprise came from all three cats, with an edge of annoyance from Willowshine.

"*I* had to wait until I had my name before Mothwing allowed me to come here alone," she mewed.

I bet Mothwing lets you come alone all the time now. It's a wasted journey for her. Jaypaw itched to make the retort, but he stopped himself. The RiverClan medicine cat didn't believe in StarClan; she could spend the night of the half-moon in her den without all the trouble of the journey to the Moonpool.

"It doesn't look as if Littlecloud is coming," Barkface muttered. "I thought he at least would stay faithful to StarClan."

He's trying, Jaypaw wanted to tell him, but there was no way he could reveal his expedition into ShadowClan territory. Littlecloud had protested against what Sol was telling his Clan, but it hadn't made any difference. ShadowClan had turned their back on their warrior ancestors, and Blackstar must have forbidden his medicine cat to come to the meeting.

"Perhaps he can share tongues with StarClan from his own territory," Willowshine murmured.

"And maybe StarClan will show us what to do about Sol," Jaypaw suggested, though privately he didn't think it was likely.

Barkface grunted agreement. "We'd better go on without him. We're wasting moonlight."

Jaypaw could hear the sound of falling water and the soft pad of paw steps as he followed the others down the spiral path to the Moonpool. He felt very close to Rock and Fallen Leaves and the other ancient cats as he felt his paws slip into the hollows they had made so long ago.

I hope I get a good dream tonight, he thought. *It's about time.*

Ever since his vision in ShadowClan territory and his talk with Leafpool he had hoped to meet the strange badger Midnight again. If she didn't come here, in this special place under the half-moon, then maybe she didn't mean to come at all.

The other cats were settling down at the edge of the pool. Jaypaw took his place beside Barkface. Kestrelpaw crouched on the other side of his mentor, while Willowshine found a spot farther around the rim of the water.

Jaypaw stretched out his neck and dipped his nose into the Moonpool; its cold touch shivered through him. Curling up, he let sleep take him.

When he opened his eyes he found himself on a rough stretch of open ground; a precipice plunged down at his paws and he took a pace back, dizzy from his glimpse of the depths. Wind whined among the rocks, and Jaypaw dug his claws into the gritty soil, scared that he might be blown away. Dim light illuminated the mountaintop; peering around him, Jaypaw couldn't decide whether it was twilight or early dawn. He thought at first he was alone until something moved on top of one of the boulders, and he recognized the bald, distorted body and unseeing eyes of Rock.

"You're here!" Jaypaw gasped. "Do you have something to tell me?"

Rock shook his head. "I have brought someone who wishes to meet you."

A black shape loomed up behind Rock, moving slowly into the open. Jaypaw gripped even harder with his claws, and his neck fur began to bristle. He was gazing into the berry-bright eyes of the badger.

"Midnight?" he meowed, furious that he couldn't stop his voice from quivering. "You're the badger who helped ThunderClan?"

The huge creature dipped her head; the pale stripe down her head gleamed in the half-light. "Is nothing to fear, small one. Speak with me you will?"

"Yes, I . . . I wanted to ask why you appeared to me the night we went to ShadowClan. It was you, wasn't it?"

Midnight nodded. "I went that way, find out what Sol say to Clans."

"You *know* Sol?" Jaypaw was astonished.

"Past my den near the sea he came. He had heard of cats by the lake, and many questions he asked."

"And you *answered* him?" Was this how Sol had known so much about the Clans? "Why? Leafpool told me you were our friend!" Jaypaw protested.

Midnight shrugged her heavy shoulders. "Is more than one way to be friend. True, I give Sol knowledge. But knowledge not always bring power."

"It's brought Sol enough power," Jaypaw mewed bitterly. "He's already convinced one Clan to give up their faith in StarClan."

"Perhaps will be StarClan's task to restore faith of Shadow-Clan."

Jaypaw blinked. He thought Rock had been teaching him that StarClan didn't have that kind of power. "How can they?"

Midnight's eyes shone with black light. "Faith is strong enough, it achieve anything," she assured him.

"That's no answer!" Jaypaw cried, frustrated. "Why did you talk to Sol and not to me?"

There was no reply. Midnight's bulky body was fading, melting into the shadows. Her white stripe glimmered for a heartbeat longer, and she was gone.

Jaypaw glanced wildly around. Rock had vanished as well, and he was alone on the bleak mountaintop. He struggled to wake up, blinking in the hope of opening his eyes to darkness, but it was no use. *Am I stranded here?* he wondered, beginning to panic.

Then he spotted two other cats approaching him across the open ground, the wind buffeting their fur. The first was a muscular tabby with one shredded ear; the cat who followed him was a small gray-and-white tom with a drop of moisture gleaming on his nose. The shimmer of stars at their paws was very faint; both of them were advancing nervously, casting swift glances into the shadows as if they expected enemies to leap out at them.

The tabby halted in front of Jaypaw and dipped his head. "Greetings, Jaypaw," he meowed. "My name is Raggedstar; once I was leader of ShadowClan. And this is Runningnose, who was our medicine cat."

Jaypaw stared at the two of them; Leafpool had told him about Runningnose, and it looked as if even in StarClan the former medicine cat couldn't cure his own cold. "Why have you come to speak to me?"

"For the sake of our Clan," Raggedstar replied, his voice hollow with sadness. "If no cat can help them, then Sol will tear them apart. They will scatter and become rogues! All their honor and pride will be gone!"

"I have spoken to Littlecloud in dreams," Runningnose added, resting his tail-tip on his leader's shoulder. "He keeps faith, but few cats will listen to him, and now Blackstar has forbidden him to speak of StarClan. He is not allowed to leave the camp to share tongues with us at the Moonpool."

"But . . . what do you expect *me* to do about it?" Jaypaw asked, bewildered. "I can't go into ShadowClan to talk to Blackstar, and if I did he wouldn't listen. He would send me back to ThunderClan one piece at a time."

"I can't tell you what to do," Raggedstar admitted. "I just know my heart tells me you might be the cat to save my Clan."

He shared a look of despair with Runningnose. Seeing it, Jaypaw realized that not only had ShadowClan rejected StarClan, but their warrior ancestors were almost ready to give up on them, too.

Anger pierced his belly like a thorn, and set his neck fur

bristling again. *All right,* he snarled silently. *If they won't do anything,* I *will! There must be some way to defeat Sol and restore ShadowClan's faith in their warrior ancestors. And then Sol can keep his promise and help us fulfill our prophecy.*

"I'll try," he promised, not bothering to keep his fury and contempt out of his voice. "At least I'm not sitting back and wailing like a lost kit."

"Thank you." Raggedstar dipped his head once more. "Your warrior ancestors . . ."

His voice began to die away, as if the vision was fading, though Jaypaw could still see him and Runningnose clearly. Bewildered, he glanced around and down, and froze with terror; he could see the rough surface of the rock *through* his own paws.

I'm fading!

His eyes snapped open on darkness; he was curled up beside the Moonpool, with the gentle plash of falling water in his ears and the other medicine cats waking around him.

Following Barkface, Kestrelpaw, and Willowshine down the ridge once more, Jaypaw thought about what he had seen. Midnight had told him next to nothing, except that it was she who had given Sol his knowledge about the Clans. Had she told Sol that the sun would vanish, too? Jaypaw wouldn't be surprised. But Midnight hadn't said anything that would help him with the problem of ShadowClan now. She seemed to think that StarClan would be able to restore their faith, but StarClan obviously wasn't going to do anything, except plead for help from a medicine cat apprentice.

Jaypaw paused to say good-bye to the other cats on the WindClan border. A soft breeze was blowing from the moor, bringing with it the scents of herbs and rabbits. Willowshine padded up to him and brushed his shoulder with her tail.

"StarClan walk with you, Jaypaw, until next time."

"Thanks," Jaypaw grunted. "You too." She needn't think he was going to start being friendly, not after that smart remark when they met. She was far too smug about receiving her name before him. Besides, he didn't want to talk; he had to think.

The only way to defeat Sol was to make ShadowClan recover their belief in the power of their warrior ancestors. *How am I going to do that?*

He thought back to when he had visited the Tribe of Rushing Water. He remembered how grief-stricken Stoneteller had been when he discovered that the Tribe of Endless Hunting had given up on the cats behind the waterfall. Jaypaw didn't trust Stoneteller, but he had felt sorry for the old leader then.

Stoneteller had lied to the Tribe to persuade them to go on battling against the invaders. His lies had filled them with courage, and they had beaten the intruding cats. The Tribe of Rushing Water had been made stronger because they had faith in what their warrior ancestors wanted for them.

But there aren't any easy lies that will convince ShadowClan, Jaypaw told himself. *Or are there?*

By the time he reached the stone hollow, Jaypaw could feel a freshening breeze that told him dawn was breaking, and hear birds beginning to twitter in the trees. *I could do with a good fat blackbird,* he thought hungrily.

His worries about Millie and Briarkit returned as he crossed the clearing, but when he entered his den he could hear the deep, regular breathing of all three cats. *That's good. They all need sleep.*

Instead of joining them, Jaypaw crept quietly out again. He didn't feel tired; instead, he was quivering with excitement. On the way home the beginnings of a plan had come to him, and he needed to talk to his littermates. He tasted the air, trying to find his brother and sister, and quickly tracked down Hollyleaf crouched beside the fresh-kill pile with Mousewhisker and Berrynose.

"Hey, Hollyleaf!" he called; he didn't want to go over to her and get stuck talking to the others.

Hollyleaf came bounding over to him; his belly rumbled as he caught the scent of fresh mouse clinging to her pelt. "Did something happen?" she asked; he could feel her urgency crackling like lightning.

"We've got to talk. Where's Lionblaze?"

"Still asleep in the warriors' den," Hollyleaf mewed.

"Get him. I'll meet you in back."

Jaypaw slid into the gap behind the warriors' den, his claws flexing impatiently until Hollyleaf and Lionblaze squeezed into the narrow space beside him.

"We've got to find a better place to meet," Lionblaze grumbled. "If we get any bigger we'll never fit in here."

"Stop complaining," Jaypaw snapped, wriggling to make

sure he got his fair share of the space. "This is important."

"Tell us, then!" Hollyleaf meowed.

Jaypaw told them about his dream at the Moonpool, his meeting with Midnight the badger and then with Raggedstar and Runningnose.

"StarClan asked *you* for help?" Hollyleaf queried, awe in her voice. "That's amazing!"

Jaypaw gave a faint hiss of annoyance. "You don't have to sound so surprised."

"Do you think you can do what they want?" Lionblaze asked. "We'll help, you know that."

"I had an idea," Jaypaw began. "We have to make Shadow-Clan believe in their warrior ancestors, right? So what they need is a sign from StarClan—a clear sign that every cat can see."

"If StarClan could do that, wouldn't they have done it already?" Hollyleaf asked doubtfully.

"Yes, I think so." Jaypaw's pelt prickled with excitement. "So, if StarClan can't do it, we'll have to do it for them."

There was a short silence. Then Lionblaze mewed, "*Make* a sign from StarClan?"

"Why not?"

"I dunno." Lionblaze sounded puzzled. "It just seems . . . wrong, somehow. Besides, if we're more powerful than Star-Clan, why does it matter that ShadowClan believe in their warrior ancestors?"

"Of course it matters, mouse-brain!" Hollyleaf spat. Jay-paw felt all her muscles bunch as if she would have leaped on her brother for a couple of mouse tails. "All four Clans *have* to stick to the warrior code."

"Okay, calm down," Lionblaze muttered.

Hollyleaf ignored him. "Jaypaw, I don't know how we're going to do this, but I know we can. I'll do whatever it takes to save ShadowClan from Sol!"

Her voice shook with intensity, and Jaypaw could imagine fire blazing in her green eyes. A shiver crept on mouse feet down his spine. It was clearer and clearer that *nothing* mattered to Hollyleaf more than the warrior code, and for the first time in his life he felt a little afraid of her.

Chapter 6

The sound of coughing woke Hollyleaf. Raising her head, she peered across the warriors' den. A few tail-lengths away, Thornclaw was sitting up, his head bent as he coughed.

His sister Brightheart pressed her muzzle into his shoulder fur. "Don't worry," she murmured. "I'll fetch you something from Leafpool to make you feel better."

"Get a move on," Spiderleg rasped. "Then maybe the rest of us can get some sleep."

"Yeah, it's like trying to sleep with a monster in here," Berrynose added.

Brightheart gave them a furious glare, her teeth drawn back in a snarl. "See if I help you if *you* get ill," she snapped, and slid out between the branches.

Thornclaw coughed again. "Sorry."

"Don't apologize to the stupid furballs," Hollyleaf told him. "If they don't like it, they can go out and do something useful."

Both Spiderleg and Berrynose ignored her, curling up again and wrapping their tails over their ears. Thornclaw lay down, too, but a cough shook him every time he tried to breathe.

Hollyleaf was too anxious to go back to sleep. She curled up in her nest, listening to the rain beating steadily on the branches of the den. How many more cats would fall ill before Leafpool got the greencough outbreak under control?

Her thoughts jumped to what she and Lionblaze had discussed with Jaypaw the day before. Did they truly need to fake a sign to make ShadowClan believe in StarClan again? Wouldn't that make StarClan angry with them? Perhaps they ought to find another way to show that Sol wasn't a worthy leader.

Unwillingly, Hollyleaf remembered how she had felt when Sol talked to her; she had basked in the warmth of his gaze, and his calm, deep voice made her feel as if everything would be fine as long as she listened to him.

And yet he had taken a whole Clan away from StarClan. That couldn't be right! *StarClan has always been there! None of the Clans should turn away from them.*

Arguing with herself was making Hollyleaf dizzy. In spite of the pounding raindrops, she got up and squeezed out through the branches of the den. Rain had turned the floor of the clearing to mud; it splashed up over Hollyleaf's legs and belly fur as she sprinted across to the thorn tunnel and stood shivering in its shelter. Her paws itched to race through the forest, as if she could find the answers she was looking for by tracking them down like prey.

Gray dawn light seeped reluctantly into the hollow. No other cat was stirring, until Brightheart emerged from Leafpool's den and pelted back across the clearing with some leaves in her mouth. Soon after, movement on the Highledge caught Hollyleaf's eye and she spotted Sandstorm leaping down the tumbled rocks. The ginger she-cat headed for the dirtplace tunnel, then swerved when she saw Hollyleaf and bounded over to join her.

"What are you doing up so early?" she meowed. "There won't be any patrols until the sun is up." Twitching her tail, she added, "With any luck, the rain will ease off by then."

"Thornclaw was coughing," Hollyleaf replied, aware that she wasn't telling the whole truth.

Concern filled Sandstorm's green eyes. "The last thing we need is illness in the camp. A lot of the cats are still weak from the battle—especially Squirrelflight."

Hollyleaf flinched. Her mother had been terribly injured in the battle; her wound was only just beginning to heal. Although she wasn't sleeping in Leafpool's den anymore, she wasn't allowed to leave the camp. If she caught a bad cough she wouldn't have the strength to fight it.

Sandstorm bent down and nuzzled Hollyleaf's head; for a heartbeat Hollyleaf felt like a kit again, safe and comforted. "Don't look so worried," the older cat purred. "There are plenty of warriors to take care of the Clan, and Leafpool's a great medicine cat. You just need to concentrate on learning everything you can to serve ThunderClan."

"That's what I try to do," Hollyleaf meowed, painfully aware of how far she fell short of what she would like to be.

"You made a great start in the battle," Sandstorm encouraged her. "Firestar is very proud of you. But you mustn't take on more responsibility than you need to."

Hollyleaf stifled a snort of bitter laughter. Sandstorm had no *idea* what responsibilities she had to cope with.

"Don't forget what I said." Sandstorm stroked her tail-tip gently over Hollyleaf's shoulder, then pushed her way out of the tunnel and headed for the dirtplace.

The morning light was growing stronger, though clouds still covered the sky and rain still hissed down into the clearing. Hollyleaf saw Graystripe bound across the clearing to Leafpool's den, though he didn't go farther than the bramble screen.

Checking on Millie, Hollyleaf guessed.

A couple of heartbeats after Graystripe, Ashfur emerged from the warriors' den, closely followed by Cloudtail and Cinderheart. All three cats headed for the tunnel.

Ashfur gave Hollyleaf a nod as they approached, curiosity in his blue eyes. "You look frozen," he meowed. "Do you want to come on the border patrol to warm up?"

"Sure!" She didn't want to go back to the warriors' den, and she knew Jaypaw wouldn't plan anything about the fake sign without her.

Ashfur led the way out into the forest, making for the old Twoleg path. The rest of the patrol followed him, the rain muffling their paw steps. Cinderheart fell in beside Hollyleaf. There was a hint of nervousness in her blue eyes. "I don't like going this way," she confessed. "It reminds me too much of the battle."

Hollyleaf let out a murmur of agreement. Her memories

disturbed her, too, especially when they came in sight of the abandoned Twoleg nest. The blood had been washed away from the stones, but it was easy to imagine that the stench still hung in the air, and the shrieks of battling cats still echoed from the crumbling walls. Hollyleaf's neck fur rose as she eyed the moss-covered walls and thick clumps of bracken, half expecting WindClan warriors to leap out at them.

"Stop!" Cloudtail's command jerked her back to the present. The white warrior was standing with his tail raised to halt the rest of the patrol. "There's something up ahead."

"Can you tell what it is?" Ashfur asked softly. "WindClan?"

Cloudtail shook his head; his jaws gaped as he tasted the air.

Ashfur signaled with his tail for Hollyleaf and Cinderheart to fall back and let Cloudtail take the lead. Hollyleaf knew that the white tom was the best tracker in ThunderClan; he would soon find out what was waiting for them.

Cloudtail slunk along the edge of the Twoleg path, close to the rain-battered undergrowth, and slid under the overhanging stems to disguise his white pelt. Ashfur followed him, with Hollyleaf and Cinderheart in the rear. As she crept behind the senior warriors, Hollyleaf caught a trace of unfamiliar scent. She stiffened, her pelt beginning to bristle, and exchanged an alarmed glance with Cinderheart.

ShadowClan!

Hollyleaf tried to convince herself that the scent was left behind from the battle, but she knew that it was fresh, and it grew stronger as she padded forward. Her belly churned. Surely Sol wouldn't have ordered ShadowClan to invade ThunderClan's territory?

Wouldn't he? Hollyleaf thought she could hear Jaypaw's voice, drily sarcastic.

Cloudtail and Ashfur dropped into a crouch, ready to leap into battle; Hollyleaf and Cinderheart hastily copied them. The rain had almost stopped, though the wind still blew spatters into Hollyleaf's face. She could hear sounds now, of cats pushing their way through the rain-soaked undergrowth, heading for the Twoleg path.

Then she heard a plaintive squeak. "Mother, that fern dripped water all the way down my neck!"

"Hush," came the reply. "We'll be there soon."

"Tawnypelt! Flamepaw!" Hollyleaf bounded forward, ignoring Ashfur's hiss of anger.

Fronds of bracken parted at the side of the path, and the ShadowClan she-cat pushed her way through. All three of her kits followed, shaking water from their pelts as they reached the open ground.

"It's you!" Tawnypelt exclaimed in relief, touching noses with Hollyleaf. "Thank StarClan it's some cat I know." Turning away, she dipped her head to Cloudtail and Ashfur. "Greetings," she meowed. "I've come to—"

"You've no right to be here," Ashfur interrupted, the fur along his spine sticking straight up. "What do you want? Are you alone, or have you brought the rest of your Clan?"

"Hang on." Cloudtail slapped his tail over the gray warrior's mouth. "Let her get a word in edgewise."

Tawnypelt blinked gratefully at Cloudtail. "I've brought my kits to ThunderClan." Her voice was low, so that her kits couldn't hear; all three of them were huddled together at the side of the path, staring around with huge eyes. "I don't want to be part of a Clan that doesn't listen to their warrior ancestors anymore."

While she was speaking, Hollyleaf noticed how tired and hungry she looked. Her voice quivered; she was far from the tough, resourceful warrior Hollyleaf had known on their journey to the mountains.

"And what makes you think—" Ashfur began, still hostile.

"Try not to be more of a mouse-brain than you can help." Cloudtail spoke over him. "What have we got to be afraid of? It's only a queen and her kits."

"We're *apprentices*!" Flamepaw piped up indignantly.

Cloudtail twitched his ears. "Whatever. In any case, you can all come back to the camp. Firestar will be interested to hear about what's going on in ShadowClan." He shot a glance at Ashfur. "And it's Firestar who'll make the final decision."

Fury still burned in Ashfur's blue eyes. "All right," he snapped. "We go back to camp. And if WindClan decides to cross the border because we didn't finish our patrol, don't blame me."

He led the way back along the path, stalking ahead of Cloudtail and Tawnypelt. Cinderheart followed, while all three apprentices crowded around Hollyleaf.

"Hi, Hollypaw!" Tigerpaw mewed.

"I'm Hollyleaf now," she told them.

"Wow, you're a warrior!" Dawnpaw's eyes stretched wide. "Congratulations."

"Hollyleaf! Hollyleaf!" Flamepaw called out, and his brother and sister joined in.

Cinderheart glanced back, blue eyes brimming with amusement. "It sounds as if you've got three new apprentices," she murmured.

"Stop that," Hollyleaf mewed. Every hair on her pelt felt hot with embarrassment. "I can't move without tripping over you. We'll get left behind."

The young apprentices stopped squeaking and began trotting along beside Hollyleaf with their tails stuck straight up in the air.

"What's that?" Dawnpaw asked, as they passed the abandoned nest.

"Twolegs used to live there," Hollyleaf explained. "But they haven't been there for a long time," she added, as the three apprentices exchanged anxious glances. "Can you scent any Twolegs here?"

All three of them opened their little mouths to taste the air, then shook their heads solemnly. "Not a thing!" Tigerpaw announced.

"Well done," Hollyleaf meowed, wondering if this was how it felt to be a mentor.

"Where is the rest of your Clan?" Flamepaw asked as they hurried to catch up to the other cats.

"In camp, mostly," Hollyleaf replied. "We were the dawn

patrol. There might be patrols out hunting by now, but it's still pretty early."

"Can *we* hunt?" Dawnpaw asked. "We're starving!"

"Don't be such a stupid furball," Tigerpaw scolded her, flicking her ear with the tip of his tail. "You don't hunt in another Clan's territory."

"Well, I *asked*," Dawnpaw retorted.

"There's no time to hunt now," Hollyleaf replied, wondering how skillful the apprentices would be. They were still very young; they couldn't have had much training. "I expect you'll be able to eat when we get to camp."

Flamepaw's eyes gleamed. "Thank you!"

Looking at them more closely, Hollyleaf realized that Dawnpaw might have really meant it when she said they were starving. They were all very thin; every one of their ribs was visible through their pelts. Tawnypelt, too, looked thin and hollow, and her fur looked as if it hadn't been groomed for a moon. Was there a problem with the prey in ShadowClan?

"Do you think Sol knows we're here?" Tigerpaw asked as they veered off the Twoleg path toward the stone hollow.

Hollyleaf wasn't sure what to answer. Sol had known all about her and her littermates, and he had known that the sun would vanish. But Jaypaw had told her that he'd found out a lot of things from Midnight. Could he possibly know where Tawnypelt and her kits were now? And would he be angry that they had left for another Clan?

"I don't know what Sol knows," she admitted. "Your mother didn't tell him you were leaving?"

"No way!" Dawnpaw shuddered, her eyes wide with fear. "He would never have let us go."

Hollyleaf was saved from having to find a response, as they rounded a stand of hazel bushes to see the thorn barrier across the entrance to the camp. Brambleclaw was standing outside, tasting the air, his dark tabby fur still rumpled from sleep. When the patrol came into sight he stared at Tawnypelt for a heartbeat, then bounded over to her and pressed his muzzle into his sister's shoulder.

"It's good to see you," he meowed. "Are you and your kits okay? How are things in ShadowClan?"

"Everything's fine," Tawnypelt replied with a cautious glance at Ashfur. "Prey is running well in ShadowClan territory."

Brambleclaw narrowed his eyes and gave his sister a long look. Hollyleaf could see that he didn't believe Tawnypelt was telling them everything. If there was plenty of prey, why did she and her kits look so thin? "You'd better come into camp," he mewed eventually. "I'll tell Firestar you're here."

He led the way through the barrier. The three apprentices dived eagerly after their mother, but when they stepped into the clearing they hesitated, their fur bristling as they gazed around.

"It's okay," Hollyleaf reassured them. "Brambleclaw said you could come in, so no cat will hurt you."

The three young cats relaxed a little; Tigerpaw's eyes gleamed as he spotted the fresh-kill pile. "Can we have some?" he asked Hollyleaf. "We're *so* hungry!"

"You'd better ask Brambleclaw," Hollyleaf replied.

Brambleclaw, who was talking to Tawnypelt a tail-length away, had heard the plaintive question. "Help yourselves," he invited with a wave of his tail. "There's plenty."

Hollyleaf followed the three apprentices as they bounded across to the fresh-kill pile. "Don't gulp your food or you'll get bellyaches," she warned them.

Flamepaw gave her a hasty nod and dived into the pile beside his brother and sister. They clawed away the soaking wet fresh-kill on top of the pile to find the drier, juicier pieces underneath, and crouched down to eat with purrs of enthusiasm.

Taking a mouse for herself, Hollyleaf was just starting to eat when Lionblaze emerged from the warriors' den, followed by Jaypaw. Both her littermates padded across the clearing toward her; their ears flicked up in surprise when they noticed the ShadowClan apprentices.

"What's going on?" Jaypaw asked. Hollyleaf picked up the tang of herbs from his pelt; he must have been to see Thornclaw. "ShadowClan cats?"

"Hi, Lionblaze!" Dawnpaw mumbled around a mouthful of vole. "It's good to see you again."

"It's good to see you, too," Lionblaze responded, surveying the scattered fresh-kill pile. "I can see you're making yourselves at home."

"Where's our mother going?" Flamepaw asked as Tawnypelt padded past with Brambleclaw, heading for the Highledge.

"Brambleclaw is taking her to see Firestar," Hollyleaf

explained. "His den is up there on that ledge."

"Right up there?" Tigerpaw exclaimed. "Cool!"

"But why are they here?" Jaypaw insisted, an edge to his voice.

Hollyleaf explained how the dawn patrol had met Tawnypelt and her kits in the forest, and brought them back to camp. "She said she didn't want to be part of a Clan who didn't look to their warrior ancestors anymore," she finished.

Jaypaw said nothing, but looked thoughtful, his whiskers quivering as if he had scented prey. Hollyleaf guessed he was wondering how many more cats wanted to leave, and whether Tawnypelt and her kits would be any help in his plans to make a sign from StarClan.

More cats had begun to appear from the warriors' den. Dustpelt padded across to the fresh-kill pile, followed by Mousewhisker and Honeyfern. Foxpaw and Icepaw bounded across from the apprentices' den.

"In StarClan's name, what's going on here?" Dustpelt asked, his lip curling. "What has happened to the fresh-kill pile? It looks as if a horde of badgers has trampled through it."

"Er . . . we've got visitors," Hollyleaf mewed.

Dustpelt's tail shot straight up as he stared at the apprentices. "ShadowClan cats?" He let out an irritated sigh. "Have they left *any* dry prey?"

Tigerpaw spoke up. "We didn't want to eat the soggy pieces."

"No other cat wants to eat them, either," Honeyfern pointed out, pawing through the remains of the pile to see if she could find a drier piece.

"And what are we supposed to do?" Icepaw demanded, flicking a sodden rabbit with her tail. "Mousefur will claw our ears off if we take her *that*!"

Hollyleaf turned to the three ShadowClan apprentices. "That wasn't a very polite thing to do, was it?"

All three young cats studied their paws, their tails drooping. "We're sorry," Flamepaw mumbled.

"Sol says we can only rely on ourselves to take the best care of us," Dawnpaw explained. "He says we shouldn't spend all our time thinking about fighting and marking the borders. Then there'd be time for every cat to catch enough prey for themselves, and there wouldn't be any problem."

Hollyleaf exchanged a shocked glance with Lionblaze. Where was the warrior code in the way of life Sol had imposed on ShadowClan?

"What about cats who can't hunt for themselves?" she asked Dawnpaw.

The apprentice looked uncertain. "Well . . . we wouldn't let any cat starve."

You might not, but others would, if it kept them from going hungry, Hollyleaf thought. *And you three look as if you're pretty close to starving.*

"Dawnpaw, you shouldn't listen to that dumb ol' patchy cat," Tigerpaw declared, giving his sister a shove. "He won't let us train to be warriors anymore. I *want* to fight for my Clan!"

"And I'd really like to be a medicine cat," Flamepaw added, scoring his paw angrily through the wet earth. "But Sol says we wouldn't need special cats if every cat knew about herbs and stuff. I was going to be Littlecloud's apprentice, but now we don't even have mentors anymore."

"Blackstar says we have to call him Blackfoot," Dawnpaw added, her tail drooping.

"It sounds as if ShadowClan is breaking up," Dustpelt remarked, gulping down the last of a blackbird and swiping his tongue around his jaws. "I never thought I'd say this, but I'd be sorry to see it happen. Your Clan has some fine warriors." He signaled to Mousewhisker and Honeyfern with a wave of his tail. "Come on—let's get some patrols organized and see if we can find some prey that's fit to eat."

He stalked off toward the warriors' den. Icepaw and Foxpaw picked up the rabbit and carried it between them toward the elders' den.

"You can explain why it's wet," Icepaw meowed.

"No, *you* can," Foxpaw retorted.

Hollyleaf watched them go. Her paws were trembling, yet she felt rooted to the ground. "What can we do?" she asked, hardly expecting a reply. There *was* nothing they could do to restore ShadowClan's faith in their warrior ancestors. Even Jaypaw's plan to fake a sign from StarClan didn't hold out much hope now they'd heard how much Sol had poisoned ShadowClan against the code.

Lionblaze shook his head; his amber eyes were uneasy. "I don't know."

"Tell us more about Sol," Jaypaw prompted. "Does he—"

"Hey, I look like you, don't I?" Tigerpaw interrupted, stretching out a paw to compare his golden pelt with

Lionblaze's. "That must be because we share kin."

"That's right," Lionblaze mewed, giving the smaller cat's ear a friendly lick. "Your mother and our father were littermates."

Tigerpaw nodded proudly. "Tigerstar was their father. I'm named after him. He was the greatest warrior *ever*!"

Lionblaze twitched his ears. "We should all try to be the greatest warriors ever."

Dawnpaw was gazing up at the Highledge, as if she was waiting for her mother to reappear. "Are we going to join ThunderClan?" she asked; she didn't sound enthusiastic. "After all, it's where our mother was born."

Flamepaw sighed. "I don't want to. Leafpool already has an apprentice, and besides, I want to be the *ShadowClan* medicine cat."

Tigerpaw touched his nose to his brother's ear. "I know. I want to fight for ShadowClan."

Hollyleaf's heart was torn with sympathy for the three young cats. Of course they all wanted to go home. ShadowClan still held their loyalties, even though everything had changed. A tiny flicker of warmth grew inside her. Sol had tried to destroy the warrior code, but he had failed. It lived on inside these apprentices. Sol couldn't change every cat's mind about what they had believed for so long.

She sank her claws into the wet earth. Somehow, they had to find a way to get rid of Sol and bring ShadowClan back to the way of the Clans.

CHAPTER 7

From the corner of his eye, Lionblaze spotted movement on the Highledge. Firestar had appeared with Brambleclaw and Tawnypelt.

"Let all cats old enough to catch their own prey join here beneath the Highledge for a Clan meeting," he yowled.

He ran nimbly down the tumbled rocks, halting on a boulder just above the heads of the assembling cats. Even on such a gray day, his flame-colored pelt gleamed. Brambleclaw and Tawnypelt picked their way down more slowly, until they stood just behind him.

Mousefur and Longtail emerged from the elders' den; Foxpaw and Icepaw followed them, each with a bundle of soiled bedding. Lionblaze noticed Mousefur's bristling fur and suspicious gaze, and realized that the apprentices must have told her what was going on.

Graystripe appeared from the dirtplace tunnel and padded over to join the group around the fresh-kill pile, giving the ShadowClan apprentices a friendly nod. Leafpool came to sit outside the bramble screen in front of her den, while Daisy appeared at the entrance to the nursery with the four kits peering curiously from behind her. Whitewing and Birchfall pushed their way out of the warriors' den, and bounded across the camp to sit at the foot of the boulder where Firestar stood. Lionblaze spotted Thornclaw poking his head out between the branches of the den. Sorreltail and Squirrelflight stood side by side, flicking the tips of their tails.

As the cats gathered, Lionblaze was aware of uneasy looks cast at Tawnypelt and the three apprentices. He could hear muttering, too, as if many of the warriors were unhappy at seeing ShadowClan cats in their camp.

Berrynose stalked over to the fresh-kill pile. "Surely Firestar's not bringing *more* outsiders into the Clan?"

"I hope not," Spiderleg agreed. "That's what caused the battle with RiverClan and WindClan in the first place."

"And where would you be, Berrynose," Lionblaze asked, his neck fur beginning to rise with annoyance, "if Firestar hadn't taken you in when you were a kit?"

Berrynose snorted and turned his back. "That's different."

Jaypaw leaned over to whisper into Lionblaze's ear. "Yeah, he's such a *special* cat."

"Cats of ThunderClan," Firestar began when all the Clan had gathered around him, "you can see that Tawnypelt of ShadowClan has come here with her kits—"

"We're *apprentices*," Flamepaw muttered.

"—and she has asked for shelter because of the way her own Clan has changed."

"And are you going to agree to that?" Mousefur called out from her place in front of the elders' den. "Hasn't there been enough trouble because of taking in other cats?"

Before Firestar could reply, Graystripe sprang to his paws. "These cats are part of ThunderClan," he hissed. "They deserve to have a home here."

"No cat forced Tawnypelt to leave," Mousefur retorted. "If you ask me, cats should decide where they want to live and stay there."

There was a murmur of agreement; Lionblaze saw dismay in the eyes of the three apprentices.

"They don't want us here," Tigerpaw muttered.

"Some cats don't," Lionblaze admitted, resting his tail-tip on the young cat's shoulder. "But it'll be okay. Firestar will talk them around, you'll see."

"I understand your worries," Firestar went on. "But Tawnypelt isn't asking for a permanent home in ThunderClan. She and her kits—"

Dawnpaw rolled her eyes. "How many *more* times?"

"—are only here while Sol holds sway in ShadowClan. If she has seen through his lies, others will too, and he won't be allowed to stay for long."

"Then we should take a patrol across the border and drive him out," Cloudtail meowed. "The lake would be well rid of him."

"Yes!" Birchfall agreed. "ShadowClan helped us, so we should—"

Yowls of protest drowned out his last few words. "There's been enough fighting," Sorreltail meowed, glancing at Squirrelflight. "Some cats are still recovering from their wounds."

"ShadowClan should deal with their own problems," Spider-leg added. "It's no business of ours."

Cloudtail whipped his head around to stare at the black warrior. "If ShadowClan cats are moving in here, then it's *not* their own problem anymore."

"That's enough!" Firestar raised his tail for silence. "Tawnypelt is welcome to stay for as long as she wants. The apprentices—"

"At last!" Tigerpaw muttered.

"—will train and perform duties alongside Foxpaw and Icepaw."

Lionblaze saw the two ThunderClan apprentices exchange delighted glances, and he heard some of the younger warriors let out sighs of relief at being freed from helping with the apprentice tasks.

"Tawnypelt will have a place in the warriors' den, and take part in patrols," Firestar went on.

"Can she be trusted?" Ashfur called out. "Especially along the ShadowClan border?"

Lionblaze saw Brambleclaw's fur start to bristle, but Fire-star raised his tail, warning him not to retaliate. "It's time for the regular patrols," he meowed, ignoring Ashfur's comment. "The fresh-kill pile needs restocking, and we need to keep a close eye on the border with WindClan."

Brambleclaw leaped down from the rocks and began calling cats to him, splitting them up into patrols. "Lionblaze, Holly-leaf, I want you on a hunting patrol with Dustpelt and Sorreltail. And you apprentices go over there and talk to Firestar."

Tigerpaw, Flamepaw, and Dawnpaw sprang up, looking a bit daunted at the thought of meeting the Clan leader. "You'll be fine," Lionblaze promised them as he padded off to join Sorreltail and Dustpelt.

As Sorreltail led her patrol toward the camp entrance, Lionblaze glanced back to see Firestar arranging mentors for the three ShadowClan apprentices. Flamepaw was paired with Cloudtail, Tigerpaw with Brackenfur, and Dawnpaw with Spiderleg. Sandstorm and Whitewing beckoned their apprentices, Foxpaw and Icepaw.

"We'll all go to the clearing for some hunting practice," Sandstorm announced.

Following Sorreltail through the tunnel, Lionblaze couldn't help feeling relieved that the ShadowClan apprentices weren't receiving any battle training—at least, not yet. If they learned ThunderClan skills, wouldn't that give them an unfair advantage in future battles?

Curiosity burned like a flame inside him. He wondered whether any of the three were being visited by Tigerstar in dreams. Tigerpaw would be an obvious choice; he was big and strong, and he seemed most interested in their shared kin, especially the warrior whose name he bore. Even though he wanted to be rid of Tigerstar's menacing influence in his dreams, Lionblaze couldn't suppress a flash of jealousy that the dark warrior might choose another cat to mentor, a cat in a different Clan.

Perhaps I should warn Tigerpaw, he thought. *But then I would have to tell him that Tigerstar visits me. I can't do that.*

Lionblaze shook his head in confusion. It seemed that since Sol came to the lake, nothing was simple anymore.

Sorreltail led them toward the top of the territory, where the border gave way to open moorland not claimed by any Clan. Although the rain had stopped, the ground was muddy and the undergrowth was soaked; all the scents were damped down and hard to detect. Lionblaze shivered as he plodded along; every fern or clump of grass that he brushed against released a shower of raindrops and his pelt was soon sodden, the fur plastered against his body.

Hunching his shoulders, he wished he could be training for battle instead of trying to track down soggy little mice. *They'll all be deep inside their burrows, hiding from the rain. Sometimes I think they have more sense than we do.*

Head down, he blundered into a clump of bracken, letting out a hiss of annoyance as it dumped its load of water drops all over him.

"Lionblaze!" The yowl came from Sorreltail. "Look where you're going, won't you? You just scared off the vole I was stalking."

"Sorry." Lionblaze's paws tingled with frustration and embarrassment.

"Sorry fills no bellies," Sorreltail retorted.

She stood still, head raised and jaws apart as she tried to locate the vole again. Lionblaze backed off to give her space, and spotted Hollyleaf appearing from behind a bramble thicket with a mouse hanging from her jaws.

"Well done," he mewed as she padded up to him and dropped her prey at his paws.

"Lionblaze, we need to talk." Hollyleaf ignored his praise; her eyes were wide and distraught. "We *have* to stop what Sol is doing in ShadowClan. He's destroying the warrior code!"

"Keep your fur on." Lionblaze was startled by his sister's intensity. "We—"

"We have to do what Jaypaw suggested, and make a fake sign from ShadowClan. And we have to do it soon! I'll do *anything* to remind ShadowClan cats of their warrior ancestors."

Lionblaze's surprise deepened to uneasiness; the passion in Hollyleaf's eyes unnerved him. "Steady," he murmured, pressing his muzzle against her shoulder. "Why does it matter so much? We have our own destinies, and they don't have anything to do with the other Clans."

"Of course it matters!" Hollyleaf flashed back at him. "Sol was supposed to be helping us, remember? And what will happen to the rest of us if ShadowClan abandons the warrior code?"

"I know," Lionblaze responded. "But how can we fake a sign when ShadowClan is bound to be hostile? They'll defend their beliefs because they won't want to admit they're wrong. Great StarClan, we don't even know the territory!"

"We don't." Hollyleaf's eyes narrowed. "But there are three new apprentices in ThunderClan who do."

"Hollyleaf, that's brilliant!" Lionblaze exclaimed. "But will they—"

An annoyed hiss interrupted him; he whirled around to see Dustpelt standing a tail-length away.

"Are you going to stand there gossiping all day?" the senior warrior inquired with a lash of his tail. "Or do you think that you might possibly find time to do some hunting?"

"Sorry," Lionblaze muttered. *I can't do anything right today!*

"It might have escaped your notice," Dustpelt went on with biting sarcasm, "but we have four new mouths to feed. And several of our own cats are sick, so they can't help with patrols."

Lionblaze nodded. He realized that the tabby warrior was angry because he was worried. "I'm really sorry," he repeated. "We'll get going right away."

"See that you do," Dustpelt sniffed as he stalked off.

As he tasted the air, ears pricked for the sound of prey, Lionblaze knew Hollyleaf was right. They had to help ShadowClan so that Tawnypelt and the apprentices could go home, and ThunderClan could concentrate on making itself strong again.

Lionblaze worked hard for the rest of the hunt, but most of the prey was still hidden in their holes. By sunhigh, when the patrol returned to camp, he had only caught two mice and a shrew. He dropped the meager offering on the fresh-kill pile and padded off to find Jaypaw. After checking the medicine cats' den and not finding him there, Lionblaze finally tracked him down in the elders' den.

"Look, Mousefur," Jaypaw was saying as Lionblaze ducked under the low branches of the hazel bush, "these tansy leaves should stop you getting greencough. Why don't you want to eat them?"

Mousefur gave the leaves a push with one paw. "I told you, I don't need them. Stop fussing over me and keep them for cats who are really sick."

"Jaypaw doesn't want you to get sick," Longtail tried to explain.

Mousefur gave him an angry flick with her tail. "Since when were you a medicine cat?"

Jaypaw let out an exasperated sigh. "Mousefur, for the last time—"

"The last time?" Mousefur snapped. "Good. Go away." She pointedly turned her back.

Jaypaw dug his claws into the floor of the den and spoke through gritted teeth. "Mousefur. I am not leaving this den until you eat these herbs." He was obviously trying hard to hang on to his temper.

"Come on, Mousefur," Lionblaze meowed cheerfully. "Stop being such a grump and just eat the stuff."

Mousefur whipped around and glared at him. Lionblaze tensed, ready to feel her claws raking his pelt. He couldn't fight back if an elder of his own Clan attacked him. Then Mousefur gave him an abrupt nod, bent her head, and licked up the leaves, chewing and swallowing with a disgusted expression on her face. "Satisfied?" she grunted, then curled up and wrapped her tail over her nose.

"I don't believe it," Jaypaw muttered, as Longtail let out a tiny snort of amusement and curled up beside the dusky brown elder. "Thanks for helping," he added as he and his brother emerged from the den.

Lionblaze shrugged. "No problem. We need to talk about the fake sign."

Jaypaw's neck fur started to bristle. "I wish there were ten of me, I've got so much to do. Our den is full with Millie and Briarkit, but we really need to take Thornclaw out of the warriors' den because he's sick, too, and Foxpaw has started coughing. I don't know how we're going to cope."

Anger surged through Lionblaze; he lashed his tail and dug his claws into the earth. He could fight an ordinary enemy, but there was no way he could protect his Clanmates against the sickness.

"It'll be easier if we don't have the extra ShadowClan mouths to feed," he pointed out. *And if Sol leaves ShadowClan so he can mentor us like he promised.*

Jaypaw gave a grudging nod. "True. Okay, what about the sign?"

Lionblaze padded beside his brother as he headed for the medicine cats' den. "Hollyleaf had an idea. She thought the ShadowClan apprentices might help us make the sign, because they know the territory."

Jaypaw looked dubious. "Help us fool their own Clan?"

"You heard them when they arrived," Lionblaze persisted. "All they want is to go home—to the *real* ShadowClan, not the mess that Sol has made of it. Don't you think they would help any cat who could make that happen?"

Jaypaw hesitated outside the bramble screen, his head on one side. "Maybe you're right," he agreed. "Okay, we'll talk to them later." Then he whisked out of sight into the den.

As Lionblaze turned away, he noticed that the thorns blocking the entrance to the hollow were shaking. The apprentices and their mentors were returning from hunting practice. All three of the ShadowClan apprentices looked bedraggled, their fur clumped together and stuck with bits of leaf and moss. Dawnpaw carried a mouse; she padded across the clearing, her tail straight up in triumph, and laid it on the fresh-kill pile.

"But that can't be right." Tigerpaw was arguing with Foxpaw as they came up. "If you stalk the prey until you're nearly on top of it, you give it the chance to know you're there. *We* pounce when we're a lot farther away."

"That's because there's thick undergrowth in our territory," Foxpaw explained. "That hides us and our scent until we get close, then it's easier to pounce."

"Oh." Tigerpaw thought about that for a moment. "Well, it still seems mouse-brained to me," he decided.

"Hey, Lionblaze!" Hollyleaf bounded out of the nursery, distracting Lionblaze from the apprentices' chatter.

"How's Daisy coping with all the kits?" he asked.

"Pretty well," Hollyleaf replied. "Ferncloud is with her, helping to keep the kits amused. I just took them some fresh-kill." Glancing around to make sure that no cat was listening, she added, "Did you have a word with Jaypaw?"

Lionblaze nodded. "He says we can talk to the apprentices."

Hollyleaf's whiskers twitched with satisfaction. "Good. I'll get Foxpaw and Icepaw away, then you can take the others behind the warriors' den. No cat will hear us there."

The mentors and apprentices were standing in the middle

of the clearing; Cloudtail was explaining something about following a scent trail. Hollyleaf bounded up to them. "Foxpaw, Icepaw, can you fetch some clean moss for the elders' den?"

Foxpaw and Icepaw exchanged a sullen glance. "Why can't *they* do it?" Icepaw asked, flicking her ears toward the Shadow-Clan apprentices.

"Because they're not here to do all the jobs that you don't like," Hollyleaf retorted. "Besides, the elders will appreciate having the respect of their *own* Clanmates."

"Yes, when you're warriors you get to decide who does what," Sandstorm added. "Not before."

"Okay, okay, we'll do it," Foxpaw muttered, stifling a cough as he headed back toward the thorn barrier. "It'll all be wet through, you know that."

"Like *they* know the best moss places anyway," Icepaw mewed with a twitch of her tail-tip as she followed her brother.

Hollyleaf turned to the group of mentors. "Shall I take Flamepaw, Tigerpaw, and Dawnpaw to get cleaned up?" she asked. Lionblaze's whiskers twitched at the helpful tone in her voice. "Any cat can see they're not used to hunting in thick woodland."

"Not thick *soaking-wet* woodland," Flamepaw agreed. He gave himself a thorough shake, scattering water drops and scraps of leaf, twigs, and moss. "I'd rather hunt in our own territory. It's a lot cleaner there."

Cloudtail leaped back as drops from Flamepaw's fur spattered his white pelt. "You do that, Hollyleaf. The sooner the better."

At the same moment, Lionblaze noticed that more cats had emerged from the tunnel: The border patrol was returning, led by Ashfur, with Honeyfern and Brackenfur.

"Yes, carry on, Hollyleaf," Sandstorm meowed, heading toward the newcomers. "We need to find out what's been happening along the ShadowClan border." Whitewing, Cloudtail, Sorreltail, and Spiderleg crowded close behind her.

"Do you think any more cats will have crossed into our territory?" Spiderleg asked.

Lionblaze didn't listen to Sandstorm's reply. He padded over to meet his sister, who waved her tail at the three ShadowClan apprentices and led them across the clearing.

"Come with us," Hollyleaf said. "We need to talk to you."

Suspicion glimmered in Tigerpaw's amber eyes. "This isn't just about cleaning our pelts, right?"

"No, but it's nothing to worry about," Lionblaze assured him. "We've thought of a way to help your Clan."

As they passed the entrance to the medicine cats' den, Hollyleaf paused. "Hey, Jaypaw! Meet us in the usual place."

The only reply was a bout of exhausted coughing.

"Is that the medicine cats' den?" Flamepaw asked curiously. "Can I look inside? I really wanted to be a medicine cat," he added.

"Not right now," Lionblaze replied. "It's a bit crowded in there."

The sound of more coughing drifted through the bramble screen. Dawnpaw's eyes stretched wide. "Gee, those cats sound sick!"

Lionblaze exchanged a glance with Hollyleaf. It was natural to hide problems from a rival Clan; if he told the apprentices there was greencough in the camp, it would make Thunder-Clan sound weak. Still, the young cats were hardly likely to launch an attack. That could only happen if ShadowClan started to believe in StarClan again. Lionblaze sighed. Everything led back to the fake sign. . . .

"Jaypaw?" Hollyleaf called again.

"Okay!" Jaypaw sounded irritable. "I heard you the first time. I'll come as soon as I can."

Hollyleaf led the way to the space behind the warriors' den. It was sheltered from the wind, but it felt even more cramped with the three apprentices in there. "You'll manage better if you clean each other up," she advised. "Get all the twigs and burrs out of your fur; then you can give yourselves a good wash."

"This is *such* a pain," Dawnpaw sighed, tugging at a stubborn knot in Tigerpaw's fur. "I wish we were back on nice soft pine needles."

"With any luck you will be," Lionblaze promised.

"What do you mean?" Flamepaw asked.

"Wait until Jaypaw comes," Hollyleaf meowed.

"I'm here." Jaypaw appeared around the edge of the warriors' den. "Great StarClan, it's more crowded than ever," he added, shoving his way in beside Lionblaze and wriggling until he'd made himself a space.

"Lionblaze says we'll be back in our own territory soon." Dawnpaw was quivering with curiosity. "But I don't see how we can be."

"We've had an idea," Jaypaw began, "but we haven't much time. The longer Sol stays in ShadowClan, the harder it will be to get rid of him."

"No cat can get rid of him," Flamepaw mewed dejectedly.

Jaypaw tensed his muscles. "*We* can. We're going to make a sign from StarClan to persuade ShadowClan that Sol is lying to him. Blackstar—I mean Blackfoot—will kick him out pretty quickly after that."

All three apprentices stared at Jaypaw with baffled faces. After a few heartbeats, Flamepaw whispered, "Won't that make StarClan angry?"

"I doubt it." Jaypaw flicked his ears. "StarClan themselves *asked* me for help. They can't object to how I go about it."

The three young cats' eyes stretched wide. "Wow!" Dawnpaw breathed.

"We want to know the best place to create a sign." Lionblaze took up the explanation. "And we have to bring Blackfoot and Littlecloud to see it, so they'll be convinced StarClan is still watching over them."

"And don't forget, your Clan will know by now that you've left," Hollyleaf reminded the apprentices. "Any plan we make will have to take that into account."

"I get it," meowed Tigerpaw. "A place near the border would be best, so that you don't have to trespass too far on our territory."

"Maybe that marshy place near the edge of the territory," Dawnpaw suggested. "Not many cats go there. We don't want to be disturbed—"

"No, I think by the lake would be best," Tigerpaw interrupted. "Then you could have a StarClan cat coming out of the water and—"

"Great," Jaypaw grumbled. "And how do you suggest we do that?"

"And how do we get Blackfoot and Littlecloud to come and see it?" Dawnpaw added.

"We could tell them we saw cats trespassing," Flamepaw suggested.

"Or a fox," Tigerpaw put in. "We could lay a trail of fox scent."

"What?" Dawnpaw's neck fur fluffed up. "Are you mouse-brained? Are you just going to ask the fox nicely if—"

"We could use fox dung," Flamepaw meowed.

Dawnpaw's whiskers twitched in disgust. "*You* can. I'm not going near any fox dung, thanks very much." Then her eyes sparkled mischievously and she added, "Why not feed them poppy seeds and carry them to the place?"

"No way!" Tigerpaw protested. "Blackfoot's a seriously big cat. I'm not lugging him across half the territory."

"There are useful herbs growing near the oak tree by the stream," Flamepaw pointed out. "Littlecloud would come for those." His tail curled up in amusement. "Then we could pelt Blackfoot with acorns, and he'd think they came from StarClan."

"That's *stupid*!" Dawnpaw exclaimed, leaping on her brother. They wrestled together; in the confined space one of Flamepaw's hind legs jabbed Hollyleaf in the belly.

"Watch it!" she snarled. When the two apprentices sat up, she went on more calmly. "You're not taking this seriously. This isn't a game. It's about preserving the warrior code. Do you *want* your Clan to break up and become a collection of rogues? Because that's what will happen if we can't make them believe in StarClan again."

Serious now, wide-eyed with anxiety, all three apprentices exchanged uncomfortable glances. "Sorry," Tigerpaw muttered.

"Well, what about that marshy place?" Dawnpaw went back to her original idea. "Not many cats will be anywhere near, especially after all this rain. We wouldn't be disturbed there while we were setting up the sign. And Sol never goes that far; he doesn't want to get his paws wet."

"That sounds pretty good," Lionblaze meowed. "What do you think?" he asked his littermates.

Hollyleaf nodded, and Jaypaw murmured, "It's worth checking out."

"But what will the sign be?" Flamepaw mewed eagerly.

"We'll work that out when we get there," Jaypaw replied. "We'd better go right away."

Lionblaze stuck his head out into the open. Watery sunlight was gleaming through the clouds. Outside the warriors' den, Sorreltail and Brackenfur were sharing tongues, with Squirrelflight drowsing in the sunlight nearby. The four remaining kits were playing at the entrance to the nursery, with Daisy and Ferncloud looking on. Otherwise, everything was quiet; Lionblaze guessed that most cats were sleeping in their dens, either sick with the cough or building strength for the next patrol.

"All clear," he reported. "Let's go."

"But I'm hungry," Flamepaw complained. "Can't we eat first?"

"There's barely enough for ThunderClan," Jaypaw growled.

Seeing the guilty looks on the faces of the apprentices, Lionblaze rested his tail-tip on his brother's shoulder. "It's not their fault," he murmured. "There's no time to eat now," he told Flamepaw, "but we'll see if we can pick up some prey on the way back."

Seeing the shock in Hollyleaf's green eyes, he added, "Okay, I know, the Clan must be fed first. But faking a sign from StarClan isn't exactly part of the warrior code, is it? Anyway, we're not a hunting patrol. I reckon the territory can spare a few mice."

Hollyleaf didn't reply, just flicked her tail.

"I'll go and tell Leafpool that I'm going to collect herbs," Jaypaw meowed. "We're low on almost everything, and I can pick some up on the way back." He whisked out of their hiding place and behind the bramble screen into the medicine cats' den.

Lionblaze waited for him to emerge, then took the lead as they headed out of the camp and into the damp forest.

Chapter 8

Every hair on Dawnpaw's pelt was quivering. "This is like being sent on a real warrior mission!"

Hollyleaf could sympathize; she remembered very well how it felt to be a new apprentice, doing something to help her Clan.

"Do you think we'll get to be warriors, after it's all over?" Tigerpaw mewed. "Because we saved our Clan?"

"No," Hollyleaf replied gently. "Don't forget, no cat must know we're doing this. Besides, you're too young to be warriors yet. You still have a lot to learn."

The six cats were heading toward the far end of ThunderClan territory, following the same route Hollyleaf and her littermates had taken when they went to find Sol. Already the ShadowClan scent marks were fading along the border, and there was no sign of cats from either Clan. The only sounds were the drip of water from leaves and the rustle of ferns and grasses as the cats brushed through them.

All three of the apprentices were bouncing with excitement, rushing off into the undergrowth or dabbing at one another in the beginnings of a play fight.

"That's enough," Lionblaze ordered, rounding up Flamepaw with his tail and nudging him forward. "Do you think warriors chase each other around like that?"

The young ShadowClan cats settled down and padded along quietly, but Hollyleaf could see that their paws were still itching. They were acting as if Blackfoot had already seen the sign and decided that his Clan would return to StarClan and the warrior code.

But it's not as easy as that.

Hollyleaf's belly churned as she wondered what would happen if they failed. They would only get one chance. If Blackfoot realized he was being tricked, he would be twice as careful afterward. ShadowClan would be lost forever. Even worse, Blackfoot might decide to invade ThunderClan, to punish them for interfering.

What if cats die because of what we're doing?

"Jaypaw, have you decided what—"

Her brother flicked his ears irritably. "I can't decide anything until we get to where we're going. Now keep your tail over your jaws and let me think."

"This is where we should cross the border," Tigerpaw announced, stopping and looking around. "The marshy place is only a few fox-lengths away."

Even though she could hardly taste the ShadowClan scent marks, Hollyleaf still felt guilty as she crossed into the rival Clan's territory.

I don't know why. If they cared about their border, they would mark it. They couldn't care less about the warrior code.

But we do, she answered herself. *Going into another Clan's territory is wrong.*

Tigerpaw led them through some trees where brambles snagged their fur, then into a more open patch of ground. "Here we are," he declared.

Water welled up around Hollyleaf's paws as she gazed at the marsh ahead. Long-stemmed clusters of reeds grew around pools covered with bright green pondweed. Between them were tussocks of brittle grass and sedge, and a few spindly saplings grew with their roots in the water. There was a dank, musty scent, and the air was heavy with silence.

"What can you see?" Jaypaw mewed as the cats drew to a halt.

"Marshy ground and water," Lionblaze replied.

"Any cover?"

"Yes, reeds and long grass. And a few trees."

"What are the trees like? How big are they?" Jaypaw was beginning to sound excited. "What are their roots like?"

"Small trees," Hollyleaf replied, wondering what was going through her brother's mind. "Their roots look quite long and shallow, at least as far as I can see."

Jaypaw fell silent, motionless except for his whiskers quivering.

"I don't see what we can do here," Hollyleaf mewed anxiously, wondering if they should have chosen somewhere else. "There's nothing to—"

"Shut up, I'm thinking," Jaypaw snapped.

Hollyleaf exchanged a glance with Lionblaze.

"Leave him alone," her brother whispered. "If any cat can work this out, he can."

Hollyleaf hoped he was right. Trying to push down her impatience, she kept an eye on the three apprentices, who were stalking around the edge of the marshy ground, looking for prey.

"Nothing but pond flies!" Dawnpaw exclaimed indignantly.

"These trees." Jaypaw broke his silence at last. "Do any of them look as if they could be knocked over?"

What? Has he gone completely mouse-brained? Hollyleaf flexed her claws and forced herself not to speak.

"I'll check," Lionblaze mewed. "There might be a few."

He splashed off into the marsh with water brushing his belly fur and pondweed sticking to his golden pelt. The three apprentices left their hunt to watch, and Hollyleaf waited anxiously while Lionblaze circled several of the trees, giving their trunks a good sniff, then came splashing back.

"I think we could do it," he reported. "I could feel roots under my paws, so we should be able to dig them up."

"But *why*?" Hollyleaf only just stopped herself from wailing like a frustrated kit.

Jaypaw's sightless blue eyes gleamed. "We're going to make it look as if ShadowClan's territory is falling down around them."

Hollyleaf's heart thumped harder. Only Jaypaw would have thought of digging up *trees* as a message from StarClan. If it worked, it should really convince Blackfoot that following Sol was wrong.

Under Jaypaw's direction, Hollyleaf and Lionblaze chose two saplings, not too far from each other.

"I want them still upright, but ready to fall. And when I give the word, I want them to fall toward each other, so their branches are joined together," Jaypaw explained. "Okay, get digging."

Hollyleaf waded out into the marsh, flinching as cold mud and water soaked into her fur. Dawnpaw joined her at one of the trees, while Lionblaze and Tigerpaw tackled the other.

As Lionblaze had said, Hollyleaf found that she could easily feel the roots of the tree under her paws. She clawed at them vigorously, trying to dislodge them from the mud. At first she thought she wouldn't be able to shift them at all.

"This is hopeless!" Dawnpaw gasped. She was belly deep in the thick mud, and drops of it were spattered over her head and shoulders. "We'll never do it."

"Yes, we will," Hollyleaf growled, clawing even harder. "We've got to!"

She staggered as the root she was tugging at gave way, barely saving herself from sliding under the mud. Her pelt burned with urgency as she scrabbled around to find another root and dug her claws into it.

A few fox-lengths away, Lionblaze was struggling with the other tree. Tigerpaw worked alongside him, but Flamepaw was standing back with a troubled look in his eyes.

"What's the matter with you?" Tigerpaw asked, flicking mud from his ears. "Come and help!"

"I still don't know . . ." Flamepaw mewed doubtfully. "I'm not sure it's right to fake a sign from StarClan."

Dawnpaw glanced over her shoulder. "We've been through this," she hissed in exasperation. "We already agreed to try anything. This might just work, and let us go back to our own Clan."

Flamepaw hesitated, then took a deep breath. "Okay." He floundered forward into the mud beside Lionblaze and his brother.

Hollyleaf couldn't shift the next root however hard she clawed. Growing desperate, she gulped in air, then plunged her head below the surface of the mud and bit down on the stubborn tendril. Mud oozed into her mouth as she gnawed at it. Her chest ached with the need to breathe, but at last the bitter strands parted. Hollyleaf resurfaced, coughing and spitting out mud. Her fur was plastered with it and a foul taste clung to her tongue, but she didn't care. Triumph flared through her from ears to tail-tip. *I'll do whatever it takes to save ShadowClan!*

"I think we've done it!" Dawnpaw exclaimed. "The trunk feels unsteady."

Hollyleaf gave the sapling an experimental push. The trunk tilted and a sucking sound came from under the surface of the mud.

"Stop!" Jaypaw ordered. He had been sniffing at Lionblaze's tree; now he splashed across to Hollyleaf and stretched out a paw to touch the trunk of her tree. Hollyleaf saw it wobble again.

"That's it," Jaypaw meowed. "You can stop now."

"Thank StarClan!" Dawnpaw sighed.

Jaypaw splashed back to Lionblaze, while Hollyleaf and Dawnpaw headed for the nearest dry spot where they could crawl out and shake some of the mud from their pelts.

"I thought I was going to turn into a frog!" Dawnpaw gave her chest fur a couple of quick licks. "Ugh! It'll take moons to get this stuff off."

Lionblaze and the other two apprentices were still struggling with their tree, while Hollyleaf flexed her claws impatiently. Rays of weak sunlight slanted through the forest; if they didn't manage to uproot the trees before nightfall, Jaypaw's plan would fail. Several sunrises seemed to pass before Jaypaw announced, "That'll do."

"Now one of us has to fetch Blackfoot and Littlecloud," Lionblaze meowed, hauling himself out onto dry ground.

"I'll go," Tigerpaw offered immediately.

"No, I will," Dawnpaw protested.

"I'd be best at talking to Littlecloud," Flamepaw pointed out.

"But I'm the strongest," Tigerpaw insisted. "And the best fighter. If some cat attacks me I'm most likely to get out alive."

Lionblaze nodded. "But you need a warrior for backup. I—"

"*I'll* go," Hollyleaf interrupted. She didn't think she could stand waiting here wondering what was happening, while some other cat went deeper into ShadowClan territory to fetch Blackfoot. "You know I'm the best at stalking and keeping hidden. I've got light paws and a black pelt."

"No, a mud-colored pelt." Dawnpaw's eyes glimmered with amusement.

"Whatever. The mud should help disguise my scent." Hollyleaf sprang to her paws. "Let's go, Tigerpaw."

The ShadowClan apprentice led the way, skirting around the marsh and heading deeper into ShadowClan territory.

"I'll be a few paces behind you," Hollyleaf murmured. "Don't expect to see me unless there's trouble."

Tigerpaw nodded. "I'm going to try for Littlecloud first. If he listens to me, he'll help persuade Blackfoot."

"Okay. Good luck."

Hollyleaf fell back a few tail-lengths, keeping the apprentice in sight as he slid through the undergrowth in the direction of the ShadowClan camp. Her ears were pricked for the sound of other cats, and she paused now and again to taste the air. The silence of the forest raised the hairs on her pelt. Usually she would have expected to spot a patrol by now; her muscles were braced to leap into hiding, but the ShadowClan scent trails wandered faintly here and there, as if cats were hunting by themselves, and she caught a glimpse of only one tabby pelt, so far away that she couldn't tell which cat it was.

This isn't the way for warriors to live.

Tigerpaw headed for the stream and leaped lightly across on stepping-stones. Hollyleaf followed, more cautious than ever as the trees she was familiar with on ThunderClan territory gave way to pines, and the undergrowth became sparser. Her paws made no sound on the soft covering of pine needles.

At last she began to pick up the mingled scents of herbs.

Tigerpaw trotted briskly up a rise and paused at the top. Without looking back, he raised his tail to beckon before vanishing down the other side of the ridge.

Hollyleaf crept after him, then clawed her way up a tree that grew near the top of the slope and crouched on a branch from where she could look down. The ground fell away below her into a shallow bowl, thickly carpeted with bushes covered in bright green leaves. Littlecloud, the ShadowClan medicine cat, was standing near the bottom, biting off some stems and laying them carefully to one side.

"Littlecloud!" Tigerpaw bounded toward him.

The small tabby tom leaped to his paws, his neck fur bristling in surprise. "Tigerpaw! Are you okay? And Tawnypelt and the others?"

"Yes, we're all fine, thanks." Tigerpaw halted in front of the medicine cat and dipped his head. "Littlecloud, I need to ask you something."

The medicine cat bit off one more spray of leaves and laid it with the others. "Go ahead."

"I brought Flamepaw and Dawnpaw to the border," Tigerpaw began, gesturing with his tail. "We all want to come back to ShadowClan, but . . . well, we're scared that we'll get into trouble with Blackfoot."

Littlecloud nodded. "I see."

"Will you help us? Please?"

"What does Tawnypelt think about this?" Littlecloud asked.

"She doesn't know we're here. If Blackfoot will take us back, then we'll talk to her about it. But she might not come. She's really unhappy that ShadowClan doesn't follow the warrior code anymore."

Littlecloud heaved a deep sigh. "She's not the only cat to feel like that."

Hollyleaf tensed, digging her claws into the rough bark beneath her. Tigerpaw might be tempted to share the plan with Littlecloud, and that would ruin everything. But the apprentice said nothing about it, only repeating, "Please help us."

"Of course I will," Littlecloud purred. "Wait here. I'm not sure Blackfoot will listen to me, but I'll do my best to bring him." Picking up his bundle of stems, the medicine cat turned and bounded up the opposite side of the hollow.

"Don't let Sol know what's happening!" Tigerpaw called after him.

Littlecloud glanced back and nodded in acknowledgment, then trotted off among the pine trees.

Tigerpaw looked up into Hollyleaf's tree and waved his tail excitedly.

Thank StarClan! Hollyleaf thought. *The plan's working!*

Chapter 9

Lionblaze and Jaypaw crouched with the two remaining apprentices in a clump of spiky grass. Dawnpaw kept wriggling and bobbing her head up to see over the top of the stems.

"For StarClan's sake, keep still," Jaypaw grumbled. "And keep your head down."

"The grass is sticking into me," she complained. "And I want to see if any cat is coming."

Lionblaze laid his tail-tip on her shoulder. "We'll hear and scent the cats before we see them," he reminded her. "Keep still or you'll give us all away."

Dawnpaw settled down, though Lionblaze could feel excitement quivering through her as she pressed close to his side. His belly churned with better-hidden anticipation. *What's taking so long?* The sun was slowly sinking, and Blackfoot was unlikely to come after nightfall, if he came at all.

Suddenly Lionblaze heard rustling from the other side of the marsh. He pricked his ears and opened his jaws to taste the air. *ShadowClan scent!*

"Get to the trees," Jaypaw whispered.

Lionblaze was just about to creep into position when

Flamepaw hissed, "Wait! That's not Blackfoot!"

Lionblaze froze. The lower branches of a bush at the edge of the marsh waved up and down; then a dark brown tom emerged, sniffing the air suspiciously.

Dawnpaw's claws dug into the ground. "Toadfoot!"

"Fox dung!" Jaypaw spat.

Flamepaw's eyes stretched wide with dismay. "*Now* what do we do?"

For a few heartbeats Lionblaze felt as helpless as a piece of prey under a warrior's claws. He guessed that the Shadow-Clan warrior was following the scent trail left by Tigerpaw and Hollyleaf. What would they do if Blackfoot turned up now? Then he gave himself a mental shake. This was no time to panic!

"Flamepaw," he whispered, signaling with a twitch of his ears. "Creep around the marsh on that side, and make sure Toadfoot doesn't see you. I'll go this way. When I leap on him, you come and help."

The apprentice gave him a tense nod and crept away, his belly flat to the ground. Lionblaze headed in the opposite direction, and took cover in a clump of bracken a couple of tail-lengths from Toadfoot. He caught a glimpse of Flame-paw's ginger pelt under a bush opposite.

The ShadowClan warrior stalked forward, an aggressive light in his eyes. A low growl came from his throat. "I know you're there. Come out!"

"Now!" Lionblaze yowled.

He leaped out of the clump of bracken and bowled over the

astonished Toadfoot. At the same moment Flamepaw hurtled across the boggy ground and flung himself on top of his Clanmate. Lionblaze pinned Toadfoot down with both forepaws on his belly.

Toadfoot battered at Lionblaze with strong hindpaws. His forepaws flailed, scoring down Flamepaw's neck and shoulder, but the apprentice held on, stretching himself across Toadfoot's neck and shoulders.

"Get him into cover!" Lionblaze ordered.

Together he and Flamepaw dragged the struggling ShadowClan warrior behind the clump of bracken. Toadfoot lashed out with his claws, landing a painful blow on Lionblaze's flank, but he couldn't free himself. His screeches of fury were cut off when Flamepaw pushed his head to the ground and kept a paw over his jaws.

As soon as the thrashing and yowling stopped, Lionblaze heard the sounds of more cats approaching through the trees. Breathing heavily, he raised his head. Through the bracken fronds he could see Tigerpaw with Littlecloud pacing alongside him, and Blackfoot a tail-length or so behind.

The ShadowClan leader paused and looked suspiciously around him. "I heard something," he growled.

"Some cat hunting, maybe," Tigerpaw lied easily. "This way, Blackfoot. Flamepaw and Dawnpaw are waiting by the border."

At the sound of his leader's voice, Toadfoot heaved himself up in another attempt to escape. Lionblaze thrust him down again.

"Keep quiet if you want to save your Clan!" he hissed,

planting a paw on Toadfoot's neck.

Toadfoot glared at him furiously, but couldn't move.

While Lionblaze and Flamepaw were fighting with Toadfoot, Jaypaw and Dawnpaw had slipped back into the marsh and taken up their positions by the saplings they had loosened. Almost covered by the mud, they were hardly visible to any cat who wasn't looking for them.

The thin branches were waving as though the trees could fall at any moment. Tigerpaw led Blackfoot and Littlecloud forward as if he was going to skirt the marsh at the very edge. Lionblaze caught a glimpse of Hollyleaf creeping from behind a gorse bush and plunging into the mud to help Dawnpaw. His chest heaved. *Now! Now!*

Jaypaw raised his tail and slapped it down on the surface of the mud; then he thrust at the trunk of his tree with outstretched forepaws. Hollyleaf and Dawnpaw pushed their tree. Slowly the trunks tilted. There was a sucking noise and the surface of the marsh churned with brown bubbles.

Blackfoot let out a yowl of alarm, but it was too late to flee. The trees crashed down, their branches locking together as they fell, the roots rising out of the mud and lashing the air like enormous tails. Peering through the bracken, Lionblaze spotted Tigerpaw scrambling through the branches and taking refuge underneath one of the trunks. He could see Blackfoot, clawing vainly at a mesh of twigs; for a moment he was worried that Littlecloud was hurt, but then he heard the medicine cat's voice.

"Blackfoot? Are you okay?"

"No, I feel as if my pelt's torn off," the ShadowClan leader growled. "What happened? Where's Tigerpaw?"

"I can't see him. Tigerpaw!"

Jaypaw hauled himself out of the mud and balanced among the roots of the nearest tree, out of sight of the trapped cats. "Tigerpaw has vanished . . ." he whispered, loud enough for the ShadowClan cats to hear.

"What? Who's that?" Blackfoot demanded.

"I am one of the spirits you have denied. More cats than Tigerpaw will be lost if you go on rejecting your warrior ancestors." Jaypaw's whisper became more intense. "The forest will fall. . . ."

"What do you mean?" Lionblaze could just make out Blackfoot's face, his lips drawn back in a snarl, and Littlecloud peering out of the branches beside him. The medicine cat's eyes were wide with awe.

"A StarClan warrior is speaking to us!" he meowed.

Toadfoot started struggling again; Lionblaze crouched down on top of him while Flamepaw lay across his neck and shoulders, keeping a paw over his jaws. Keeping the writhing cat pinned down, Lionblaze peered out from hiding.

Blackfoot was clawing furiously at the branches. "Superstitious nonsense!" he spat, though Lionblaze thought there was uncertainty in his voice.

"We must listen," Littlecloud insisted. "StarClan has a message for us. What if they've taken Tigerpaw and we never see him again?"

Blackfoot let out a snort of contempt. "If that's a StarClan warrior, let it show itself."

Lionblaze's belly churned. Jaypaw wasn't a warrior with stars in his fur, just an undersized tabby apprentice, covered with mud. If Blackfoot wouldn't believe him without seeing him, their plan would fail.

"The forest will fall . . ." Jaypaw repeated. Lionblaze could just see him, crouched among the roots, his muscles tensed and his claws digging into the bark. "The trees will die. Your warriors will be scattered, and when they die they will never find a place among the stars."

It's not working, Lionblaze thought hopelessly. Blackfoot still wasn't listening, just making more and more frenzied efforts to claw his way into the open. "Show yourself!" he snarled.

"The forest will fall. . . ." Jaypaw's voice had an echoing quality, as if another voice had joined it. "The forest will fall. . . ." Now there was a third, all the voices twining together.

Lionblaze thought he saw a shimmer on the surface of the marsh. He blinked; then every hair on his pelt stood on end. Two cats balanced on the surface of the mud: one a big tabby with a torn ear, the other a small gray-and-white tom. Frost sparkled at their paws and starlight was reflected in their eyes.

"Raggedstar! Runningnose!" Littlecloud exclaimed from among the uprooted trees.

Blackfoot stopped his frantic clawing and stared, his mouth dropping open.

"Sol's time in ShadowClan must come to an end," Raggedstar meowed, his gaze locked with Blackfoot's. "He is like the darkness that covered the sun."

"He seems to have taken over your Clan," Runningnose put in, "but he will pass and be forgotten in the brightness that follows. Brightness that will shine on ShadowClan for countless moons."

"I . . . I hear you," Blackfoot stammered. "I'll do as you say."

Littlecloud dipped his head as respectfully as he could with twigs clutching at his pelt. "ShadowClan will return to our warrior ancestors," he promised, and added, "What have you done with our apprentice?"

"He is safe," Raggedstar replied.

The gaze of the StarClan warriors swept around to rest on Hollyleaf, Jaypaw, and finally Lionblaze, who forced himself not to flinch. Would these starry cats be angry at what he and his littermates had done?

The StarClan cats did not speak, just bent their heads in a dignified nod. Their glimmering forms began to fade until they were no more than wisps of starlight above the marsh. Then they were gone. Lionblaze let out a breath he hadn't realized he was holding.

Blackfoot broke through the branches that held him without much trouble; Littlecloud followed him through the gap he had made, and both cats scrambled onto dry ground at the edge of the marsh. Their pelts were clumped with mud and bits of twigs and debris, and blood was trickling from one of Blackfoot's ears.

"StarClan hasn't abandoned us!" Littlecloud's voice was shaken, but ecstatic.

Blackfoot shook his head. "They spoke to us," he murmured. "You were right, Littlecloud. We can't ignore the spirits of our warrior ancestors. Not when they're still watching over us."

"What will you do now?" Littlecloud asked.

"Get rid of Sol, to begin with." Blackfoot flexed his claws until the tips disappeared into the wet ground. "I can't believe I let myself listen to that mange-ridden trickster. He told me StarClan didn't care what happened to us! But they brought us here, made the trees fall so that we had to hear them. I'll make sure that no ShadowClan cat is led astray by Sol again. You don't think I've left it too long?" he added anxiously.

"I know you haven't," Littlecloud reassured him, touching his leader's shoulder with the tip of his tail. "The warrior code lives within every one of the cats born in ShadowClan. One cat alone cannot quench that flame."

"Then let's go," Blackfoot meowed, turning toward the ShadowClan camp.

Littlecloud hesitated. "Tigerpaw, are you there?"

Lionblaze saw the apprentice clamber out of his hiding place under the trunk and splash his way through the mud to his Clanmates.

"Are you okay?" Littlecloud asked. "Did you see what happened?"

"Yes." Tigerpaw's amber eyes were shining. "I never thought I'd get to see real StarClan warriors!"

Nor did I, Lionblaze thought.

Tigerpaw dipped his head to Blackfoot. "Can we come back now?"

Blackfoot nodded. "Of course. ShadowClan needs you."

Tigerpaw straightened proudly. "Then I'll go and find Flamepaw and Dawnpaw."

"Get back to camp as soon as you can," Blackfoot ordered. Waving his tail to Littlecloud, he added, "Let's go. I can't wait to tell our Clan they can look to their warrior ancestors again."

"I know they'll all be glad to hear it, Blackfoot," Littlecloud meowed.

The white cat drew himself to his full height, his muscles rippling beneath his ruffled pelt. "Black*star*," he corrected. "My name is Blackstar."

Raising his tail, the ShadowClan leader stalked off into the forest, with his medicine cat padding behind him.

From the moment when the StarClan warriors started to speak, Toadfoot had lain still as a stone under Lionblaze's paws. When Lionblaze and Flamepaw let him get up, he sat staring at the marsh as if he couldn't believe what had happened. "Were those really cats from StarClan?" he whispered.

"Yes, they were," Flamepaw replied solemnly. "Our warrior ancestors are still watching over us. They want the warrior code to be preserved."

Toadfoot blinked, still stunned.

"What are you going to do now?" Lionblaze asked him. If Blackstar knew what they had done, would he still want his Clan to look to their warrior ancestors?

Toadfoot's glance flicked from Lionblaze to Flamepaw

and back again, a low growl beginning to build in his throat. "You *faked* that sign!"

"Only to start with." Flamepaw faced his Clanmate. "We made the trees fall and brought Blackstar here. But we didn't make the StarClan cats appear. They came of their own accord, and that made it a real sign after all."

Toadfoot shook bits of bracken off his dark brown pelt, his eyes still indecisive. "You're lucky they did come," he muttered. "Otherwise ShadowClan would have torn ThunderClan apart for interfering and *lying*."

"You could try," Lionblaze meowed, his fur bristling.

"But StarClan really did come," Flamepaw persisted. "They proved that they are still watching over us, that we should still listen to them and live by the warrior code. They have the Clan's best interests at heart; we have to believe what they say for our own sake."

"Isn't that what you *want*?" Lionblaze demanded.

Toadfoot paused, then nodded. "I suppose I should thank you," he meowed grudgingly.

"No," Lionblaze replied, "it's StarClan you should thank."

Hollyleaf padded up, mud dripping from her pelt, and gave Toadfoot a disapproving sniff. "What are we going to do about him?" she asked Lionblaze.

It was Toadfoot who answered. "I promise I won't tell any cat what I saw."

Hollyleaf's ears flicked up. "Can we trust him?"

"It's trust him or kill him." Jaypaw joined them and sat down with a gusty sigh. "I don't know about you, but I didn't go through all this to start killing ShadowClan cats."

"Then we have to trust you." Lionblaze turned to Toadfoot. "Swear by StarClan that you'll keep the secret."

"Of course I will, mouse-brain." Toadfoot lashed his tail. "I swear it. Unless keeping your secret will harm my Clan," he added instantly.

"Which it won't." Lionblaze gave Toadfoot a brusque nod. "You can go."

Toadfoot turned and stalked away, with a last fearful glance at the marsh where the two StarClan warriors had appeared.

"Come on." Tigerpaw waved his tail at his two littermates. "We've got to get back, too."

The apprentices dipped their heads to the ThunderClan cats.

"We'll never be able to thank you enough," Flamepaw mewed.

"We did this for ThunderClan, too. And we couldn't have done it without you," Lionblaze replied.

"What are we going to do about our mother?" Dawnpaw asked her brother and sister.

Tigerpaw and Flamepaw looked blankly at each other.

"Don't worry about that now," Lionblaze assured them. "We'll tell Tawnypelt what happened. You need to get back to your camp right away, and we need to get off your territory."

"Yeah." Tigerpaw's eyes gleamed. "Don't you dare cross our borders once we renew the scent marks!"

The apprentices bounded off through the trees. Lionblaze watched them until they were out of sight, then headed back toward his own territory with Hollyleaf and Jaypaw at his side.

"I can't believe our fake sign turned into a real message from StarClan!" Hollyleaf exclaimed. "Jaypaw, do you think that StarClan needed us to set the trap before they could appear?"

Jaypaw shrugged. "I don't know, but I doubt it."

"I think they wanted the apprentices to show them how desperate they were to save their Clan," Lionblaze suggested. "Tigerpaw and the others wouldn't have gone through all that if they didn't want to bring ShadowClan back to StarClan and the warrior code."

"We were desperate, too." Hollyleaf lashed her tail. "Nothing matters more than preserving the warrior code."

"And what in the name of StarClan are we going to tell Tawnypelt?" Jaypaw asked. "The truth would be a really bad idea—I can feel it in my pelt."

"I don't know." Hollyleaf sounded worried. "I don't want Firestar to know what we did, either. He would put me and Lionblaze back on apprentice duties before you could say 'mouse.'"

Lionblaze drew ahead a few paw steps, his mind drifting from the conversation behind him. His paws were itching to know what Sol would do after Blackstar told him to leave ShadowClan.

Will he keep his promise? he wondered. *Will he come to mentor the three of us to our true destiny?*

CHAPTER 10

Hollyleaf leaped, sinking her claws into the vole and dispatching it with a quick nip to the neck. Straightening up with her prey in her jaws, she spotted Lionblaze approaching through the bracken, dragging the limp body of a rabbit.

"Hey, great catch!" she mumbled around the vole.

Twilight had fallen, and deep shadows lay on the forest floor. Hollyleaf and Lionblaze had stopped near the dead tree to hunt on their way back to camp, while Jaypaw looked for fresh herbs.

"Let's get back," he meowed, padding up with a bunch of tansy. "I'm worried about the sick cats. Leafpool can't do everything, and if I'm any later she'll have my pelt for bedding."

"Okay." Hollyleaf retrieved the mouse she had killed earlier and led the way back to camp, carrying her prey.

Every hair on her pelt was tingling with relief that they had been able to save ShadowClan. Only one problem remained: What were they going to tell Tawnypelt?

Lionblaze pushed through the thorn tunnel ahead of her, the hind legs of his rabbit leaving faint scars in the dust. As she emerged into the camp, Hollyleaf could see that the clearing was almost empty. Many cats would already be in their dens. She spotted Sandstorm and Squirrelflight sharing a thrush beside the fresh-kill pile, while Poppyfrost was padding toward the dirtplace tunnel.

"Hey, Poppyfrost!" Lionblaze bounded forward, letting his rabbit fall. "Have you seen Tawnypelt?"

Poppyfrost nodded. "She's in Firestar's den with Brambleclaw."

"Hang on," Hollyleaf meowed to her brother as he padded back to her. "We haven't decided what to tell her yet."

"We can't talk now," Jaypaw stated. "I have to check in with Leafpool. I'll find you later." Without waiting for a reply he bounded over to the medicine cats' den and disappeared behind the brambles.

Lionblaze yawned and arched his back in a long stretch. "I'm worn out. Let's drop off this prey and go to our den for a rest. We don't need to worry about Tawnypelt right now; she's busy."

"Okay."

The two young warriors picked up their prey and carried it over to the fresh-kill pile.

"You've been hunting," Squirrelflight mewed approvingly. "Well done."

"How did you get that mud all over you?" Sandstorm narrowed her eyes suspiciously. "Were you hunting for frogs?"

"It's just a bit wet out there," Lionblaze mumbled, not looking at the older she-cat.

Amusement glimmered in Sandstorm's green eyes; she opened her mouth to reply, only to be distracted by the sound of cats pushing their way through the barrier. Birchfall emerged; Hollyleaf's fur tingled with surprise when she saw that Littlecloud was following him, with Whitewing and Icepaw bringing up the rear.

Sandstorm leaped to her paws. "What's this?" She bounded across the clearing to confront the ShadowClan medicine cat.

Squirrelflight rose more slowly. "I'd better let Firestar know," she murmured, and headed for the tumbled rocks that led to the Highledge.

Hollyleaf and Lionblaze followed Sandstorm across the clearing. More cats were appearing from the warriors' den, Cloudtail loudly proclaiming that he would know ShadowClan scent anywhere. He and Brightheart joined the group around Littlecloud, followed by Berrynose, Hazeltail, and Mousewhisker. Mousefur poked her head out of the elders' den but stayed where she was, her whiskers twitching in disapproval.

"What's *another* ShadowClan cat doing in *our* camp?" Berrynose demanded.

No cat answered him, though his littermate Hazeltail gave him a sharp nudge with her shoulder, nearly knocking him off his paws.

"Greetings." Sandstorm gave Littlecloud a curt nod. "Birchfall, what's going on here?"

Hollyleaf thought that Birchfall seemed embarrassed. "We were patrolling the ShadowClan border," he began.

"*I* spotted Littlecloud," Icepaw broke in. "Birchfall and Whitewing were too busy gossiping."

"That's enough." Whitewing scolded her apprentice; she looked flustered. "Littlecloud says he needs to talk to Tawnypelt."

Littlecloud dipped his head respectfully to Sandstorm. "With Firestar's permission. Things have happened in ShadowClan that she needs to know."

Before Sandstorm could reply, Hollyleaf saw Firestar, Brambleclaw, and Tawnypelt appearing on the Highledge, with Squirrelflight just behind. Sandstorm waved her tail, inviting Littlecloud to follow her; she led him across the clearing to stand at the foot of the stones. Hollyleaf and Lionblaze padded after them with the rest of the ThunderClan cats; more were emerging from their dens and gathering around to listen. Rosekit and Toadkit frisked across the clearing from the nursery, their ears pricked curiously, while Daisy followed more slowly.

"Greetings, Littlecloud," Firestar meowed. "Welcome to our camp. How can we help you?"

"Thank you, Firestar," the medicine cat replied. "It's Tawnypelt I need to speak to."

The tortoiseshell warrior's ears flicked up in surprise. "I've nothing to say to ShadowClan anymore." There was the hint of a snarl in her voice. "They are not my Clan."

"I'm sorry you feel like that." Littlecloud blinked sympathetically. "But I think you might change your mind when you hear what I've come to tell you."

"Go on, then." Tawnypelt still sounded hostile.

"Blackstar wants you to come back," the medicine cat went on. "Your three kits have already returned—"

"What!" Tawnypelt's jaws gaped wide in shock. Hollyleaf could see she wanted to spill out a whole cascade of questions, but her gaze flickered around the listening ThunderClan cats, and she clamped her jaws shut again.

"Blackstar wants me to tell you that no cat will blame you for leaving." Littlecloud gazed up at his Clanmate. "ShadowClan is returning to the warrior code, and to their faith in their warrior ancestors."

Tawnypelt drew in a long breath. "If that's true . . . what about Sol?"

"Sol has decided to leave ShadowClan," Littlecloud replied.

"Decided?" Lionblaze whispered into Hollyleaf's ear. "Look out for flying hedgehogs."

"His place is not with us," Littlecloud continued. "Blackstar bears him no ill will, but he is not a Clan cat."

"This is good news," Brambleclaw meowed to his sister. "I'd welcome you as my Clanmate again, but I know you'll always be a loyal ShadowClan cat in your heart."

Tawnypelt touched her nose to Brambleclaw's ear, then nodded. "Okay, Littlecloud. I'll come. But you'd better be telling me the truth."

"A medicine cat doesn't lie," Littlecloud replied.

Tawnypelt turned to Firestar. "Thank you for everything, Firestar."

"I'm just glad it's ended so well," Firestar meowed. "Goodbye, and good luck."

The tortoiseshell warrior pressed her pelt against Brambleclaw's, then leaped down the rocks to join Littlecloud. Together the two ShadowClan cats padded across the clearing and disappeared into the thorn barrier.

"I never thought that would happen!" Cloudtail burst out as soon as they were gone. "Do you think Blackstar really changed his mind just like that?"

Hollyleaf deliberately didn't look at her brother.

"I'd bet a month of dawn patrols those apprentices had something to do with it," Birchfall meowed. "Why else would they disappear back to ShadowClan without their mother?"

Dustpelt let out a snort of amusement. "I can just picture those three holding Blackstar down until he agreed."

"Maybe losing them made Blackstar realize what he was doing to his Clan," Hollyleaf suggested carefully.

Hazeltail nodded. "You could be right."

"Well, whatever changed Blackstar's mind, it's a good thing for the rest of the Clans," Sandstorm mewed. "No cat wants a Clan on their borders that doesn't follow the warrior code."

"True," Ferncloud purred, brushing against the ginger she-cat's side. "There should always be four Clans around the lake, all following the warrior code."

"I just hope Tawnypelt won't tell Blackstar too much about our camp," Daisy murmured, with an anxious look at her kits.

Hollyleaf began to bristle at the suggestion that her kin

would betray the Clan who had helped her, especially when it was her brother's Clan. Before she could speak, Sandstorm touched her nose to Daisy's ear. "I'm sure you don't need to worry. Tawnypelt would never do that."

"And what about Sol, that's what I'd like to know." Mousefur stalked up to join the group of cats. "Where will he go now?"

"Who cares?" Berrynose mewed.

"Because he might start causing more trouble, mousebrain," Dustpelt pointed out. "I just hope he'll leave the Clans alone now."

"He'd better." Hollyleaf clawed fiercely at the ground. Even the thought of Sol made her pelt bristle. "He has no place here if he tries to destroy the warrior code."

Lionblaze opened his jaws as if he was about to protest, then closed them again. Hollyleaf didn't like the doubtful look in his eyes. Surely he wasn't going to defend Sol, after what the loner had done to ShadowClan?

Hollyleaf jerked her head to draw her brother away from the excited cats. "You don't still believe in that crow-food-eating menace, do you?" she hissed.

Lionblaze shrugged. "He's not as bad as all that. I was hoping he'd come back to mentor us."

Hollyleaf stared at him in disbelief. "Why should he help us? Why do you even want him to? Look at what he did to ShadowClan. He persuaded them to give up the warrior code!"

"But our destiny has nothing to do with the warrior code,"

Lionblaze argued with a glance over his shoulder to make sure no cat was listening.

Hollyleaf snorted. "Sol is a dangerous cat. If he turns up again, you should stay away from him. Our destiny will come, whatever we do or don't do. Isn't that the point of a prophecy?"

Lionblaze looked away. He didn't protest anymore, but as Hollyleaf padded over to the warriors' den, she wasn't sure she'd managed to convince him.

Hollyleaf stood on a steep bank overlooking the lake, and tasted the air for signs of prey. Behind her, Dustpelt and Sorreltail, the other members of the hunting patrol, were stalking through the undergrowth. A cool breeze was blowing the leaves from the trees; they whirled past Hollyleaf, fluttering scraps of scarlet and gold. Though the sun was up, the ground underpaw still crackled with frost.

Hollyleaf's ears flicked up as she caught a trace of vole on the wind. Heartbeats later she spotted a good plump one, under a root halfway down the slope that led to the lake. She dropped into the hunter's crouch and glided toward it, trying to keep her paw steps as light as a falling leaf.

She was sure that she hadn't made a sound, but before she had covered half the distance, something spooked the vole and it scurried down the bank toward the lake. *Mouse dung!* Hollyleaf sprang after it, but when she reached the pebbly shore her prey had vanished.

Furious, she began sniffing at the holes in the bank; there

was a strong scent of vole, but no way of getting at it.

"Hello, Hollyleaf."

Hollyleaf froze at the sound of the quiet voice. She spun around to see Sol sitting on the pebbles with his tail wrapped neatly over his paws. His white pelt with its black, brown, and ginger patches was sleek and well groomed, and his pale yellow eyes gleamed.

"What are you doing here?" Hollyleaf demanded. She could feel every hair on her pelt bristling, her tail fluffing out to twice its size, and her belly churning with her distrust of this powerful cat. "I thought you'd gone."

Fury flashed in the loner's eyes, and his claws dug into the ground. Yet a heartbeat later he was cool and controlled again, so that Hollyleaf almost believed she had imagined the anger he had betrayed.

"I left ShadowClan, but I cannot leave the lake yet," Sol meowed calmly. Hollyleaf had never met a cat, not even Firestar, who sounded so sure of himself. "The Clans need me. They just haven't realized it yet. You need me, Hollyleaf."

Hollyleaf swallowed, realizing that she was in danger of falling under the power of Sol's voice once again. "You're wrong," she insisted. "I don't need you, and neither do Lionblaze and Jaypaw."

"Are you sure of that?" Sol's amber gaze was fixed on her; for a heartbeat Hollyleaf felt like a piece of cowering prey, transfixed under a warrior's claws.

"Quite sure." She forced herself to sound certain. "We'll achieve our destiny without your help, because the warrior code will set our paws in the right direction."

She braced herself for Sol to argue, but the loner only dipped his head a little, acknowledging what she said. He rose to his paws and turned away without another word.

Hollyleaf stood watching him, determined to make sure that he left ThunderClan territory. Before he had gone more than a couple of tail-lengths, Sol glanced back over one shoulder.

"Are you sure you have found the three?"

"What do you mean?" Hollyleaf took a pace toward him, her vision blurring with anger. "Lionblaze, Jaypaw, and I are the three. We're kin of Firestar's kin, and there are three of us. And Jaypaw knows things that no other cat does."

"But Jaypaw didn't know about the vanishing sun." Sol's voice echoed around Hollyleaf, but when she focused her gaze again he was already far away, padding along the shore of the lake in the direction of WindClan territory.

"Good riddance," she whispered, but her pelt still quivered and in her heart she knew that she had not seen the last of Sol.

Hollyleaf managed to track down another vole and carried it back to where the hunting patrol was gathering, ready to return to camp. She was determined not to say anything about meeting Sol, and she hoped no other cat had seen him; the sooner her Clanmates forgot about him, the better.

Dustpelt, who was leading the patrol, was scraping the earth off their cache of fresh-kill when Hollyleaf padded up.

"The Clan will eat well today," he meowed. "Let's go."

There was a rasp in his voice, and he ended with a cough. Hollyleaf gazed at him in dismay. There was a feverish glitter in the tabby warrior's eyes; it sounded as though he had been coughing for some time.

"You should see Leafpool as soon as you get back," Sorreltail told him.

"I'm fine," Dustpelt retorted, with another painful cough.

"You are not fine, and you *will* see Leafpool," Sorreltail flashed back at him. Dustpelt had been her mentor for a while, when Sandstorm was away journeying with Firestar; Hollyleaf knew she wasn't as apprehensive of the short-tempered warrior as many of the other ThunderClan cats.

"All right, no need to be so bossy," Dustpelt grumbled, grabbing up a squirrel and stalking through the undergrowth toward the camp.

Hollyleaf exchanged an anxious glance with Sorreltail as the two she-cats followed.

Back in the stone hollow, she dropped her prey on the fresh-kill pile and bounded across to Leafpool's den to tell her about Dustpelt. She wouldn't put it past the tabby warrior to conveniently forget that he should visit the medicine cat.

"Don't come in!" Leafpool's voice came urgently from behind the brambles. A moment later she appeared, the scent of herbs clinging to her pelt. "Oh, it's you, Hollyleaf. What can I do for you?"

"Nothing for me," Hollyleaf replied, worried to see how tired the medicine cat was looking. "But I was out hunting with Dustpelt, and I heard him coughing. I thought you should know."

"Oh, no—not another cat!" Leafpool's eyes stretched wide with anxiety. "Longtail started coughing last night, and Daisy and Honeyfern this morning, and Rosekit is feverish."

Fear gripped deep in Hollyleaf's belly, not just because of the bad news, but because she had never seen Leafpool this distraught. "Are we all going to get sick, one by one?"

"I don't know." Leafpool shook her head. "I'm doing all I can, but what if it isn't enough?"

Hollyleaf couldn't remember ever seeing Leafpool so full of doubt, so frightened for her Clanmates. She pressed her muzzle into the fur on the medicine cat's shoulder. "You're a great medicine cat, Leafpool. I know every cat will be fine with you to take care of them."

"It means a lot to me, hearing you say that." Leafpool's amber gaze was fixed on Hollyleaf. "I just wish it was true." She straightened up and gave her pelt a little shake. "Go and get something to eat. You need to keep your strength up, or you'll get sick, too."

Hollyleaf dipped her head. "Okay."

As she returned to the fresh-kill pile, she felt confidence gradually filling her up like rain in an upturned leaf. Sol had gone; she had watched him leave, and she had made it clear that he wouldn't be welcome in ThunderClan. ShadowClan was keeping the warrior code once more, and looking for guidance from the spirits of their warrior ancestors. As for the sickness—it was bad, but Leafpool would cure it.

Crouching down to take the first bite of her vole, Hollyleaf felt some of her old excitement about the prophecy coming back.

I'm ready, StarClan! Just tell me what I have to do!

Chapter 11

Jaypaw let out a sneeze as dust from the dried herbs got up his nose. Squeezing himself even farther into the storage cleft in the medicine cats' den, he stretched out a paw and scrabbled at a few brittle stems that lay right at the back. The faint scent that lingered told him they were coltsfoot, collected the previous newleaf.

"Jaypaw!"

The apprentice started at the sound of Leafpool's voice and bumped his head on the roof of the cleft. "Mouse dung!" he muttered, wriggling out backward with the dried coltsfoot leaves in his claws.

"What have you managed to find?" Leafpool asked.

"Coltsfoot, and a few juniper berries," Jaypaw reported, dropping the stems at Leafpool's paws.

"So little . . ." Leafpool murmured.

Jaypaw could hear her sorting through the pitiful collection. "Better than nothing," he mewed, trying to sound optimistic.

"But it's not enough. Jaypaw, we're losing the battle."

Every hair on Jaypaw's pelt prickled and he dug his claws into the packed earthen floor. "We can't be!"

"We are." Leafpool let out a despairing sigh. "There isn't enough room to separate the sick cats from the rest of the Clan, and we can't treat greencough without catmint."

"I've been looking after the catmint plants at the old Twoleg nest," Jaypaw meowed. "Shall I go and see if there are any new shoots?"

"No, there can't possibly be enough." Jaypaw felt his mentor's hopelessness as if it were his own. "Besides, we need to let that supply grow for next season."

"Then what are we going to do?"

"I don't know. Things will only get worse as the weather gets colder. Cats will get weaker as prey runs short. And if more cats get sick, there won't be enough warriors left to hunt for the Clan."

Jaypaw lifted his chin. "Then we need to find more catmint."

"There is no more," Leafpool insisted. "I know of one patch, just outside the RiverClan border, by a Twoleg nest, but I can't leave the Clan long enough to fetch it, and—"

She broke off, but Jaypaw knew well enough what she had meant to say. *You can't go because you're blind.* He sensed Leafpool watching him in despair, and felt the strength of her desire that he could see. Briefly he struggled with a surge of bitterness. *Because then I'd be more useful, right?*

"No, Jaypaw." Leafpool answered his unspoken resentment. "It's not because you're blind that you can't go. If that was the problem, I could send you with a warrior."

"Then why don't you?"

Leafpool sighed. "Because you would need to cross ShadowClan territory, and go along the RiverClan border to get to the place. There has been too much fighting recently. We can't risk you and a warrior when so many cats are sick. What if another Clan attacked us? We need all the paws we've got, here in our own territory."

"Then what about asking the other medicine cats?" Jaypaw suggested. "If they've got catmint, they'd give us some."

"Yes, they would." Leafpool's voice grew sharper, as if she was annoyed by his insistence. "But I can't ask without the other Clans finding out how weak we are. Firestar would have my pelt if he found out I'd done that."

Reluctantly Jaypaw had to admit she was right. "So what can I do to help?" he asked.

"I've sent Millie and Briarkit out for some fresh air and sun." Leafpool sounded relieved to turn to something more practical. "They're in that space between here and the warriors' den. It's sheltered there, and they should be far enough away from the other cats to stop the cough from spreading. Could you take out their old bedding, and bring in some fresh?"

"Sure." Jaypaw padded to the side of the den and started scraping up the used moss and bracken, collecting it into a ball.

"Make sure you take it a long way from camp," Leafpool reminded him. "And when you've finished, you can fetch Millie and Briarkit back in, before they get too tired and cold."

Jaypaw rolled the ball of soiled bedding out through the

thorn barrier, and dumped it several fox-lengths away from the hollow. Nearby he found more moss growing thickly around the roots of a tree. To his relief, it had dried out since the heavy rain of a few days before. Tearing off some fronds of bracken, he bundled the whole lot together and staggered with it back into camp.

When he went to fetch the sick cats, he found Millie lying stretched out in a sunny spot beside the wall of the stone hollow. Her breath rasped in her throat and when he rested a paw on her chest, Jaypaw could feel it heaving rapidly up and down. Briarkit pushed up beside him, nudging at her mother. "I want to play," she whimpered. She had to catch her breath as she spoke, and Jaypaw could feel her legs wobbling. "Be a mouse, and I'll catch you!"

Millie let out a weary sigh, and Briarkit's pleading ended in a cough.

"Come on," Jaypaw meowed, trying to sound cheerful. "I've put down some fresh bedding for you. You'll be able to have a really good sleep."

"Don't want to sleep!" Briarkit protested.

"Yes, you do," Jaypaw informed her. "Sleeping will make you feel better."

He slipped his shoulder under Millie's as she struggled to her paws; her chest wheezed with the effort and her coughs were weak, as if her strength was ebbing fast. Jaypaw's belly twisted with frustration. The prophecy said he had the power of the stars in his paws, but what good was that if he had to witness the cats in his care die?

He helped Millie back into her nest, with Briarkit getting under his paws until he shooed her into the moss beside her mother. He straightened up and headed back to the cleft, wondering if he could have possibly missed any stores of herbs.

Suddenly his eyes filled with dazzling sunlight, so bright that he flinched and bent his head, trying to shut out the rays. When his vision cleared, he looked up again, blinking. He was standing in a glade, thick with rustling leaves. The warm air was heavy with the scent of growing herbs.

Is there catmint here? That was the first thought that jumped into his head.

As he tasted the air, the smell of cats flooded over him, drowning the scents of the herbs. Starlight glimmered in the undergrowth under the trees, and warriors of StarClan began to emerge into the clearing. Jaypaw recognized Bluestar, her tail twitching with anxiety; she glanced back at the muscular figure of Whitestorm, who followed her into the open.

"They are coming," the old ThunderClan leader whispered. "So many of them . . ."

"Maybe not," Whitestorm meowed reassuringly. "ThunderClan couldn't have better medicine cats."

Jaypaw heard a disgusted snort as yet another starry cat pushed her way through the ferns: Yellowfang with her ragged gray pelt and burning amber eyes. "Are you mouse-brained, Whitestorm? What can medicine cats do if there aren't any healing herbs?"

"Is there no way we can guide them?" A soft mew announced the arrival of Spottedleaf, her tail waving gracefully as she padded out into the open. "No way to help?"

"You tell me," Yellowfang snapped. "There's no more catmint on ThunderClan territory, and that's that. I'd give them my pelt if I could, but what use would that be?"

"Will sickness destroy my Clan?" Bluestar wailed, her claws working furiously, tearing up clumps of grass.

One last cat slipped into the clearing: the silver tabby whom Jaypaw had seen in Graystripe's memory, her lifeblood gushing out onto stones as she gave birth to a pair of tiny kits.

"Millie is close to joining us," she murmured. "What can we do? Graystripe doesn't deserve to have his heart broken again."

None of the other StarClan cats could answer her. They began to circle distractedly, their pelts quivering with distress. None of them seemed to have noticed Jaypaw.

Why am I here? he wondered. *If there's nothing useful in this vision, I've got sick cats to look after.*

A cool breeze swept over the clearing, ruffling the moon-colored fur of the restless cats. Starlight gleamed again in the shadows under the trees, and three more cats padded into the open. The first was a young she-cat—barely old enough to be a warrior—her silver tabby pelt glimmering with a pale light.

The second cat was older, a silver tabby so like the first that Jaypaw guessed she was her mother, while the third was a broad-shouldered tabby tom.

"Brightspirit." Bluestar dipped her head respectfully to the young she-cat. "It has been a long time."

"Shiningheart. Braveheart," Whitestorm greeted the two

older cats. "Your presence honors us."

Jaypaw stared at the three newcomers. Where had these cats come from? He had never seen them before, or heard their names in any of the Clans. Their scent was different too—faintly of StarClan, and of something else carried on wind and in starlight. He sensed that they had traveled a long distance. *Is this why I'm here? To meet these cats?*

The two older cats remained at the edge of the trees, their tails twined together, but Brightspirit bounded across the clearing and halted in front of Jaypaw. Her green eyes glowed with love and sympathy and her sweet scent wreathed around him.

"Greetings, Jaypaw," she mewed. "You are troubled."

Jaypaw crouched to the ground. This was no ordinary StarClan cat; he couldn't imagine telling this cat she was merely a Clan cat in a different place. Something about her, the way she tipped her head to one side and studied him as if they were the only cats in the clearing, made him spill out the truth. "ThunderClan cats are dying. I don't know what to do."

Brightspirit stretched out her neck and rested her muzzle against her ear, warming him with her breath.

"Seek for the wind," she whispered. "The wind holds what you seek."

Jaypaw took a step back and stared at her. "What do you mean? I don't understand."

With a hiss, darkness slammed down over his eyes as if night had suddenly fallen, and he found himself surrounded by the scents of stale herbs and sick cats once more. He bit back a yowl of frustration.

She was going to tell me something!

For a few heartbeats he could still make out Brightspirit's scent, and a distant echo of her voice. "Seek for the wind. And may StarClan light your path." Then she was gone.

"Come on, Millie." Leafpool's voice sounded close by him. "Lie down here. Jaypaw fetched fresh bedding for you."

"Thanks, Jaypaw," Millie rasped.

Jaypaw tensed. Had the whole of his vision taken only a couple of heartbeats? He helped Leafpool settle Millie and Briarkit, longing all the while for a bit of peace so that he could think about Brightspirit and her mysterious words.

As the sick cats curled up in their nest, Jaypaw heard the sound of racing footsteps drawing closer. *What now?* He picked up Sandstorm's scent as she halted by the bramble screen.

"Leafpool, come quickly!" she gasped. "Firestar's ill!"

Chapter 12

Leafpool let out a yelp of horror. "I'm coming!" She slipped past Jaypaw and raced after Sandstorm.

Jaypaw snatched up a couple of the coltsfoot stalks and dashed after her, scrambling up the rocks leading to Firestar's den without stopping to think about where to put his paws.

When he reached Highledge the smell of sickness struck him like a blow. Inside his den, Firestar was coughing, and as Jaypaw padded up to him he could feel the heat of fever pulsing from his body. Every hair on Jaypaw's pelt stood on end. What would happen to ThunderClan now that their leader was ill?

"Thanks, Jaypaw," Leafpool mewed, taking the coltsfoot from him. "Here, Firestar, eat these."

"I'm not that sick," Firestar protested, his voice already roughened from coughing. "You should keep the herbs for cats who need them."

"Don't be ridiculous!" Leafpool snapped. "*You* need them. I'm your medicine cat now, and don't you forget it."

"You were so quiet when you were a kit." Weary amusement

crept into Firestar's voice. "I never thought you would turn out this bossy."

"Well, I did, so do as you're told." Leafpool sounded full of affection for her father. "Come on—you know the Clan needs you to be strong and fit."

As Firestar chewed up the herbs, Jaypaw slipped out of the den and down into the clearing. Halting at the foot of the rocks, he tasted the air, hoping to find an apprentice to fetch fresh bedding for Firestar. At least the Clan leader could be kept apart in his den, so that he wouldn't pass on the sickness to healthy cats.

But instead of an apprentice's, the first scent Jaypaw picked up was Brambleclaw's.

"What's going on?" the deputy asked.

"You shouldn't go up there." Jaypaw blocked Brambleclaw from climbing the rocks. "Firestar has greencough."

"Oh, great StarClan!" Brambleclaw's voice was shocked. "You are helping him, aren't you?"

"Leafpool's with him," Jaypaw meowed. "She'll do her best."

"I know." His father sounded a little reassured. "Let me pass, Jaypaw. I've got to speak to Firestar about the patrols."

"Okay." Jaypaw moved out of the way. "Stay out on the Highledge, though, and talk to him from there. Don't get too close."

Jaypaw tasted the air again as Brambleclaw's paw steps receded up the rocks, but he still couldn't pick up Foxpaw's or Icepaw's scent. This time, it was Graystripe who padded up to him.

"Jaypaw, how is Millie?" he demanded. "She's really sick, isn't she?"

Jaypaw would have liked to find a comforting lie, but he knew that Graystripe would never believe it. He nodded, and was almost knocked off his paws by the strength of the agony that surged over him from the gray warrior. *Is that love?* he wondered. *Does Graystripe care about Millie that much? It's as if his own life was in danger!*

"The silver cat who died," he mewed. "You loved her, didn't you?"

Graystripe caught his breath, startled. "Y-yes. Her name was Silverstream. She was Stormfur and Feathertail's mother." He fell silent, wreathed in sad memories.

"You couldn't have done anything to save her," Jaypaw told him. "She lives in StarClan, and she's watching over Millie now. She doesn't want Millie to join her in StarClan yet, not when she has your kits to care for."

"You know all this?" Graystripe asked, shocked.

Jaypaw nodded. "I heard her in a vision."

"It's so like Silverstream to care," Graystripe murmured, "but it's not much comfort right now. StarClan can't fight greencough any better than we can here." He sounded defeated, as if he had made up his mind that he was going to lose Millie as he had lost Silverstream.

Anger scorched through Jaypaw like a devouring flame. *Cats won't die! I'll do something!* He wanted to battle the sickness, not only for the dying cats of his own Clan, and for warriors like Graystripe who loved them, but for all the cats of StarClan, who didn't want any more cats in their ranks, not so many and so soon.

And for Brightspirit, he added. *She came to help me. And somehow I'll work out the meaning of what she said.*

Still looking for Foxpaw and Icepaw, Jaypaw padded over to the apprentices' den. Before he reached it, he scented a hunting patrol returning through the thorn tunnel: Brackenfur, Lionblaze, Cloudtail, and Cinderheart. All four of them were carrying prey, but Jaypaw could sense their weariness and discouragement.

It's happening just like Leafpool said, he thought. *So many cats are sick, there aren't enough for all the patrols.*

Jaypaw stuck his head through the bracken that grew against the entrance to the apprentices' den. Little snuffling sounds told him Foxpaw was asleep. His breathing was even; the day before, Leafpool had given him a dose of tansy, and it seemed to have cleared up his cough.

One less cat to worry about.

"Hey!" Jaypaw slipped inside the den and poked Foxpaw with one paw. "Wake up!"

"Wha . . . ?" Foxpaw raised his head.

"I need you to fetch fresh bedding for Firestar."

The ginger apprentice let out a huge noisy yawn. "Can't some other cat do it? I did the dawn patrol, *and* a hunting patrol with Sandstorm. She said I could have a rest."

Jaypaw couldn't help feeling a twinge of sympathy. "Every cat is overworked," he meowed. "Icepaw could help you if you can find her."

"She's out hunting with Whitewing," Foxpaw told him, scrambling to his paws and grunting as he stretched. "Okay, I'm coming."

"Make sure the bedding's dry," Jaypaw instructed as Foxpaw brushed past the ferns into the clearing. "And get rid of the old stuff well away from camp. Firestar's sick."

"Why didn't you say so?" Foxpaw's voice was full of dismay. His paw steps receded, racing toward the tunnel.

Jaypaw padded over to the fresh-kill pile and collected a squirrel for the elders. Before he reached their den under the hazel bush, he could hear Longtail coughing, and a comforting murmur from Mousefur.

"Here you are." Jaypaw dragged the squirrel into the den and dropped it beside Mousefur. "How are you, Longtail?"

"His cough's getting worse," Mousefur snapped. "When are you going to fetch him some catmint?"

When hedgehogs fly. Jaypaw suppressed the sharp comment. "We haven't got any," he told Mousefur. "I'll fetch him some tansy, though, and borage for the fever."

Mousefur snorted. "A poor medicine cat you turned out to be, if you haven't even got catmint."

Once again Jaypaw stopped himself from snapping back at her. He knew that the cranky elder was worried about her denmate. At least the tansy leaves Mousefur had eaten had kept her from getting sick . . . so far.

"Longtail, try to eat some of the fresh-kill," he urged. "You need to keep your strength up."

"Okay," Longtail croaked between bouts of coughing. "Thanks, Jaypaw."

With a nod to Mousefur, Jaypaw left the den and padded back to the fresh-kill pile to fetch prey for the sick cats in the warriors' den. When he pushed his way through the branches, he located Thornclaw and Dustpelt in nests to one side. Ferncloud was curled up close to her mate.

"This is ridiculous," the tabby warrior was mewing. "I'm perfectly able to go out on patrol."

"No, you're not," Ferncloud told him. "You're staying here if I have to hold you down." Jaypaw heard her tongue rasping affectionately over her mate's pelt.

Jaypaw dropped a mouse in front of Dustpelt and another beside Thornclaw. The golden tabby had been ill for longer than any cat except Millie, and his breathing sounded fast and shallow. He lay on one side, and didn't respond when Jaypaw checked him with a paw. His pelt was rough and Jaypaw could feel every one of his ribs. Jaypaw's muscles tensed. Thornclaw could already be on his way to StarClan.

"Is there anything I can do?" Jaypaw felt Ferncloud's breath warm against his ear.

"Not much, but thanks," Jaypaw meowed. "Try to get him to eat that mouse when he wakes."

"I will." Ferncloud touched her nose to Jaypaw's muzzle, then went to curl up again beside Dustpelt.

"Jaypaw." Squirrelflight's voice came from the other side of the den. "I want you to tell Leafpool that I'm fit enough to go hunting." Her paw steps approached; Jaypaw could feel pain and stiffness in every movement.

"So you want me to lie to my mentor?"

"Lie? Nonsense! You can tell her my wound has healed."

Jaypaw sniffed at his mother where claws had slashed down her side in the battle with WindClan and RiverClan. The wound had closed and there was no smell of infection, but her fur had yet to grow back and Jaypaw could tell that her muscles were still stiff.

"You're not ready," he growled. "And Leafpool would tell you the same. I'll ask her to come and check you, and maybe you can start some gentle exercises, but that doesn't include chasing squirrels."

Squirrelflight snorted. "ThunderClan needs every warrior we have right now."

"Yes, we do." Jaypaw's patience with his mother was rapidly running out. "But can't you see you'll make more work for us if you go back on patrol before you're ready?"

Squirrelflight's reply was cut off by the sound of another warrior pushing into the den; Jaypaw picked up Mousewhisker's scent, which had an edge of urgency. "Foxpaw told me that Firestar's ill!" he exclaimed.

There was a stir of movement among the other cats. "StarClan forbid!" Ferncloud wailed. "What will we do if our leader dies? WindClan and RiverClan will attack us again for sure."

"He won't die," Jaypaw insisted, putting all the conviction he could into the words. "And if he does lose a life, he still has plenty more."

"That doesn't mean he can throw them away," Squirrelflight

snapped. "And Brambleclaw will need to do even more patrols. What if our leader *and* our deputy get sick?"

"We're doing everything we can to fight the sickness," Jaypaw meowed. "And Firestar is a strong, fit cat."

"I know, but . . ." Squirrelflight's voice died away. Jaypaw could sense the same anguish coming from her as he had picked up from Graystripe earlier. Without another word she turned away and padded back to her nest.

Worry surged over Jaypaw again as he thrust through the branches of the warriors' den and went to collect fresh-kill for the cats in the nursery. He was afraid Leafpool had been right when she said that they were losing the battle. Without catmint, there was nothing they could do.

I have to find some. Somehow I must work out what Brightspirit was trying to tell me.

By the time Jaypaw had finished reporting to Leafpool and taking what few herbs they had to the sick cats, night was falling. He curled up in his nest in the medicine cats' den, wriggling deep into the moss to block out the sound of Millie and Briarkit snuffling and wheezing close by.

Maybe now I can figure out what I have to do.

Jaypaw remembered his meeting with the beautiful silver tabby, and the warmth in her gaze as she spoke to him. *Seek for the wind.* But there was wind everywhere; you didn't have to look for it. It rustled through the branches of the trees, swept over the lake, flattened the moorland grass on the way to the Moonpool. If only it was as easy to find catmint!

Seek for the wind . . . and you'll find catmint. Was that what Brightspirit meant for him to understand? Excitement tingled through Jaypaw from ears to tail-tip; he flexed his claws, snagging the moss beneath him. Where did the wind blow harder than anywhere else? *Of course! Over WindClan territory!*

There was no catmint on ThunderClan territory; the RiverClan supply was too far away, and the sparse undergrowth under the pines of ShadowClan made it unlikely that there was any there. If there was more catmint around the lake, it must be in WindClan.

Jaypaw wanted to leap out of his nest and go charging through the forest, but he knew that would be totally mouse-brained. He didn't know his way around WindClan territory, and even if he could see, he had no idea where to start looking for the herb.

You're a medicine cat. You have powers. Use them.

Curling into a tight ball, Jaypaw closed his eyes. He had never walked in the dreams of a cat who was so far away, but Kestrelpaw, the WindClan medicine cat apprentice, had always been open and friendly toward him. *Dumb, but friendly . . .* Maybe that would make it easier to step into his dreams.

Jaypaw pictured himself heading out of the camp and through the woods toward WindClan territory. Leaping the stream that marked the border, he swooped across the moorland on featherlight paws, until he reached the top of the hollow where WindClan had their camp. Letting the dream carry him onward, he padded among indistinct shapes of rocks and bushes, focusing on the wide crack in a boulder where Barkface and Kestrelpaw had their den.

Inside the crack, the medicine cat and his apprentice were curled up in nests of moorland grass and feathers that stirred with each breath. Jaypaw's shadowy form curled up beside Kestrelpaw, touching his warm, soft fur. He slowed his breathing to match the other cat's; heartbeats later he felt wind buffeting his fur and found himself in Kestrelpaw's dream.

The young medicine cat was padding over the moor with the scents of grass and sheep all around him. Clouds scudded across a pale blue sky, and dew glittered under the rays of the early morning sun.

"Hi, Jaypaw!" Kestrelpaw sounded surprised but warm. "What are you doing here?"

"I just thought I'd visit you." Jaypaw tensed, wondering if Kestrelpaw would realize how weird that was. If he was too disturbed he might wake, and Jaypaw would be thrown out of the dream and back into his own nest.

"Great." Kestrelpaw flicked his ears in welcome. "Isn't it a beautiful day? I thought I'd come out early and look for a few herbs."

Jaypaw longed to ask Kestrelpaw what kind of herbs he hoped to find, but he was still wary of spooking the other apprentice. Instead, he just followed Kestrelpaw across the moor.

"Does this stream flow down toward ThunderClan?" he asked casually as they leaped across a trickle of brown, peaty water fringed by reeds.

"Yes, it joins the border stream," Kestrelpaw replied.

He's not suspicious at all, Jaypaw thought. *After all, it's just a dream, right?*

"I don't suppose you find much prey up here," he went on, anxious to keep the WindClan cat talking.

"Then you suppose wrong!" Kestrelpaw's tail shot up and he raised his head proudly. "Can't you smell all the rabbits? And sometimes we catch birds; Crowfeather taught us how the Tribe hunts in the mountains."

"I guess you've got to be fast," Jaypaw commented.

Kestrelpaw gave his chest fur a couple of quick licks. "That's what WindClan cats are best at."

"So what about herbs?" Jaypaw went on, his belly churning as he asked the question that really mattered. "It looks pretty bleak up here. Not the right place for growing most kinds of plants."

"Wrong again. We've got good stocks tucked away along the streams, and in that bit of woodland next to the Thunder-Clan border."

"That must be good for water mint," Jaypaw remarked. "What about catmint?"

"Oh, yes, we've got plenty of that." Kestrelpaw pointed with his nose toward a spot where the moor dipped down sharply to a tumble of rocks. "Down there."

"Really?" Jaypaw forced himself to sound mildly interested, when what he really wanted to do was bounce up and down caterwauling in triumph.

"Yes, there's—"

Just in front of the two apprentices, a rabbit started up out of a gorse thicket and streaked away across the moor. Kestrelpaw broke off what he was saying and raced after it, his belly fur brushing the coarse grass.

"Thanks, rabbit," Jaypaw murmured.

He waited until the WindClan apprentice had disappeared, then scrambled down the slope to the rocks. Sniffing the air, he picked up the scent of water and a strong smell of catmint. A few heartbeats later he found it: a spring welling up between two of the rocks, with thick clumps of catmint growing all around it.

For a moment Jaypaw stood still, breathing in the scent of the precious herb. He wished desperately that he could tear off a bundle of the stalks and carry them back to his Clan, but he was still dreaming. Some cat would have to come here in the waking world, and steal some of the herb from WindClan.

It's not really stealing, he told himself. *Not when we need it so badly. And WindClan has plenty.*

Gradually Jaypaw realized that the catmint was not all he could smell. A familiar scent clung around the rocks, the scent of caves and earth and deeply buried water. Scrambling among the stones, he tried to find where the scent was strongest. Finally he found it: a narrow gap between the rocks, leading down into darkness.

This must be an entrance to the underground tunnels! Maybe this is the way WindClan came when they raided our territory.

In the mud in front of the gap he could see the traces of several paw prints. Taking a quick glance around, he padded forward and squeezed himself through the gap. The passage quickly grew wider, and Jaypaw could make out the scent of WindClan cats clinging to the stones.

"Jaypaw! Jaypaw!"

Jaypaw stiffened; had Kestrelpaw spotted him going into the tunnel and become suspicious?

"Jaypaw!" A paw prodded him sharply in the side. "Jaypaw, Millie's fever is worse. Can you fetch her some moss soaked with water?"

Jaypaw opened his eyes on darkness and scrambled out of his nest, shaking himself to dislodge scraps of moss and bracken from his pelt. The chill of early dawn filled the den, together with Leafpool's fear scent; at the other side he could hear Millie's harsh breathing and Briarkit mewling pitifully.

"She's going to die, isn't she?" The little kit sounded terrified. "And I'll never see her again, 'cause I don't know the way to StarClan."

"We're doing all we can." Leafpool moved away, and Jaypaw pictured her bending her head to comfort the frightened kit. "And even if she does die, you'll see her again one day. When she's in StarClan, she'll know the right time to come and fetch you."

"Are you sure?" Briarkit still sounded uncertain.

"I promise you," Leafpool reassured her.

Jaypaw's legs started to shake with fear. Leafpool was acting as if she was resigned to watching every one of her Clanmates die. *We have to get that catmint now!* "I'll fetch the moss," he mewed, and whisked out of the den.

As soon as he had delivered the dripping moss to Millie,

he slipped out again and crept through the branches into the warriors' den. The air was full of the warm scent of sleeping cats; it was so early that hardly any of them were stirring.

Jaypaw located Lionblaze by his scent, and woke him with a sharp prod in the shoulder.

"Uhhh . . . ?" Lionblaze's muscles flexed and he raised his head. "Jaypaw? Is something wrong?"

Jaypaw bent his head to whisper in his brother's ear. "I know where there's a supply of catmint."

"Really?" Jaypaw could sense Lionblaze's excitement. "Where?"

"In WindClan, near the entrance to a tunnel. You have to go and fetch some."

The excitement Jaypaw could feel in Lionblaze changed abruptly to horror and disgust. "No," he mewed hoarsely. "I'll never go to WindClan. Never!"

Chapter 13

Lionblaze felt cool grass brushing his belly fur as he crept forward. The scent of WindClan was in his nostrils. Leaves scraped his pelt and left raindrops on his ears and whiskers, but he was concentrating too hard to flick them away. Every muscle in his body was focused on what he could see in front of him.

Now! Pushing off with his powerful back legs, Lionblaze leaped. The squirrel fled, but it was too late. Lionblaze's claws sank into its shoulders and he killed it with a swift bite to the throat.

As the squirrel went limp, Lionblaze's vision blurred. A lake of scarlet, sticky blood spread out across the grass and leaves of the forest floor; he could taste the stench of it. The squirrel became a gray-furred she-cat. Lionblaze found himself looking down at Heatherpaw's dead body; her blood clogged his paws.

"No . . . oh, no," he whispered.

Ever since Jaypaw had asked him to fetch the catmint from WindClan, two sunrises before, Lionblaze had felt guilty. But he couldn't do it. He was too scared that his dream would come true, and he would end up killing Heatherpaw.

He shuddered, staring at the dreadful vision of the dead cat he had once loved. Yet again, he wished that he could be an ordinary warrior, without the powers that terrified him more and more as they grew stronger.

If only I could tell Jaypaw how I feel . . . But he couldn't show weakness to his brother, not when Jaypaw was depending on him to fulfill his part of the prophecy. He only knew that he couldn't risk going into WindClan territory, especially not through the tunnels. Heatherpaw had betrayed him; Lionblaze desperately wanted to believe her story that it was the kits who had given away the secret of the tunnels, but he couldn't be sure that was true. Heatherpaw was his enemy now, because he was completely committed to ThunderClan. Why should he trust a cat from another Clan? He would never forgive Heatherpaw, but he still didn't want her blood on his paws.

As the vision faded, Lionblaze straightened up with his prey in his jaws. Ashfur was approaching through the bracken from the stream that marked the WindClan border, carrying a couple of voles by their tails. Spiderleg followed him with a mouse.

"Well done." Ashfur nodded at Lionblaze, dropping his prey nearby. "Have you seen Sorreltail? We've caught as much as we can manage."

"Here." Sorreltail staggered through the undergrowth, dragging a rabbit nearly as big as she was. "Whew!" Dropping her prey, she spat out a clump of fur. "Some other cat can carry that back."

As they padded back to the stone hollow, Lionblaze's

worries started to creep back into his mind. So far leaf-fall had been mild and prey was running well, but there weren't enough warriors fit to hunt. When he had left the camp that morning, Brightheart was coughing, and he had spotted Honeyfern heading toward the medicine cats' den. *How long before so many cats are sick that there aren't enough of us left to take care of them?*

The fresh-kill pile was ominously low when Lionblaze dropped his prey on it.

"We'll go out again right away," Ashfur announced, "but we should all eat something first, to keep our strength up."

"I'm fine," Sorreltail meowed. "One of the sick cats can have mine."

Ashfur padded up to her. "You will eat. What good will you be to your Clan if you get sick too?"

Sorreltail stared back at him rebelliously for a heartbeat, then dropped her gaze. "Okay. You're right." But Lionblaze noticed that she chose the smallest mouse from the pile.

As he gulped down a vole, he spotted Jaypaw emerging from the warriors' den. Swallowing the last mouthful, he bounded across to him.

"How's Brightheart?" he asked. "I heard her coughing this morning. And Honeyfern was on her way to your den."

"Like you care!" Jaypaw snapped at him.

"I do!" Guilt and indignation battled inside Lionblaze. *That's not why I won't go to WindClan!*

"They both have greencough," Jaypaw mewed curtly. "Cloudtail, too. I've told them not to leave their nests. *Now* will you go and fetch the catmint?"

"I can't." Lionblaze flinched from the fury in Jaypaw's eyes. He wished that he could explain to Jaypaw about his dreams; then he would understand why it was impossible for him to go to WindClan. "Why can't you send another cat instead?" he asked.

"You know why!" Jaypaw spat, his fur bristling up. "You know what it's like in the tunnels."

"So does Hollyleaf," Lionblaze argued. "She could go—"

"Hollyleaf!" Jaypaw interrupted. "You know what she's like about the warrior code. Do you think she'd agree to trespass on another Clan's territory and steal their herbs? She'd claw our ears off if we even mentioned it. No, it has to be you. Besides, you're the best fighter we've got, and if you get caught you'll need your powers to escape."

"Then why can't Leafpool ask Barkface for some catmint?"

"Stupid furball!" Jaypaw hissed. "Which cats did we just fight? Barkface might give Leafpool catmint, but Onestar would have to know, and if he found out ThunderClan is weak, he'd attack again before you could say 'mouse.'" Lashing his tail, he added, "It's useless talking to you. I never thought my own brother would stand by and let his Clan die." Spinning around, he stalked toward his den.

Lionblaze watched him go, then padded sadly back to the patrol by the fresh-kill pile. Brambleclaw and Squirrelflight had appeared, and Graystripe bounded up to choose a piece of fresh-kill and head for the medicine cats' den.

"Take some for yourself as well," Squirrelflight called after him, but Graystripe gave no sign that he'd heard her.

"Okay, Ashfur," Brambleclaw meowed, "when you take your patrol out again, go along the ShadowClan border. You can combine the border patrol with some hunting. But when you get back, that's it for today. You need to rest."

"Take your own advice, then." Squirrelflight gave her mate a flick on the shoulder with her tail. "You need to rest, too."

"I can't." Lionblaze's heart sank when he saw how bright Brambleclaw's eyes were, and heard the rasp in his voice. "I need to fix up more patrols."

Sorreltail leaned in to Lionblaze and murmured in his ear, "If your father gets ill . . ."

Lionblaze nodded, but didn't reply. There was no need. With Firestar sick, ThunderClan depended on their deputy to protect them.

Oh, StarClan, Lionblaze thought, *why are you letting this happen?*

Gray clouds covered the sky, but the air was still mild; wind rustled through the trees above the hollow, but down below the cats were sheltered. Lionblaze had just returned from a hunting patrol with Brambleclaw, Hollyleaf, and Cinderheart. Brackenfur and Sorreltail were sprawled near the fresh-kill pile, sharing tongues, while Sandstorm crouched beside them, eating a thrush.

As Lionblaze and the others dropped their prey on the pile, Leafpool and Jaypaw appeared to choose fresh-kill for themselves.

"How is Millie?" Sandstorm asked, looking up from her thrush.

"If she doesn't get some catmint soon, she'll die," Leafpool meowed flatly.

Jaypaw shot a furious glare at Lionblaze as he snatched a mouse from the pile; Lionblaze felt it like a claw raking across his pelt. *Stop blaming me! I can't go to WindClan!*

Out of the corner of his eye, he caught the flicker of a flame-colored pelt up on the Highledge. Looking up, he saw that Firestar had appeared. Every hair on his pelt tingled with shock. What was the Clan leader doing out of his nest? He looked unsteady on his paws, and when he opened his jaws to speak all that came out was a cough.

"Firestar!" Sandstorm leaped to her feet. "What do you think you're doing?"

"Go back to your nest right now!" Leafpool sprang up and raced for the rocks, closely followed by Sandstorm.

Firestar stretched out a paw to halt them. "Don't come any closer," he rasped. "The sickness spreads too easily. We have to get the sick cats out of the camp to keep the others healthy."

"But we can't do that," Leafpool objected, halting at the foot of the tumbled rocks. "There's nowhere for them to go."

"Yes, there is," Firestar told her, his too-bright eyes shining with triumph. "The old Twoleg nest has walls and a roof to shelter us, and there's a stream nearby where we can drink."

"But I can't be in two places at once," Leafpool pointed out; she sounded anguished, as if she hated to refuse the hope that Firestar offered.

"You won't need to be," Firestar meowed. "I shall look after the sick cats. You can tell me which herbs to use, and keep me supplied without coming too close."

Sandstorm let out a gusty sigh, fluttering her whiskers. "This is ridiculous! You're putting yourself in danger. You need rest just as much as the other sick cats."

Firestar looked down at her, love glowing from his green eyes. "I have lives to lose; my Clanmates do not. I have to do this, for their sake."

Murmurs of surprise came from the cats gathered around the fresh-kill pile. Brambleclaw looked up at his leader, then slowly nodded, as if he was making a promise.

"It might work," Brackenfur remarked.

"I think it's worth a try," Cinderheart agreed. "If we don't do something, every cat will get sick."

The more Lionblaze thought about Firestar's suggestion, the more sense he could see in it. The sick cats would have a safe, dry place to stay, and those who were left could look after them better. Leafpool and Jaypaw would have more chance of keeping well. And maybe Jaypaw's catmint plants at the Twoleg nest would have grown enough to provide some healing leaves.

"There aren't enough yet," Jaypaw growled as if Lionblaze had spoken aloud. "We need more! Half the Clan is sick."

Lionblaze felt as if his littermate's glare was scorching his pelt. Turning away, he padded over to Hollyleaf.

"Isn't Firestar great?" she meowed. "I'm so proud he's our kin. I wonder if I'd have the courage to do what he's doing."

Lionblaze touched his nose to her shoulder. "I'm sure you would." *And what about* my *courage?* he asked himself. *I should be brave enough to fetch the catmint. But I can't do it, I just can't!*

On the Highledge, Firestar straightened up and lifted his head. "Let all cats—" His attempt to raise his voice ended in a bout of coughing.

Brambleclaw bounded up to the Highledge and spoke rapidly to his leader. Lionblaze couldn't hear what they said, and a moment later Firestar staggered back into his den. Brambleclaw looked down at the clearing.

"Let all cats old enough to catch their own prey join here beneath the Highledge for a Clan meeting," he yowled.

Foxpaw and Icepaw appeared from the elders' den, each with a bundle of soiled bedding. Mousefur followed them and stalked across to where Sandstorm and Leafpool stood at the foot of the tumbled rocks.

Ferncloud and Squirrelflight emerged from the warriors' den and padded over to the fresh-kill pile. Berrynose and Graystripe pushed their way out after them, and stayed sitting just outside the den.

Lionblaze's heart sank to see how few cats answered the summons. So many of the Clan were sick, and the rest of them must be out on patrol.

Brambleclaw began by explaining to the cats who hadn't heard Firestar's plan. "We'll need to collect a lot of moss and bracken—and dried leaves and feathers, anything to keep the sick cats comfortable and warm," he continued. "Lionblaze and Hollyleaf, you can do that, and take the apprentices with you."

Lionblaze flicked his tail in acknowledgement of his father's order.

"Brackenfur, you're good at mending den walls," Brambleclaw went on. "Find some warriors to help you, and block the holes in the Twoleg nest so that there aren't any drafts."

"Sure, Brambleclaw," the ginger warrior replied.

"And there'll need to be a new fresh-kill pile. Sandstorm, you're best at hunting; can I put you in charge of that?"

Sandstorm gave him a tense nod, her green eyes narrowed as if she was already planning her hunt.

"Leafpool, you'll need to transport herbs for Firestar to use. Get another warrior to help you if you have to collect more."

"I'll do that," Leafpool replied. "And every cat should keep a lookout for catmint. It's just possible there are a few clumps we've overlooked."

Lionblaze could tell that the medicine cat didn't believe what she was saying, but he knew that they couldn't ignore even the smallest chance of discovering more of the precious herb. *And if we did find some, I wouldn't feel so guilty anymore.*

"Right," Brambleclaw began. "Then—"

"What about me?" Squirrelflight interrupted, her green eyes blazing a challenge. "You don't expect me to sit around in camp doing nothing?"

"You're not fit to leave yet," Leafpool retorted instantly.

"You'll leave when our medicine cat says you can," Brambleclaw told his mate. "But you won't be doing nothing. As the cats out on patrol come back, you can explain to them what's happening, and give them jobs to do."

Squirrelflight hesitated, as if she was going to argue, then gave a reluctant nod, muttering something under her breath as she scraped her claws in the earth.

"Okay, the meeting's over," Brambleclaw meowed crisply. "Let's get moving."

Lionblaze beckoned the apprentices with a wave of his tail and led the way to the thorn tunnel with Hollyleaf padding at his shoulder. His paws tingled with urgency; even the apprentices didn't complain at the task.

"It feels weird." Hollyleaf was looking worried as they headed deeper into the forest. "The Clan has never been split up like this before."

"It's the best way to save lives," Lionblaze answered.

"There's nothing about this in the warrior code. Except . . . we all swear to defend our Clan, so I guess this is one way of doing it." Her anxious look faded.

Lionblaze led the other cats farther from camp, into a clearing where the moss lay deep and undisturbed.

"Thank StarClan it hasn't rained lately," Foxpaw muttered as he tugged a huge swath of moss away from a tree root and started to bundle it up.

"Be careful to squeeze all the water out," Hollyleaf instructed him. "And dig as deep as you can to find the driest bits."

"Hey, look what I've found!" Icepaw came bounding across the clearing with a bunch of gray-and-white feathers in her jaws. "There's a whole lot more over there," she added. "A fox must have killed a pigeon."

"That's good," Lionblaze meowed. "They'll be soft to lie on. Collect as many as you can."

When they had as much bedding as they could carry, he and the other cats headed for the Twoleg den. Lionblaze pricked his ears in surprise as they approached. The place that had always been eerily quiet was now swarming with activity like a disturbed ants' nest.

Poppyfrost bounded past him with a bundle of sticks in her jaws, followed by Birchfall, who was dragging a long tendril of bramble. When Lionblaze reached the entrance to the den, he saw Cinderheart stuffing more bramble into a gap between the stones.

"Great, Poppyfrost," she meowed as the young tortoiseshell dropped the sticks at her paws. "That's just what we need."

"I'll fetch some more." Poppyfrost spun around and whisked past Lionblaze, back into the forest.

"Let's have that moss over here!" Sorreltail called. She was helping Ashfur drag branches into place, separating the floor of the den into separate nests. "Put it there," she continued, waving her tail toward a wide space at the back of the den, already surrounded by thorns woven together. "That's going to be the nursery."

Foxpaw and Icepaw followed Lionblaze and his sister and dropped their bundles in the place Sorreltail had shown them. Both the apprentices stared around uneasily, as if they expected something to leap out at them from the shadows in the corners of the nest. Lionblaze could understand how they felt. The straight lines and hard angles of the Twoleg nest were uncomfortably strange; the floor was hard and cold under his paws and it didn't feel right to have a solid roof overhead, without gaps for sunlight or moonlight to shine through. *That might be why Poppyfrost dashed off so quickly,* he thought. *Will the sick cats really be able to settle down here?*

"Well, why are you standing there?" Sorreltail asked. "Go and fetch us some more moss." She gave Lionblaze an affectionate prod with her muzzle, softening her sharp tone. "Make sure it's good and dry, and we'll need all you can find."

When Lionblaze and the others returned the second time, he spotted Sandstorm approaching at the head of a hunting patrol. Berrynose and Whitewing followed her; all three cats had their jaws stuffed with prey.

Sandstorm headed for a hollow tree trunk a few fox-lengths from the entrance to the Twoleg nest, among thick growths of fern and long grass. She dropped her fresh-kill just inside the opening. "I'm glad I found this," she commented. "The prey will keep dry here."

"And we can stay away from the sick cats," Berrynose added as he dumped his own catch.

"Foxes might come and steal it," Whitewing mewed, adding her fresh-kill to the growing pile. "Would it help if we scent-marked the opening?"

"Good idea," Sandstorm replied. "And we'll set markers around the edges of the old Twoleg garden. If the foxes think a lot of cats are around here, they might stay away."

They won't know the cats are too sick to fight, Lionblaze thought as he led his patrol inside the den with their bundles of moss.

By now the Twoleg nest was looking much more welcoming. Ashfur had finished dividing up the area into nests separated by branches. The first load of bedding was spread neatly in the nursery area. Brackenfur and Cinderheart were sniffing along the walls, pushing twigs and leaves into any cracks they had missed. Leafpool was there, too, checking for drafts in the nursery area.

"Over here!" she called to Brackenfur. "The wind's cutting through me like a claw."

Brackenfur bounded over with a bundle of dry leaves and shoved them into the gap the medicine cat had pointed out.

"Much better." Leafpool waved her tail approvingly.

Sorreltail showed Lionblaze and the others where to put their moss. "That's great!" she meowed, flexing her claws into the fresh bedding. "But we still need more."

"I know." Lionblaze twitched his whiskers. "We're on our way."

Leaving the den, he saw Jaypaw and Mousewhisker approaching from the direction of the camp with bundles of herbs in their jaws. They laid them on a flat stone near the entrance to the den, and Jaypaw separated them neatly into piles.

"Pity there's no catmint," he commented to Mousewhisker, loudly enough for Lionblaze to hear. "The sick cats would stand a much better chance if we had some."

"What about the plants growing here?" Mousewhisker asked.

"I've checked," Jaypaw replied, swinging his head around to glare at Lionblaze from sightless blue eyes. "They're starting to grow again, but only a tiny bit."

Guilt stabbed Lionblaze again, sharp as thorns, but he said nothing. He couldn't explain to Jaypaw why he'd refused to go through the tunnels into WindClan territory. *But what if cats die because of your dreams?*

Unable to answer the question, Lionblaze raced off into the forest as if a horde of badgers were hard on his paws. But as he headed for the moss place, he knew that he would never outrun his guilt.

The sun was going down, filling the forest with red light barred with dark shadows, as Lionblaze and his patrol returned to the old Twoleg nest once more. He had lost count of how many loads of moss he and his Clanmates had gathered and brought to the nest.

Crossing the hard stone path, Lionblaze saw Leafpool standing in the entrance to the nest with Brambleclaw beside her. They broke off their conversation when they spotted the patrol.

"Well done," Brambleclaw meowed. "Take that inside, and then you can stop. Everything's ready."

Lionblaze led his Clanmates up to the nest, noticing that there was now a well-stocked fresh-kill pile inside the hollow tree. Inside, the nest felt warm and safe, with cozy dens big enough for two or three cats to sleep, and a bigger area for the nursery, lined with the softest moss and feathers. Ferncloud was patting the clumps into place.

Sorreltail waved Lionblaze over to the last space, and spread out the moss and bracken he and the others were carrying.

"All done," she declared, touching her nose to his. "Thanks, all of you."

Looking around, Lionblaze saw that most of the healthy cats had gathered in the nest. Brackenfur and Cinderheart both had pelts snagged by thorns and brambles, but their eyes glowed with satisfaction. Poppyfrost was busily licking one of her pads, as if she had a thorn in it. Graystripe was flexing his claws in the moss; Lionblaze guessed he was impatient to get back to Millie. Berrynose had curled up for a snooze in one of the new nests; Hazeltail gave him a sharp prod with one paw.

"Get up, stupid furball!" she hissed. "These aren't for us."

"I've been working all day," Berrynose grumbled, rising to his paws and giving his shoulder fur a quick lick to hide his embarrassment.

Leafpool appeared in the entrance, with Brambleclaw just behind her. "Everything's ready," she mewed. "We can go back to camp now. But no cat must go inside until our sick Clanmates come out. From now on, we have to stay away from them."

"What?" Graystripe's claws worked harder in the moss. "You mean we can't help them?"

"Some of them are too weak to make the journey without us," Brackenfur objected.

"The stronger ones will help the weaker," Leafpool told him in a tone that warned every cat not to argue. "You know how fast the sickness spreads. We need to stay strong and healthy to provide for ourselves and the ones who are sick."

"She's right," Brambleclaw added from where he stood at the medicine cat's shoulder. "That's why we're doing this, remember?"

There were no more objections, but Lionblaze's pelt prickled at the thought of sick Clanmates struggling along without help, and from the glances they exchanged he could see that most of the other cats felt the same.

Leafpool led the way back to the camp and vanished into the tunnel through the thorns. Brambleclaw waved his tail to set the rest of the Clan into position on either side, leaving a wide space between to let the sick cats through.

Lionblaze's belly clenched in pity as they began to emerge: Firestar led the way, his head raised proudly even though he was shaken by a bout of coughing as he padded past. Cloudtail supported Thornclaw, while Dustpelt leaned on Brightheart's shoulder. Hollow coughs came from the brown tabby; Lionblaze could see every one of his ribs, while his pelt was thin and dull. Ferncloud let out a piteous mew, instinctively starting forward; Birchfall raised his tail to bar her way.

Dustpelt turned his head, blinking eyes glazed with fever. "Keep back," he meowed hoarsely. "I'll be fine."

Ferncloud looked away and buried her muzzle in Birchfall's shoulder fur.

Daisy was the next cat to appear, carrying Rosekit, with Toadkit, Blossomkit, and Bumblekit behind her. The mischievous kits were unusually subdued, their gaze fixed on their paws as they padded quietly along.

"You can't go with Rosekit," Brambleclaw declared,

stepping out to bar Daisy's path. "You and the healthy kits have to stay in camp."

"Nonsense!" Rosekit let out a feeble wail as Daisy set her down gently to confront the Clan deputy. "Who will feed Rosekit if I'm not there?"

"Rosekit can eat fresh-kill now," Brambleclaw replied. "And Firestar will make sure she's cared for. Do you want the other kits to get sick?"

For a couple of heartbeats Daisy stood glaring at him, then dropped her gaze and padded to one side, gathering the healthy kits to her with a sweep of her tail.

"I want to go with Rosekit!" Toadkit mewed fiercely.

"You can't." Daisy stooped to touch her remaining kit on the head with her nose. "You can help her best by keeping well and strong."

Toadkit still looked rebellious, but he didn't say any more. Honeyfern, emerging from the barrier, took in the situation at a glance and stood over Rosekit. "I promise I'll look after her," she told Daisy, who gave her a grateful nod.

Rosekit batted the air with her paws and went on wailing as her Clanmate carried her toward the Twoleg nest.

More movement in the tunnel signaled Millie's approach. The gray she-cat was supported on either side by Leafpool and Jaypaw. Lionblaze caught his breath in horror when he saw her. Her paws barely moved; the medicine cats were all but carrying her. Her pelt clung to her ribs, and her sides heaved as she let out a rasping cough.

"No!" Graystripe yowled from just behind Lionblaze and

Hollyleaf. He plunged forward; Lionblaze blocked him, and Hollyleaf sank her teeth into the loose fur on his shoulder. "Let me go!" Graystripe snarled as he struggled. "She's dying! I have to go to her!"

Lionblaze braced himself; it went against everything he had learned to fight a Clanmate, but he knew that he couldn't allow Graystripe to be near his sick mate.

"Keep back!" Leafpool ordered, raising her tail in warning.

Graystripe ignored her and kept struggling, lashing out a paw to rake his claws down Lionblaze's shoulder.

"Stop!" Brambleclaw bounded up to help.

"Graystripe." Firestar's hoarse voice came from the head of the pitiful line of cats. The Clan leader had halted and turned to face his friend. "I know how you feel. But you must stay away from Millie." His voice was full of sympathy; Lionblaze knew how deep the friendship was between the two cats. "Millie needs you to stay strong and healthy."

Graystripe stopped struggling and took a long breath. "Firestar, my heart is clawed in pieces."

"I know. But what you're doing now doesn't help. Graystripe, if Millie's paws are truly set on the path to StarClan, then I'll send for you to say good-bye. I promise you."

Graystripe hesitated for a heartbeat, then bowed his head. "I'll hold you to that, Firestar," he choked out.

Lionblaze and Brambleclaw stood back, and Hollyleaf let go her grip on the gray warrior's shoulder. Graystripe stood still, his head and tail drooping; Lionblaze was close enough to feel the shivers that were running through him.

Leafpool and Jaypaw moved on, with Millie supported

between them. Her head hung; she didn't seem to have heard her mate's protests. Behind them came Longtail, guiding himself by the tip of Leafpool's tail. Briarkit dangled limply from his jaws like a piece of fresh-kill.

Lionblaze tensed. Was the tiny kit dead? Then her tail twitched, and she let out an exhausted cough. Seeing she was still alive, Lionblaze relaxed, only to have his relief swallowed up in a wave of guilt. *She needs catmint. They all do.*

When the sick cats had gone, Brambleclaw led the rest of the Clan back into the stone hollow. Mousefur and Squirrelflight, the only cats remaining, were sitting together near the fresh-kill pile; Mousefur rose and padded to meet them as they returned.

"I should be with them," she snapped at Brambleclaw. "I could help. I'm an elder; it doesn't weaken the Clan if I get sick."

Brambleclaw dipped his head. "That's an offer worthy of a warrior," he replied. "But the Clan values every cat, from the newest kit to the most senior elder." His amber eyes glinted. "I know you already asked Firestar, and he said no. Don't think you can get around me."

"Pesky young cat . . . thinks he knows everything," Mousefur muttered, turning her back.

Instead of going to their dens, the remains of the Clan huddled together in the center of the clearing, as if they were waiting for something. Lionblaze crouched beside his sister, his fur standing on end. The camp felt strange, as if it wasn't their home anymore. The stench of sickness still hung around it, and an eerie quiet covered everything.

"I don't like this," Hollyleaf whispered. "I wonder how

many of the sick cats will ever come back."

Don't. Lionblaze dug his claws hard into the ground. "It's in the paws of StarClan," he muttered, knowing how hypocritical he was being.

It seemed a long time, though the shadows had crept no more than a mouse-length across the hollow, before Leafpool and Jaypaw returned.

"Good, you're all here," Leafpool meowed, padding toward the gathering of cats. "Jaypaw, fetch me those strengthening herbs from our den." As Jaypaw bounded off, she continued, "Every scrap of bedding has to be taken out of the dens and into the forest, and fresh bedding brought in."

"What?" Icepaw, who had been grooming herself drowsily, raised her head. "I've been dragging moss around all day. Do we really have to get more? I'm worn out!"

"Every cat is worn out," Spiderleg added. "Can't it wait until morning?"

"Sure it can, if you want more cats to get sick," Leafpool retorted. Her tone softened as she added, "Every cat will be helping this time. It won't take long."

Jaypaw came back with the herbs, dropping a few leaves in front of every cat. Lionblaze felt his aching limbs fill with warmth as he swallowed them.

"Let's get going," he mewed to Hollyleaf. "The sooner we get started, the sooner we'll be done."

All the warriors headed out of the camp to fetch fresh moss and bracken, while Icepaw, helped by Mousefur and Squirrelflight, cleared the old bedding out of the dens and carried it as far as the barrier to be disposed of outside. Leafpool and Jaypaw checked the dens to make sure not a scrap of it remained behind. By the time it was all gone, and fresh bedding installed, the taint of sickness that had hung about the camp for so long had almost vanished.

"This is better," Hollyleaf murmured as she settled down inside the warriors' den beside Lionblaze. "Except it's strange with so many cats missing. I hope Firestar's plan works."

Lionblaze was already sliding into sleep, his eyes closed and his tail wrapped over his nose. He was too exhausted for his worries to keep him awake, but as he slid into darkness his mind filled with a vision of catmint: thick, lush clumps of it, growing among rocks on the edge of the moor, just as Jaypaw had described. He leaped forward to bite off the stems, only to halt, trembling, on the bank of a river.

The stream that marked the border with WindClan had swollen into a rushing scarlet torrent. The air was filled with the stench of blood, and the grasses on the edge of the river where Lionblaze stood were spattered with it.

He took a step back, horrified at the thought of blood sticking to his paws, and stiffened as he heard a familiar voice behind him.

"Are you scared, little warrior?" Tigerstar taunted him. "Where's this power of yours now?"

CHAPTER 14

Every muscle in Jaypaw's body was yowling with exhaustion as he finished sniffing around the elders' den to make sure that every scrap of the tainted bedding had been removed. He stumbled back into the clearing and padded up to Leafpool. "It's okay," he reported.

"Why don't you get some rest?" his mentor meowed. "Brambleclaw and Cinderheart have just brought us some fresh moss."

Jaypaw opened his jaws to protest that he could keep going as long as any cat, then thought better of it. His job and Leafpool's was finished for now; there was no reason why he couldn't catch up on his sleep. But tired as he was, his paws were itching and his mind whirling; he knew his thoughts would keep him awake.

"Thanks," he replied, "but I'd like to go out for a while."

"Fine." Leafpool sounded faintly surprised. "Be careful, won't you?"

"Sure." Jaypaw wished she wouldn't keep trying to mother him. He had Squirrelflight for that; Leafpool was just his mentor. He took off at a trot through the tunnel, where he passed Whitewing and Birchfall returning with bundles of bedding, and headed for the lake.

Pushing through the last of the undergrowth, Jaypaw paused at the top of the bank overlooking the water. He could hear the soothing lap of waves on the shore, and the faint scrape of pebbles. Scenting carefully, he made his way to the hollow under the tree roots where he had hidden the stick.

As he laid his paws on the scratch marks, the whispers of the long-ago warriors rose up around him. He strained to hear them clearly, but just as before, they stayed out of his reach.

"Rock, don't you have a message for me?" he meowed aloud.

His head spun with thoughts of everything that had happened: the mysterious appearance of Sol, and the fake sign that had become real and driven him from ShadowClan; the terrible sickness, and Firestar taking the sick cats away from the stone hollow . . . Jaypaw felt as if he were a leaf spinning in eddies of wind.

It's all escaping from me, like prey running too fast. I'm supposed to have power, but I can't control anything.

"Has it always been like this for the Clans?" he murmured. "Fighting one battle after another? And some battles no cat can win. I wonder if it was sickness that drove the first cats away from the lake?"

Yet again he ran his paws over the scratches, the record of the cats who had emerged victorious from their test in the tunnels, and of those who had never come out. The whispers wafted around him like faint puffs of breeze, but Jaypaw still couldn't make out their meaning.

"What's the use of you if I can't hear you?" he protested. "Speak up a little, please. Tell me how to fight the sickness, or what I can say to Lionblaze to make him fetch the catmint."

But the gentle whispering didn't change. Sighing, Jaypaw lay down with his chin on the stick, and closed his eyes.

Damp soaking into his belly fur woke Jaypaw. His muscles felt stiff and cramped with cold as he raised his head and looked around. He was in the underground cave, lit by a trickle of daylight from the roof far above his head. The river flowed past him a couple of tail-lengths away.

Jaypaw staggered to his paws. He expected to see Rock, but the ledge where the ancient cat usually crouched was empty, and there was no sign of him anywhere in the cave.

Soft paw steps sounded behind Jaypaw; he spun around to see a ginger-and-white tom standing at the entrance to one of the tunnels. His green eyes looked haunted and somber, as if he couldn't shake off the memory of drowning when rain flooded the tunnels.

"Fallen Leaves!" Jaypaw exclaimed.

"I didn't think you would come back." Aching loneliness vibrated in the ancient cat's voice. "Are you going to stay with me this time?"

Sympathy stabbed Jaypaw, sharp as a thorn in his pad. He couldn't imagine what it would be like to be trapped down here, alone, for countless seasons. The last time he had seen Fallen Leaves, the ancient cat had saved his life, and the lives of his littermates and WindClan cats, when floodwaters had risen while they were looking for the lost kits.

"What happened to your Clanmates?" Jaypaw asked. "Why did they leave the lake?"

Fallen Leaves looked down at his paws. "I don't know. I only knew that they had gone. Sharpclaws stopped coming into the tunnels, and the only sound from the moor was the wind. I have been on my own here for so long, I have lost count of the moons." He raised his head, his green eyes pleading. "You and your friends were the first cats I had seen down here since . . . since I came in."

"I have to know why they left!" Jaypaw meowed; he couldn't explain it, but he was certain that the fate of those long-ago cats was bound up with the prophecy. Meeting Rock, finding the stick, feeling the whispers of ancient cats around him when he went to the Moonpool: None of that had happened by chance, he was sure.

He bounded toward the tunnel that led up into ThunderClan territory, brushing aside Fallen Leaves, who stared after him in dismay.

"Wait!" Fallen Leaves called out. "I thought you were going to stay with me."

"I have to know what happened," Jaypaw insisted with a last glance over his shoulder. The drowned cat was standing at the end of the tunnel, his eyes wide and distressed.

Jaypaw forced anger to stifle his pity. "How can I stay with him?" he muttered as he padded forward into the thick blackness of the tunnel. "There are too many things I need to find out. I can't spend all my time hanging out with a dead cat!"

He expected to emerge in the woods above the hollow, awake and blind once more, or perhaps find himself on the lakeshore with the stick. Instead, daylight began to gleam on the walls ahead of him, growing stronger as he padded on. He could hear the sound of leaves rustling in the wind.

"I must be still dreaming," he whispered.

His paws tingling, Jaypaw headed for the light. Rounding a curve in the tunnel, he saw a circle of daylight ahead of him. Excited voices broke the silence.

"Is it him?"

"He's later than I thought he'd be."

"Do you think he got lost?"

Jaypaw slowed his pace. Even if he was coming up inside WindClan, he should have known some of the voices, but they were all strange to him. And he didn't recognize any of the scents drifting toward him from the tunnel mouth. Where was he, and who was waiting for him?

Then another voice reached him, making his paws freeze to the floor of the tunnel.

"Jay's Wing? Jay's Wing, is that you?"

CHAPTER 15

Jaypaw forced his legs to carry him forward to the end of the tunnel. As he emerged, blinking, into brilliant sunlight, several cats crowded around him, mewing excitedly.

"Jay's Wing! It *is* you!"

"Well done! You're a sharpclaw now."

"Congratulations!"

At first Jaypaw couldn't make out individual cats among the press of furry bodies. Then a ginger-and-white she-cat thrust her way through the crowd. Her fur stood on end as she danced on restless paws.

"You're lucky Jay's Wing survived the challenge!" she yowled. Her voice quivered with sorrow, and her amber eyes were full of bitterness. "Have you forgotten that Fallen Leaves never came out of the tunnels?"

A small gray-and-white she-cat, her belly heavy with kits, padded up to her side and pressed her muzzle into her shoulder. "Come on, Broken Shadow," she murmured. "Let's go find a patch of sunshine to rest in."

"You don't understand, Rising Moon!" Broken Shadow wailed, but she allowed the other she-cat to lead her away.

Jaypaw stared around him, his mind racing. He recognized the way the ground sloped down toward the entrance to the tunnels, but the trees were smaller, letting through the bright sunlight that had dazzled him. The spaces between the trees were mostly clear of undergrowth. It was like his home, yet not like it.

Where am I? And who are these strange cats? Has ThunderClan been invaded?

He spun around, looking for his Clanmates. *Looking?* Jaypaw shivered. *This feels too real to be a dream.* He could feel the wind in his fur and hear the voices of the other cats like birdsong in his ears; his belly was rumbling and his paws dragged as though he had truly been awake all night, searching for a way out of the tunnels in order to become a sharpclaw.

A pretty pale gray she-cat bounded up to him, her blue eyes sparkling with affection. She drew her tail down Jaypaw's side.

"You're a sharpclaw! It's so exciting!" she meowed, bouncing gently on her paws. Suddenly her tail drooped. "I wish our mother could see you."

Jaypaw stiffened. This she-cat was his *sister?*

Who does she think I am?

"Perhaps Falcon Swoop *can* see you." A silver-furred she-cat padded up to Jaypaw. She was slender and graceful, with long legs and brilliant blue eyes.

"Do you really think so, Whispering Breeze?" Jaypaw's sister meowed hopefully.

"Precious Dove's Wing, you know how much Falcon Swoop

loved you and Jay's Wing while she was alive. I'm sure she still loves you, wherever she may be."

"I hope so," Dove's Wing murmured.

Jaypaw didn't understand. *Don't these cats go to StarClan when they die? And why do they all seem to know me?*

"Look, there's been a mistake," he began. "I'm not who you think I am. And where's ThunderClan?"

Whispering Breeze stretched out her neck to give him a sniff. "Are you okay?" she queried. "I think your brain got scrambled down in the tunnels."

"What's ThunderClan?" Dove's Wing asked, faintly anxious. "Did Rock tell you about it?"

Rock? Jaypaw's belly lurched. Did Dove's Wing know the sightless cat who lived in the tunnels?

He was about to ask her, when another cat loomed over him, a dark ginger tabby tom with muscular shoulders and amber eyes. "Don't forget sharpclaws never talk about what goes on in the caves," he warned. "That's a secret they must keep for the rest of their lives."

"It's okay, Furled Bracken," Dove's Wing assured him. "Jay's Wing is just a bit confused."

Furled Bracken grunted. "Just so long as he remembers what he was told when he went into the tunnels two nights ago."

"I haven't been in the tunnels for two nights!" Jaypaw protested. "I—"

"We were so worried about you when you didn't come out on the first sunrise," Dove's Wing interrupted. "We thought you'd been lost."

"Like Fallen Leaves," a new voice broke in. Jaypaw turned and saw a hefty dark gray tabby tom with glittering ice-blue eyes. Sadness radiated from his pelt. Jaypaw picked up such a strong image of Fallen Leaves from his mind that he guessed this cat must be the drowned cat's father.

"Stone Song." Furled Bracken touched the tabby tom's ear with his nose. "I know how hard this is for you."

Stone Song sighed. "We waited a moon of sunrises for Fallen Leaves to emerge," he murmured. "But he never came." He glanced across at Broken Shadow, who was lying under a tree not far off. Rising Moon crouched beside her, grooming her gently like a mother with her kit. "It is time to give up waiting," Stone Song finished quietly.

Jaypaw stared at the dark gray tabby. *How can it be only one moon since Fallen Leaves disappeared? If that's true, it means this must be long ago!* Somehow he had emerged from the tunnels during the time before the Clan cats came to the lake, maybe even as far back as when the ancient cats trod the path to the Moonpool.

The stick! Jaypaw felt every hair on his pelt rise. *I'm among the cats who are marked on the stick!*

He looked back at the mouth of the tunnel. It looked different now, because it was on exposed hillside rather than surrounded by thick undergrowth, but he had sensed its shape when he walked through it to find the WindClan kits, and he was sure it was the same tunnel. Turning, he looked down at the lake, its glinting surface clearly visible through the trees. The shape of the water was familiar, but when he looked across to the flank of WindClan territory, he spotted Twolegs swarming over a mound of pale brown earth, pushing it around with yellow monsters. Their roaring hung in the air like the buzzing of bumblebees.

Jaypaw padded forward to the edge of the slope to take a closer look. A moment later, Furled Bracken joined him. "The Twolegs are still moving the earth," he meowed worriedly. "Chasing Clouds and I went down there to check it out, but we still don't know what they're doing."

"They're building nests," Jaypaw replied without thinking.

Furled Bracken gave him a sharp look. "What, nests for Twolegs to live in? There are a few in the woods on the other side of the lake, but Twolegs have never tried to live any closer than that."

"Yes, there'll be four nests." Jaypaw remembered Hollyleaf's and Lionblaze's description of the horseplace. "The Twolegs are going to keep horses there."

He realized that Furled Bracken was looking at him with a strange expression in his eyes. "How do you know that?" he gasped.

Jaypaw gulped. *Mouse-brain!* Of course these cats had no way of knowing what the Twolegs were doing with their yellow monsters. Had he just made a prophecy that was going to come true?

Furled Bracken twitched his ears; he was still waiting for an answer.

Jaypaw shrugged. "I just figure that's what Twolegs do

when they dig holes in the ground."

The ginger tom was still giving him a doubtful look. *And I can't say I blame him.* Jaypaw was relieved to see Dove's Wing bounding toward them.

"What are you doing, standing here?" she demanded as she gave him a shove back toward the deeper part of the forest. "You must be worn out and starving after being in the tunnels all that time. You need to rest. And I want Rising Moon to take a look at your pads. They're bleeding from walking on stone for so long."

Jaypaw looked down and saw spots of blood smeared on the grass where he had put his paws. Pain suddenly swept over him, and his head spun from the hunger that snarled in his belly. Maybe he really had been in the tunnels for two nights. He was glad to follow Dove's Wing into the trees, where the long shadows of early morning striped the grass.

"Are we going to the camp?" he asked.

Dove's Wing turned back, her blue eyes puzzled. "What do you mean? Are you sure you're feeling all right?"

Okay, so these cats don't have a camp, Jaypaw guessed. *Think before you ask any more questions, stupid furball!*

Looking worried, Dove's Wing nosed aside some tendrils of ivy hanging from an oak tree, to reveal a cozy scoop among the roots. The bottom was lined with moss and feathers; warm scent clung about it.

This must be a den. Jaypaw bent his head to sniff, and felt every muscle in his body tense. *That's my own scent!*

Dove's Wing nudged him forward. "Lie down. I'm going

to fetch Rising Moon."

Rising Moon must be the medicine cat, Jaypaw thought, remembering how she had comforted Fallen Leaves's mother. He watched Dove's Wing as she trotted away, trying to spot more dens among the trees and scant undergrowth. He couldn't see any, but the intensity of scent in the air suggested they were not far-off.

Worn out, Jaypaw crawled into the den, curled up, and closed his eyes. Anxiety clawed through him. *Will I ever get back to ThunderClan?* But he was so exhausted that he fell into a shallow, uneasy sleep.

". . . these are good juicy dock leaves." The voice roused Jaypaw from his doze. "Well done for finding that clump."

Relief flooded through him. He was back in his nest in the medicine cats' den, with Leafpool talking about herbs close by.

Then he opened his eyes and saw tangled brown roots and soft feathers around his head. He could still see. The voice he could hear wasn't Leafpool's, and when the ivy tendrils twitched to one side, Dove's Wing and Rising Moon looked down at him, their eyes huge with concern. Dove's Wing had a bunch of dock leaves in her jaws. Jaypaw gave himself a tiny shake. If he wasn't going to wake up back in his own Clan, in his own time, then he must be here for a reason. Maybe this was another place where he'd find answers to his questions about the prophecy—answers that StarClan couldn't give him.

"Were you hurt while you were in the tunnels?" Rising Moon asked.

Jaypaw shook his head. "N-no. I'm not injured. My pads are sore, that's all."

"Were you scared down there?"

"A bit." Jaypaw wondered if Rising Moon thought he was losing his mind. Dove's Wing must have told her about the peculiar things he'd said. "I'm really tired, though," he added, hoping she would believe that was the reason for his odd behavior. "And hungry. I . . . I guess that's made me confused."

He had to convince these cats that he really was Jay's Wing. He wasn't sure what they would do to him if they discovered he wasn't. They certainly wouldn't believe him if he told them the truth.

He had waited for so long to find out about the ancient cats, and now here he was, living among them! No other cat in the Clans or the Tribe of Rushing Water knew as much as this about the cats who once lived beside the lake. Jaypaw had always been conscious of them, felt their pelts brush against his, heard their whispers by the lake, and trodden in their paw steps on his way to the Moonpool.

And now I'm one of them!

Rising Moon blinked thoughtfully. "I guess there's nothing wrong that food and rest won't cure. Let's look at your pads." She crawled down into the den to crouch beside Jaypaw. "Have you licked them clean?"

"Uh . . . no."

Rising Moon waited while Jaypaw's tongue rasped busily at his pads, scraping off the mud and grit. Dove's Wing dropped the mouthful of dock leaves down to her.

"Oh, are you using dock?" Jaypaw asked, looking up from his licking. "I always thought horsetail was best to stop bleeding."

Rising Moon's eyes widened in surprise. "Horsetail? I've never heard of that. I don't think it grows around here. Where did you hear about it?"

Every hair on Jaypaw's pelt tingled. He'd done it again! *Think next time before you open your jaws, mouse-brain!* "Er . . . I think one of the elders mentioned it," he muttered, hoping that these cats *had* elders.

"I'll have a word with Running Horse later," Rising Moon meowed. "He taught me so much about herbs, I'm sure he'll know about it."

"I saw Dawn River using yarrow the other day," Dove's Wing added helpfully. "We could ask her advice, too."

So they don't have a single medicine cat, Jaypaw thought as Rising Moon rubbed the cooling dock leaves on his pads. *Just a few cats who share knowledge about herbs. And they don't know as much as a Clan medicine cat.*

Jaypaw remembered how uncertain Dove's Wing had been that her mother might be watching her. If these cats had no medicine cat, that could explain why they weren't aware of their ancestors. *What do they think happens when a cat dies?*

"There." Rising Moon finished rubbing the last of Jaypaw's pads. "Does that feel better?"

"It feels great, thanks." Even though he knew that horsetail would have worked better, Jaypaw was still grateful for the cooling juices on his pads.

"You can rub your feet again later," the she-cat went on, pushing the remaining dock leaves together into a pile. "But you'd better get some sleep now."

"I'll bring you something to eat," Dove's Wing promised.

Jaypaw's jaws stretched in an enormous yawn. He was barely aware of Rising Moon scrambling out of the den. Closing his eyes, he let himself drift into sleep.

CHAPTER 16

Scent tickled Jaypaw's nose. Mouse! His belly growled, and his eyes flew open to see that dusk had fallen. Dove's Wing's pale gray shape stood on the edge of the den, peering down at him. A mouse dangled from her jaws.

"You're awake!" she exclaimed, dropping the mouse at her paws. "Are you feeling better?"

"I'm fine," Jaypaw meowed, hauling himself out from underneath the tree roots.

"Hey, Jay's Wing!" A young brown tabby tom was standing just behind Dove's Wing, his amber eyes alight with curiosity. "What was it like, down in the tunnels?"

"Quiet, Fish Leap!" A white she-cat padded up on Dove's Wing's other side. "Don't pester Jay's Wing. He must be worn out already, without you asking questions."

"And don't tell me what to do, Half Moon," Fish Leap retorted. "You want to know everything as much as I do."

The white cat brushed her pelt against Jaypaw's. Her green eyes shone up at him. "Of course I do," she purred. "But I can wait while he eats."

The scent of the mouse was making Jaypaw's mouth water.

"Thanks," he meowed to Dove's Wing, and took a bite. He was aware of Fish Leap tearing impatiently at the grass beside him.

"I don't know why Furled Bracken is making us wait to go into the tunnels," he grumbled. "We're all ready to become sharpclaws. I want to get on with my challenge."

"Furled Bracken will let us go when *he* thinks we're ready," Dove's Wing meowed.

So they're all apprentices, Jaypaw figured as he gulped down the mouse. *If they call them apprentices here. It sounds as if Furled Bracken is their leader. But how can he have nine lives if they don't know about StarClan?*

"Well, come on." Fish Leap sounded irritated. "Tell us."

"I can't," Jaypaw mumbled around a mouthful of mouse, glad that he had an excuse for being mysterious. "You know sharpclaws can't talk about what happens in the tunnels."

Fish Leap grunted. "You think you're better than us now you're a sharpclaw."

"He does not!" Half Moon exclaimed indignantly.

Jaypaw wasn't sure how to defend himself. He didn't know enough about what a sharpclaw was supposed to do. He guessed they were like warriors, but if he was wrong he might be in trouble again.

To his relief, Dove's Wing nudged Fish Leap away. "Leave him alone," she meowed. "He's still tired; he needs to rest some more. We'll all find out about the tunnels soon enough. I'm just glad Jay's Wing got out safely."

Half Moon's green eyes clouded. "Not like Fallen Leaves," she murmured.

Fish Leap and Dove's Wing exchanged a sorrowful glance. Jaypaw felt hollow in his heart when he thought about how long Fallen Leaves was destined to wander through the tunnels, trying to find the way out. He wished there was a way to let these cats know that their friend was dead, drowned in a flood, and they would never see him again. It was clear that the waiting had already driven Broken Shadows mad.

Finishing the mouse, Jaypaw wriggled back into his den. He was falling back to sleep when he heard Fish Leap's voice, raised in protest.

"One lost cat doesn't mean that all the rest of us have to leave!"

"It's not just one, as you well know," Half Moon retorted. "How many cats have to die before we look for somewhere else to live? There must be other places with prey and shelter for all of us."

Jaypaw pricked his ears, keeping his eyes shut so it would look as if he was asleep. These cats were debating whether to stay here by the lake, or to find a new home. *Is that why we didn't find any cats here when the Clans came to the lake?* Fish Leap padded away, still muttering, with Half Moon arguing more and more heatedly. When he could no longer hear what they were saying, Jaypaw let the blackness of exhaustion fill his mind.

During the night he woke briefly to find Dove's Wing curled up close beside him. He hadn't slept so near another cat since he became Leafpool's apprentice; her warmth was comforting, and her scent was already becoming familiar. He let out a faint purr as sleep washed over him again.

Gray light was filtering through the ivy tendrils when Jaypaw next opened his eyes. Dove's Wing had disappeared, but two other cats were gazing down at him. One of them was Fish Leap; the other was an older tortoiseshell she-cat that Jaypaw remembered seeing when he came out of the tunnel the day before. Her amber eyes were the exact same shade as Fish Leap's; Jaypaw guessed that she was his mother.

"Hey, Jay's Wing! Come hunting!" Fish Leap exclaimed when he saw that Jaypaw was awake.

That seemed like a good chance to explore their—Thunder-Clan's—territory. Jaypaw scrambled out of his nest and stretched. "Are we going on a patrol?" he asked.

To his dismay, Fish Leap and the tortoiseshell exchanged a baffled glance. "What's a patrol?" the tortoiseshell meowed.

Mouse-dung! They don't have patrols, either.

"Dawn River, I think Jay's Wing banged his head when he was down in the tunnels." Fish Leap shrugged. "He keeps talking nonsense."

Jaypaw hid his awkwardness by licking a tufty piece of fur on his chest. "Never mind," he mumbled.

"Let's go," Dawn River urged. "Remember to watch out for badgers."

She took the lead as the three cats set off into the woods. Jaypaw shivered from ears to tail-tip when he saw how different the forest was from the territory he knew in the time of the Clans. It wasn't just that the trees were smaller and there was so little undergrowth. The biggest difference was that now he could see.

"Watch it!" Fish Leap warned him.

The exclamation came just too late. Jaypaw was so busy gazing around at the trees, their leaves taking on colors of scarlet and gold at the beginning of leaf-fall, that he hadn't noticed the rabbit hole right in front of his paws. He stumbled into it, paws flailing.

"Fox dung!" he spat.

He heard Fish Leap let out a *mrrow* of laughter, and felt the tabby tom's teeth sink into his scruff as he hauled him out.

"Are you okay?" Dawn River checked.

Jaypaw shook loose earth out of his pelt. "I'm fine."

As they padded on he made a determined effort to watch where he was putting his paws, but it was difficult. Light dazzled him, and he was distracted by the flickering of leaves and trees looming up in front of him. The senses of smell and hearing, and his awareness of nearby objects, that were usually so acute had grown dull, so that he felt as if he was blundering through a fog.

I'm never as clumsy as this, he thought crossly as he tripped over a branch.

"You'll scare all the prey away if you go on like that," Fish Leap pointed out. "Are you sure you're okay?" he added. "Do you want to go back to your den?"

"I'm fine," Jaypaw repeated through gritted teeth. But Fish Leap was right: Stumbling around like a blind badger would scare off all the prey. Jaypaw closed his eyes, and instantly felt more comfortable. His other senses grew sharp again, telling him which way to go. Scents and sounds swirled around him, calling up a far clearer picture of his surroundings than he could gain from his eyes.

"Jay's Wing?" Dawn River sounded puzzled and concerned. "Have you gone to sleep on your paws?"

Startled, Jaypaw veered away from the sound of her voice. His eyes flicked open just in time to see the rough bark of a tree in front of his nose. There was no chance to stop before he crashed right into it.

"Wow!" Fish Leap exclaimed, his voice trembling with amusement. "You caught a tree!"

Jaypaw was relieved when Dawn River and Fish Leap set off alone, each of them sniffing for prey, and left him to recover. Grooming bits of bark out of his coat, he wondered what he was going to do. If he was a sharpclaw, these cats would expect him to know how to hunt. But back in his own Clan, he had never been trained for that. He had never caught his own prey.

I'll just have to try. How hard can it be?

He began prowling through the trees with his eyes closed so that he could pick out the scents more clearly, and soon detected a trace of mouse. Pausing to listen, he heard the scuffling of tiny paws, and leaped in the direction of the sound. His paws thumped down on grass; there was no sign of his mouse.

"Bad luck!" Fish Leap meowed cheerfully behind him. Jaypaw opened his eyes and turned to see that the other cat was dragging a squirrel between his front paws. Dawn River stood behind him, a mouse clamped in her jaws.

"Haven't you caught anything yet?" Fish Leap teased. "I thought sharpclaws were better than that."

"I . . . er . . . I was looking for the horsetail that Running Horse mentioned," Jaypaw mewed, improvising wildly. "He says it's good for sore pads."

Dawn River nodded. "It must be hard for you to hunt when your pads aren't healed yet."

"All the same, you'd better catch something," Fish Leap told him. "Unless you want to go hungry."

Jaypaw wasn't surprised. He had already guessed that these cats had to hunt for themselves, even before they were sharpclaws; they didn't have patrols, and he hadn't seen any sign of a fresh-kill pile. "Should we catch something for the elders?" he suggested.

Fish Leap shrugged. "If we find something extra."

Jaypaw felt a pang of homesickness for ThunderClan, where every cat was fed, even those who didn't have the time or skill to hunt for themselves.

"I'm going to try down by the stream," Dawn River declared. "I could just eat a yummy vole."

So could I, Jaypaw thought, watching the tortoiseshell she-cat out of sight, *but I don't think I'm going to get one. What am I going to eat if I can't tell them that I don't hunt?*

"I'll see you later," Fish Leap meowed. "Good hunting!"

He bounded off in the direction of the ShadowClan border. *No,* Jaypaw reminded himself. *Where the ShadowClan border will be.*

Keeping his eyes open in an attempt to get used to seeing, he headed toward the stone hollow. Fear drew icy claws down his spine. *What if the hollow isn't there?*

Before many heartbeats had passed, the harsh tang of a Thunderpath crept into Jaypaw's nostrils. He paused, bewildered. *There's no Thunderpath across our territory!*

He pressed himself closer to the ground, creeping forward and taking advantage of what little cover there was. Eventually he came out beside the Thunderpath, its hard black surface snaking through the trees. Pricking his ears, he listened for the sound of monsters, but nothing disturbed the gentle rustling of the breeze among the branches.

Glancing up and down, Jaypaw spotted the walls of a Twoleg nest among the trees; more cautiously than ever he crept toward it, alert for the scent and sound of Twolegs or dogs. But everything was silent. The door of the nest was tight shut, and the shiny stuff in the windows was broken and scattered.

Jaypaw blinked in sudden understanding. *This is the Twoleg nest where the sick cats are staying!* There weren't any holes in the walls, and the roof was still in one piece, but the size and shape were the same.

So the Thunderpath is the old Twoleg path. Jaypaw bounded back to it. He hadn't recognized it with its black surface intact instead of broken up and covered with tiny creeping plants. *Now I know where I am!*

He trotted along beside the Thunderpath, still wary of monsters, though none of the smelly, roaring creatures appeared. Just as he knew it would, it led him to the entrance to the hollow.

Jaypaw stopped and looked around. Walls of stone stretched up around him, low near the entrance and rising to a height of many fox-lengths opposite him. There was a trace of Twoleg scent, but it was faint and stale. His gaze traveled around the hollow as he tried to imagine where the dens would be. It was hard to picture them because there was no undergrowth yet, no brambles, bracken, or hazel to soften the harsh lines of the walls. Only a few stems of willowherb had pushed their way through the earth, their feathery tops stirred by the breeze. Jaypaw thought he recognized the Highledge with the cave behind it where Firestar had his den, but there was no sign of the tumbled rocks that made a path up to it.

"Jay's Wing!"

Jaypaw jumped, startled, and whirled around to see the white she-cat, Half Moon, staring at him with scared green eyes.

"What are you doing here?" she gasped. "The badgers will get you. Quick!"

She bounded away through the trees and up the side of the hollow, heading for the entrance to the underground tunnels. Jaypaw followed her, closing his eyes so that he could match her speed. *So this is where the badgers lived,* he thought, noticing strong badger scent for the first time; his mind had been so distracted by the changes to the Twoleg path and the stone hollow that he had missed it on the way there. The hollow must be out-of-bounds to the cats because it belonged to their enemies—not rival cats, but badgers. Maybe these were the ancestors of the badgers that came back to the forest, moons and moons later, and attacked ThunderClan, killing Cinderpelt. Did those badgers know that this had been their home once?

Jaypaw was relieved when the badger scents faded and Half Moon finally slowed and flopped down on the cool grass. He wondered how she knew that they were safe here, when there were no border markings to separate their territory from the badgers'.

"I never thought so before," he began carefully, "but isn't it weird how the badgers never chase us here, when there's nothing to stop them?"

Half Moon shrugged. "I guess there's enough prey in the thicker part of the forest, so they don't need to come out this far." She glanced sideways at Jaypaw, clearly wanting to say something but not sure if she should. "I followed your scent," she admitted. "I thought you might be in trouble. And I've got this for you." She vanished under a bush and reappeared a heartbeat later with a blackbird in her jaws, which she dropped in front of Jaypaw. "I thought you might find it hard to hunt when your paws are sore."

Jaypaw nodded, glad of the excuse but still feeling a bit guilty as he crouched in front of the blackbird. "Thanks. Do you want to share it with me?"

"I already ate, but I'll have a mouthful, thanks." Half Moon settled down on the opposite side of the prey.

While he ate, Jaypaw realized that he would need to learn how to hunt if he was going to stay here for any length of time. But that could be tricky, when he was supposed to be a sharpclaw already.

"Will Furled Bracken give me any duties?" he asked Half Moon.

The white she-cat had taken one bite of the blackbird, then began to clean her face and whiskers with her paws. "You might have to hunt for the elders if no cat has any spare," she mewed. "Don't you remember how hard it rained last moon? How Whispering Breeze had to catch prey for all of us because she's the only cat who doesn't mind getting her fur wet?"

"Oh, sure," Jaypaw mumbled.

"I couldn't believe it when she caught fish!" Half Moon purred. "I'd never tasted fish before."

"Prey isn't running well, is it?" Jaypaw thought that was a safe comment to make.

Half Moon shook her head. "Maybe Stone Song isn't wrong when he says we should think about leaving." Sadness clouded her eyes. "I remember you said the same."

"Right," Jaypaw meowed, relieved to know which side of the argument Jay's Wing had taken. "There must be somewhere with more prey, and no Twolegs and badgers to bother us."

"You really think there's a place like that for us?"

Jaypaw nodded slowly. *After all, the Clans found a new home for themselves when the Twolegs destroyed the old forest.*

Except that the Clans came here.

CHAPTER 17

By the time Jaypaw was full, there was still quite a lot of the blackbird left. "Do you want any more?" he asked Half Moon.

The white she-cat shook her head. "We could take it to Owl Feather," she suggested. "Her kits are hungry, and growing fast."

"Good idea." Jaypaw wanted to see as much of these cats and where they lived before he went back to ThunderClan. *If* he went back . . .

He and Half Moon picked up the remains of the blackbird and headed farther up the hill toward the tunnel entrance. It seemed to be a popular daytime gathering place, like the clearing in the center of a camp. Several cats were scattered around it, dozing or sharing tongues; Jaypaw waved his tail at Dove's Wing and Fish Leap as he passed, hoping he looked as if he knew where he was going.

He dropped back to follow Half Moon as she climbed farther up the slope until they broke clear of the trees. On the ridge, she dropped her chunk of blackbird and stood gazing out across the moorland. She pointed her muzzle at a faint purple line in the far distance.

"Stone Song thinks we should go that way," she mewed.

As he put down his fresh-kill, Jaypaw felt the hair on his pelt start to rise and his paws tremble. Those were the mountains! Could these cats possibly be the ancestors of the Tribe? Glancing sideways at Half Moon, he saw that she was compactly built, with strong haunches that looked as if they would be good for climbing trees. She didn't have the wiry build of a Tribe cat.

"What do you think it would be like to travel so far?" Half Moon asked.

"Hard." Jaypaw tried to choose his words carefully. "The land that way could be very, very different from the land here."

"How?"

"Sharp hills of stone that stretch up into the sky," Jaypaw replied, his mind filled with memories of the journey he had taken to the mountains. "Huge birds, bigger than badgers, that have to be dragged out of the sky by many cats at once. Tumbling water, filling the air with spray even when there aren't any clouds . . ."

"You sound as if you've been there already," a new voice meowed.

Jaypaw stiffened and turned his head to see the hefty gray figure of Stone Song standing behind them. His piercing blue eyes were fixed on Jaypaw.

"I . . . er . . . I had a dream," Jaypaw stammered.

Stone Song's ears flicked up, his interest intensifying. "Really? Did you dream anything else?"

"No." Jaypaw could have told him a lot more, but he didn't want to get any more tangled up in the gap between what he knew and what these cats thought he should know.

"But you think cats could live there?" Stone Song persisted.

"It wouldn't be easy," Jaypaw warned, thinking of the harsh life of the Tribe. "But maybe."

Stone Song began to pace to and fro along the ridge, the tip of his tail twitching. When he began to speak, Jaypaw could hardly hear him above the roar of the monsters on WindClan territory, which had just begun to move their piles of earth again. He could even feel them in his paws, thrumming through the ground.

"We can't stay here!" Stone Song growled. "Listen to those monsters! What if they come here and tear up this place, too?"

Jaypaw wanted to say, *They won't,* but he remembered in time that he wasn't supposed to know that.

"It's wrong," Stone Song continued, his blue eyes clouded. "Cats are being lost and prey is disappearing. There must be a better place to live." He stopped pacing and sat down facing the purple line of the distant mountains, the wind flattening his pelt against his sides. "Maybe that place is in the stone hills you speak of. When I was kitted, my mother said the wind cried over the stones like a birdcall, giving me my name. Perhaps this means I must find a place where the wind sings over stones, and that will be our home." Sorrow crept into his voice. "My son is never coming back. I cannot wait in this place anymore."

Half Moon glanced toward him, compassion in her eyes. Then she looked at Jaypaw with her head tipped on one side. "Did you really dream of the stone hills?" she meowed. "You seem to see them so clearly."

Jaypaw shuffled his paws. "There must be lots of different places out there."

Half Moon's shining green gaze was still fixed on him. "You would go, wouldn't you? To find a new home for us, with plenty of food and no Twolegs?"

"Well . . ." Jaypaw began.

"If you went, I'd come with you," Half Moon mewed. "You know that."

Jaypaw felt overwhelmed by the strength of her gaze; he wasn't used to looking another cat right in the eyes. The emotion flowing from her pelt threatened to sweep him away. He had never felt it before, not like this, but he knew exactly what it was. *She loves me—at least, she loves the cat she thinks I am!*

For some reason a picture flickered into his mind of Lionblaze and Heatherpaw. Was this how they had felt? He had never understood before how much they had lost when Lionblaze decided they couldn't see each other anymore.

Do I love Half Moon? he wondered. *No . . . but maybe I could love her. I like the way she makes me feel.*

Half Moon took a pace toward Jaypaw, who found himself taking a step back. *We can't do this! I'm a medicine cat!* he wanted to wail aloud. *I don't belong here. You think I'm some other cat!*

To his relief, whatever Half Moon wanted to say was

interrupted by a big black tom who leaped up to the top of the ridge and halted beside Stone Song. "What's going on?" he demanded.

Stone Song turned toward him, blinking as if he had to drag himself back from some distant place. "Oh, it's you, Dark Whiskers. Jay's Wing has had a dream about stone hills and falling water, where there are huge birds to be plucked from the sky, and where Twolegs cannot go. It sounds like a place where we could live safely, with prey and shelter and nothing to harm us."

Dark Whiskers's ears flicked up. "Do you believe him?"

Stone Song nodded.

"Then we must go!" Dark Whiskers exclaimed.

Rising to his paws, Stone Song turned to Jaypaw. "If we leave, will you guide us to this place? Will your dreams show you the way?"

Jaypaw was bewildered by how quickly everything was happening. How long had they been planning to move? Surely they couldn't leave just like that? What about Furled Bracken? A decision like this was for their leader to make.

Before he could reply, a small, dusty-brown she-cat appeared on the ridge, padding in Dark Whiskers's paw steps. "You aren't talking about leaving again, are you?" she spat. "But this is our home! Why can't you understand that?"

Stone Song and Dark Whiskers exchanged a glance. "Shy Fawn, it isn't our home if we can't live here," Stone Song mewed quietly.

Shy Fawn's tail lashed once. "You seem to have forgotten

it's not your decision to make. You know what has to happen: the casting of stones."

"See, stones again!" Stone Song meowed. "We are linked always to stones; why shouldn't we live among them, and feed from the sky?"

Shy Fawn glared at him. "I came to tell you Furled Bracken wants to have a meeting."

"Then we can cast the stones now," Dark Whiskers announced.

With an annoyed hiss, Shy Fawn headed down the slope toward the trees. Stone Song and Dark Whiskers followed; Jaypaw and Half Moon picked up their pieces of blackbird and brought up the rear.

Jaypaw could feel his companion's nervousness and wasn't surprised when she paused halfway down the slope and dropped her prey. "It's really going to happen!" she exclaimed. "We're going to cast the stones to decide whether to leave our home!"

Confusion eddied through Jaypaw. It sounded as if the cats used omens from stones to make their decisions. There was a moonfull of questions he wanted to ask, but he knew enough by now to keep his jaws shut and his ears open.

Is this happening because of me? How can I influence what happened all those seasons ago? He couldn't even think straight because of the feelings that were crackling between him and Half Moon like lightning in greenleaf.

As they continued on down the slope, Dove's Wing and Fish Leap came running out to meet them, their eyes alight and their tails waving.

"Is there going to be a meeting?" Dove's Wing asked excitedly. "Will there be a casting of stones?"

Jaypaw nodded.

"About leaving?" his sister gasped, her neck fur beginning to rise.

"We'll never leave," Fish Leap declared. "This is our home. What about the Pool of Stars? And the tunnels where we become sharpclaws? How can we lose all that?"

Dove's Wing's excitement faded, but her voice was determined as she replied, "If it's a choice between water and caves, and saving our own lives, then we have to go."

Fish Leap led the way down the hill to a glade where the undergrowth grew more thickly than anywhere else Jaypaw had seen. He spotted a row of dens under a fallen tree and behind dense ferns. Several other cats were already there.

Half Moon beckoned him with a flick of her tail and led him behind a clump of spiny thistles to where a dark gap yawned at the foot of an oak tree. From inside Jaypaw could hear tiny sounds of mewling.

Half Moon poked her head inside the hollow tree. "Hi, Owl Feather. We brought you some prey."

As Jaypaw stepped forward to drop his piece of blackbird inside the hollow, he saw a skinny she-cat with pale speckled brown fur, suckling three squirming kits. *She looks just like Kestrelpaw,* he thought.

"Thanks," Owl Feather purred. "The kits are ready to try fresh-kill. Hey . . ." She nudged her kits gently. "Come have some of this blackbird. It's really good."

While the kits tasted blackbird for the first time, Half Moon told Owl Feather about the meeting.

"Not before time," Owl Feather meowed.

"You mean you'd go?" Half Moon gasped. "With the kits?"

"Of course." Owl Feather spoke as if her decision had been made for moons.

"But what about Jagged Lightning?" Half Moon blurted out, then looked as if she wished she hadn't asked that.

"My kits will come with me," Owl Feather replied in a tone that warned no cat should argue with her.

Half Moon gave her an embarrassed nod, and she and Jaypaw backed away from the hollow tree into the glade. By now more cats had arrived. Jaypaw spotted two whose graying muzzles and scant fur showed their age. One of them was a dark brown tom with long legs and knobbly joints; Jaypaw guessed he was Running Horse, who knew so much about herbs. He wondered whether Rising Moon had asked the elder about the horsetail yet; Jaypaw had meant to look for some in the forest, but he had been distracted by finding the Twoleg path and the stone hollow. The other elder was a pale ginger she-cat with green eyes; Jaypaw could see she had once been beautiful, but she was frail now, every rib showing through her pelt.

Opposite Jaypaw, Rising Moon padded into the clearing, nudging along Broken Shadow, who looked so dazed with grief that she didn't know where she was. A large gray-and-white tom flanked her on the other side; he looked enough like Half Moon that Jaypaw guessed he must be her father, Chasing Clouds.

Furled Bracken was sitting in the center of the glade, waiting for the rest of the cats to appear. Jaypaw thought he looked patient and respectful, not at all like a Clan leader who had just summoned his cats to a meeting. Furled Bracken hadn't even called to announce it; the news had spread from cat to cat, and they all seemed to be strolling in whenever they felt like it.

At last Stone Song stepped forward from where he had been standing at the side of the clearing beside Dark Whiskers. "We wish to cast the stones," he meowed.

"About leaving?" Furled Bracken asked.

Stone Song nodded. "Yes."

With a resigned look, Furled Bracken rose to his paws. "I wish it hadn't come to this," he sighed, "but I know there is only one way to decide. Before we cast the stones, I want to remind you all that this has been our home for as long as any cat can remember."

Any living *cat,* Jaypaw corrected him. *But where have all the dead cats gone? Are they here now, watching us without being able to speak?*

"Yes," Furled Bracken went on with a sad glance around the clearing, "prey is scarcer this greenleaf than it has ever been before, and yes, the Twolegs are coming closer. But are we really going to turn and flee like mice? We have found a way to survive alongside the badgers, and they have caused us far more trouble in the past than Twolegs. We should stay together and accept that we have to share the lake."

Jaypaw was almost convinced by the deep emotion behind Furled Bracken's speech. Several other cats were nodding in agreement, including Rising Moon and the frail old she-cat.

Half Moon nudged him. "Look, Jagged Lightning wants to stay." She flicked her ears toward a long-legged black-and-white tom, whose amber eyes were glowing with approval of Furled Bracken's plea. "Owl Feather won't like that."

A soft murmur of anticipation ran around the glade as Stone Song stepped forward. "What you say is true, Furled Bracken," he began, dipping his head respectfully, "but it leaves out too much. What about the cats we have lost? Falcon Swoop died under the paws of a Twoleg monster."

Jaypaw spotted Dove's Wing with head and tail drooping miserably at the mention of their mother's death; quickly he bent his own head.

"Then her mate Falling Rain left us, and no cat knows where he's gone. And a moon ago"—his voice shook—"Fallen Leaves went into the tunnels and never came out."

Broken Shadow let out a soft wail at the mention of their son, and Stone Song glanced at her for a heartbeat, his eyes full of love and pain.

"The trial in the caves isn't supposed to take sharpclaws away from us," he went on. "It's supposed to be the making of them, the sign that they're fully grown and the equal of any other cat. And that's not all. Prey is disappearing, scared off by Twolegs or taken by foxes and badgers. Even the ground is being torn up by Twolegs, with endless noise and quaking. This isn't our home now; it's a place that doesn't want us anymore."

More nods and murmurs of agreement followed Stone Song's speech. A black-and-white cat called out, "But where can we go?"

Jaypaw's heart sank when he saw Stone Song turn toward him. He could guess what was coming next.

"Jay's Wing has had a dream," the tabby tom announced. "He saw a place where we can live: stone hills teeming with prey and shelter, and free from any enemies."

Jaypaw bit back a protest. He hadn't made the mountains sound as wonderful as that! But Stone Song had a point; the Clans had made the Great Journey when Twolegs made the forest impossible to live in. And cats *had* settled in the mountains, long, long ago. If these cats were the ancestors of the Tribe, then perhaps it was Jaypaw's responsibility to *encourage* them to go there.

"It sounds a lot better than here," Dark Whiskers commented.

Rising Moon nodded. "I don't want to lose my kits down those dreadful tunnels."

"And we'd be far away from Twoleg monsters," Whispering Breeze added. "We wouldn't lose any more cats like my sister was lost."

Jaypaw saw that Dove's Wing and Fish Leap were gazing at him expectantly; their glances scorched his fur. They were waiting for him to lead them! Then he realized that *all* the cats were looking at him in the same way. For a heartbeat his head spun. *I can't do this! I want to go home to ThunderClan!*

When his head cleared, Jaypaw saw that the cats had formed into a ragged line, leading up to Furled Bracken. Their gaze was fixed on the ground in front of the line. Jaypaw padded forward to see what they were looking at.

At Furled Bracken's paws was a circular patch of bare ground, about the size of a tree stump. Beside it was a pile of small, round pebbles that looked as if they came from the lakeshore. Furled Bracken stretched out his claws and drew a line in the earth across the bare patch, dividing it into two halves. Then he pushed one of the stones into the center of one half.

"This side wishes to stay," he announced. He stepped back to let the next cat choose.

Stone Song padded up. He pushed his stone into the opposite half of the bare patch. "This side wishes to leave."

Jaypaw stared at the circle of ground in astonishment. These cats were casting the stones themselves! There were no omens, no sharing tongues with StarClan, no obeying the word of the leader. Furled Bracken was allowing the cats to make their own decision. "What sort of way is this to run a Clan?" he murmured under his breath.

And what's going to happen when all the stones are cast?

The elder Running Horse stepped up and placed a stone in the "stay" half of the circle. "My bones are too old to climb stone hills," he grunted. "Come on, Cloudy Sun, you know what to do."

The frail she-cat padded up beside him. "The sun warms me here, and that's all I want now," she murmured, pushing a stone to rest beside Running Horse's. She touched her nose to his ear. "We'll stay together."

Stone Song and Dark Whiskers led Broken Shadow up to the circle. Distractedly, as if she hardly knew what she was doing, she set a stone in the "leave" half, and Dark Whiskers added his own with it.

Jagged Lightning padded up, hesitating for a moment while he glanced at Owl Feather. But Owl Feather was absorbed in watching her kits, who were wrestling at her paws. Jagged Lightning voted to stay, and turned away.

Jaypaw realized that Owl Feather had been aware of her mate all the time. As soon as Jagged Lightning had moved off from the circle, she cast her own stone, to leave, without looking at him once.

His belly churning, Jaypaw stepped up to make his own choice, but Furled Bracken held him back with a flick of the tail. "As the newest sharpclaw, you cast the final stone," he meowed.

Jaypaw's belly churned when he saw that two straight lines of stones were forming in the half circles. They looked equal; what would happen if there was no clear decision?

Rising Moon was the next cat to step up; she paused for a moment, then took a deep breath and pushed her stone into the "stay" half. "I've reared kits here before," she murmured, "and I'll rear them again."

Her mate Chasing Clouds gave her a long, sorrowful look, but cast his stone to leave. Whispering Breeze followed him. The line for leaving was growing longer, but then Fish Leap,

Dawn River, and Shy Fawn all went up together and set their stones to stay.

Dove's Wing padded up slowly, glanced at her friends' stones, then at Jaypaw, and finally voted to leave. Only Half Moon and Jaypaw were left. Half Moon stepped forward, gazing straight at Jaypaw as she pushed her stone into the "leave" half of the circle.

The lines were equal! *Now what do I do?* Jaypaw wondered, aware that every cat was staring at him. *How can it be fair that I have to make the decision? I don't even belong here!*

His paws trembled as he walked up to the edge of the bare patch and stretched out a paw to draw a stone toward him. It felt sun-warmed under his still-sore pad. "They have to go to the mountains," he whispered. "They will become the Tribe of Rushing Water." Closing his eyes, he pushed his stone to the end of the line that voted to leave.

CHAPTER 18

A gasp like the wind in the trees rose from the cats around Jaypaw. "No! No!" Broken Shadow wailed. "Fallen Leaves, I didn't mean it! I want to stay with you!"

Another wail of distress rose from some other cat; Jaypaw felt a claw of guilt tear briefly at his heart, but he did his best to ignore it. *I know that this is the right decision for them.*

He padded away from the circle, aware of the glowing look in Half Moon's eyes. "We're going to travel together!" she whispered.

Furled Bracken stepped forward. "The stones have been cast," he announced. "I can no longer be your leader. Stone Song, it is only fair that you lead us into the mountains." His gaze traveled around the assembled cats. "If any cat thinks Stone Song should not be our leader, speak now."

They choose *their leaders?* Jaypaw wondered, astonished. *Leaders can retire, and become ordinary sharpclaws again?*

Silence followed Furled Bracken's words, except for the muffled wails of Broken Shadow. Rising Moon was beside her, comforting her by licking her ear. "Everything will be all right," she encouraged the grief-stricken she-cat. "Fallen

Leaves won't know you've gone."

You're wrong, Jaypaw thought. *Fallen Leaves will live in the tunnels for moons and moons and moons, in agony that he was abandoned.*

Stone Song dipped his head to Furled Bracken. "I will do my best to lead our cats to safety," he promised. Then he glanced around at the others, meeting the expectation in their eyes. "We shall rest until dusk," he ordered. "We will leave while the Twoleg monsters are sleeping."

Cats looked at each other, a flurry of confusion arising even among those who had wanted to leave. "So soon?" Chasing Clouds asked.

"We have waited long enough," Stone Song replied with a grief-filled glance at Broken Shadow. "There is nothing more to keep us here. Jay's Wing has told us of the stone hills that are ready for us. They will be our home."

Chasing Clouds straightened up. "Then let's hunt," he suggested. "We'll make sure that every cat is full fed before we set out."

Several cats bounded out of the glade as soon as he had finished speaking, looking relieved to have something to do. Chasing Clouds followed them, pausing beside Rising Moon to touch her ear with his nose. "We will raise strong, healthy kits in the mountains," he promised her.

Rising Moon hesitated for a heartbeat, then twined her tail with his. "I know. I'll look for some useful herbs," she added. "Running Horse will help me."

Memories flooded over Jaypaw of the preparations he and his Clanmates had made before their own journey into the mountains. He wondered if there was any more advice he ought to give these cats, like watching out for the dogs in the barn that had nearly torn Hollyleaf and Lionblaze to pieces.

Mouse-brain! he told himself. *The barn probably isn't even built yet.*

Standing alone in the midst of the flurry of activity, Jaypaw couldn't shake off the feeling that there was something missing, something essential for the cats to find their new home and establish themselves securely in the mountains. He just couldn't think what it was.

I'd better try to catch some prey, he decided. *I'll need strength for the journey. At least I'll be able to see when I leap over the gaps in the mountains!*

Before he reached the edge of the glade, he was intercepted by Stone Song. "Jay's Wing, I need to talk to you."

Puzzled, Jaypaw followed him into the shadow of the trees that fringed the glade. The dark gray tabby stood over him, an earnest expression in his blue eyes. "I need your help, Jay's Wing," he explained. "We've never had a cat like you before, who sees things in their dreams. Have you done it before? Do you think it will happen again?"

Jaypaw didn't know what to answer; certainly he couldn't tell the truth. In the end, he nodded awkwardly.

Relief crept into the new leader's eyes. "This is unknown for all of us. I know your dreams may be wrong, but I am willing to trust you—and wherever your dreams came from."

Understanding blazed down on Jaypaw like a burst of sunlight. Now he understood what these cats needed more than anything else. They needed StarClan, and a medicine cat to help them listen to the cats that had walked here before.

"Your . . . our ancestors," he blurted out. "The dreams are sent by our ancestors."

Stone Shadow looked startled. "You mean cats who have *died?*"

Jaypaw nodded. "They will guide us, if we're prepared to listen. They'll . . . they'll speak to us in dreams, and send us signs that certain cats will understand."

Stone Song's eyes widened and his neck fur began to rise. "Do you mean they speak to *you?*"

"Yes, but they'll speak to other cats, too—if they're willing to hear what they have to say."

Stone Song tipped his head on one side. "We have always wondered whether our lost cats can still see us and hear us. I know Broken Shadow wishes for that more than anything." He hesitated, then added, "You're sure it's not just dreams of your mother?"

"I know it isn't."

The new leader's blue eyes seemed more piercing than ever. "If we find the stone hills, I will know you are right." Turning to leave, he glanced back over one shoulder. "Thank you, Jay's Wing."

When he had gone, Jaypaw flopped to the ground, his head spinning. *Have I just made myself the first-ever medicine cat?* He didn't even know if these cats had the same sort of ancestors, in some kind of StarClan or Tribe of Endless Hunting. *Have I just set myself an impossible task?*

The sound of approaching paw steps roused him from his thoughts. Looking up, he saw Half Moon appearing from behind the nearest tree, a vole dangling from her jaws. She set it down in front of him.

"Here," she mewed. "I know your paws are still too sore to hunt." When Jaypaw hesitated, she pushed it closer with one paw. "Go ahead. I've had mine."

"Thanks." Jaypaw tore hungrily into the vole. "You're a great hunter, Half Moon," he mumbled around a huge mouthful.

"It looks as if we've a long journey ahead," Half Moon went on. "Do you really believe there are stone hills where we can make our home?" Her green eyes were wide, shimmering in the half-light under the trees.

Jaypaw swallowed. "Yes. I promise, they are there."

Half Moon gave him a long look, overwhelming him once more with the intensity in her gaze. "I believe you," she murmured.

Jaypaw shared the last of the vole with her and settled down to doze beside her, their tails curled around each other. Breathing in her sweet scent, he began to feel a little less homesick. A little more as if this was where—*when*—he belonged.

A paw prodded him in the side. Blinking, he looked up into the face of Whispering Breeze. "It's time," she mewed.

Half Moon was already on her paws. Jaypaw followed her through the clearing and out onto the hillside. The sun had set, leaving only a few streaks of scarlet in the sky. Jaypaw looked up to see if any of the warriors of StarClan had appeared, before he remembered that his warrior ancestors wouldn't be born for many seasons.

So are they just stars? he wondered, gazing up at the glittering points of light.

Cats were padding anxiously among the trees as if their paws itched to leave, while their hearts still drew them back to their familiar home. Jaypaw watched Owl Feather's kits tumbling around her paws. "Are we really going all the way to the top of the hill?" one of them asked, his eyes huge as moons.

"That's right," Owl Feather replied. "And even farther than that."

The tiny kit bounced with delight. "Wow!"

Running Horse and Cloudy Sun were standing together under a tree. Running Horse brushed his tail along his denmate's side. "The stones are cast, so we have to go," he meowed.

"We'll get there," Cloudy Sun replied bravely. "We'll help each other."

Admiring the elders' courage, Jaypaw hoped she was right. He was already planning the route to make it as easy as possible, hoping that now that he could see he could remember the way to the cave behind the waterfall.

"Are we ready?" Stone Song padded up, casting a glance at all the cats.

A murmur of agreement rose around him. Jaypaw noticed that Jagged Lightning and Shy Fawn were both looking unhappy, but they didn't protest. Now that the decision had been made, every cat would stand by it. This was their code of honor, their version of the warrior code.

Stone Song flicked his ears at Jaypaw. "Ready, Jay's Wing?"

Jaypaw nodded. *Am I really doing this? Am I about to lead the Tribe of Rushing Water to their new home?*

Stone Song set off up the hill, his cats following him in straggling groups. Jaypaw took his place near the back. When they reached the top of the ridge, the purple line of mountains had vanished in the gathering darkness; the land stretched flat and black in front of them as far as the horizon.

As they padded along the ridge, Half Moon hurried up, brushing against Jaypaw's side. "Look, one of Owl Feather's kits has fallen over," she mewed. "I must go help her."

She bounded on, then halted briefly and glanced over her shoulder. "Don't look back," she whispered. "It will only make it harder."

Jaypaw watched her pale shape moving away from him in the dusk. Something swelled inside his chest as he realized how much courage she had—how much all the cats had—to set out on a journey like this on the strength of a dream. He just hoped he was right, for their sakes.

His paws slowed beneath him and he stopped to gaze down the hill at the black expanse of the lake, glittering here and there under the first stars to appear in the dark blue sky. As he watched, the moon slid out from behind a cloud, shedding its silver light over the water. The lake seemed so familiar, and yet it was not his home.

"Good-bye," he whispered, wondering if he was saying good-bye to ThunderClan as well.

The rest of the cats had passed him, heading into what would become WindClan territory. As Jaypaw set out to catch up to them, he heard a cat calling his name.

"Jaypaw!"

His ThunderClan name.

He spun around. "Rock!"

The sightless cat stood close to a boulder on the hillside, his furless skin glowing in the moonlight.

"You do not belong with these cats," he rasped. "You have done what you came here to do. It is time for you to go back to your Clan."

The day before, Jaypaw would have been relieved. Now his first reaction was panic. "But—but what about Stone Song?" he stammered. "I promised him. And Half Moon . . ."

"Your time here is over," Rock insisted.

Jaypaw knew he had to obey. His destiny lay here, by the lake, not in the mountains. Thanks to him, the Tribe of Rushing Water would find their new home, and the Tribe of Endless Hunting would be found.

Padding over to Rock, he cast one last glance at the plodding line of cats, straining his eyes to pick out Half Moon's glimmering pelt. *She'll be so hurt that I left without saying good-bye.* But she was not his future. ThunderClan was, where he was a medicine cat.

He turned back to Rock. "Will the real Jay's Wing come back now?"

Rock shook his head. "No. He disappeared at the start of their journey to the mountains."

The cats were vanishing one by one into the darkness. None of them had noticed that Jaypaw was gone. Jaypaw stood rigid for a moment, then gave his pelt a shake. "Okay, let's go," he muttered.

Rock led the way behind the boulder, where the narrow entrance to a tunnel opened up. The old cat squeezed his way inside and beckoned with his tail for Jaypaw to follow.

The tunnel was utterly dark; Jaypaw guided himself by the sound of Rock's paw steps as they padded through the silent blackness. Cool air told him where other tunnels branched off, but Rock led him straight down into the hill. Jaypaw pricked his ears, alert for any sound of Fallen Leaves, but there was no sign of the lost cat. How long before he realized that the cats aboveground had gone? Would he know at once how many moons he would have to wait in the empty darkness, until cats returned to the lake? Jaypaw shuddered, hoping Fallen Leaves would have no idea of what lay ahead.

At last the tunnel began to slope upward again. The sound of Rock's paw steps faded, but now Jaypaw could smell moss and leaves again, the damp scents of the forest. Soon he found himself stepping into open air with the familiar scents of ThunderClan swirling around him. He was blind again, but he knew exactly where he was.

Slowly he picked his way down the paths that led to the stone hollow. Had he found the answers he was looking for? Had he really been one of the cats that lived here once? And had those cats left to form the Tribe of Rushing Water? Was that where the prophecy came from?

At the last moment, when he could already taste the scent of the stone hollow, he veered away and headed for the lake. A soft breeze had sprung up; the broken twittering of birds overhead told him that dawn was approaching. Reaching the lakeshore, Jaypaw padded across the soft grass and found the stick hidden under tree roots on the bank. He pulled it out and ran his paws over the scratch marks, as he had done so often before.

This time the scratches spoke to him clearly: Names and images of the sharpclaws filled his mind, and he could remember many of them from meeting them face-to-face. Jagged Lightning, Cloudy Sun, Shy Fawn, Owl Feather . . . They walked beside him at the Moonpool because he was one of them, the one cat who had returned to where they had lived long, long ago. *Is that what makes me more powerful than StarClan?*

Jaypaw wondered if Lionblaze and Hollyleaf must have been part of the ancient Clan, too, even though he hadn't met them in the past. He drew his paws down the stick again and a vision flashed into his mind: three cats standing together on the ridge, with the rising moon behind them and their shadows stretching out, vast and black, across the silver lake.

Three cats, kin of Firestar's kin, with the power of the stars in their paws. And now Jaypaw could understand how they belonged together, even after the lapse of so many, many seasons.

"We have come back," he murmured. "The three have come home."

CHAPTER 19

Lionblaze woke to the sound of coughing. For a moment he burrowed deeper into the moss, trying to remember the last time he'd had a good night's sleep. His dreams were filled with Tigerstar, taunting him about his power, sneering at him for being revolted by the sight of Heatherpaw's blood-soaked body. And when he wasn't asleep, the warriors' den was filled with choking, spluttering cats battling greencough. Then he stiffened. The sick cats had all gone to the Twoleg nest with Firestar! There shouldn't be any coughing now.

Raising his head, Lionblaze saw Spiderleg in his nest a couple of tail-lengths away, his body shaken by another fit of coughing.

Oh, no! Firestar's idea hasn't worked.

"Spiderleg," he meowed, "you'd better get along to Leafpool. She'll give you something for the cough, and then you can join the others in the Twoleg nest."

"Don't tell me what to do," the older warrior snapped. "I've just got a bit of moss in my throat, that's all."

Even in the dim light of the warriors' den, Lionblaze could see that Spiderleg's eyes were glazed with fever. "I don't think so."

At the same moment Brambleclaw raised his head from his nest nearer the center of the den. "Spiderleg, you're ill. You know how fast the sickness spreads. Go and see Leafpool *now.* Lionblaze, go with him."

"Sure." Lionblaze hauled himself out of his nest and gave his pelt a quick grooming.

Spiderleg rose to his paws with an exaggerated sigh that ended in another bout of coughing. He pushed his way into the clearing, and Lionblaze followed, padding a few paw steps behind him as they headed for the medicine cats' den. The chill of dawn still lay over the camp, and shadows crowded thickly around the sides of the hollow. A moisture-laden breeze held the promise of rain later.

Before they reached the den, Daisy came bounding over from the nursery. "Spiderleg, what's the matter?" she fretted. "Are you ill?"

"I'm fine. I just wish—" More coughing interrupted Spiderleg. "I just wish every cat would stop fussing," he finished when he could speak again.

Daisy's eyes grew wide with dismay. "You *are* ill!"

"Don't worry, Daisy." Lionblaze brushed his muzzle against the cream-colored she-cat's shoulder. "I'm taking him to Leafpool now."

He and Spiderleg headed off again, leaving Daisy to watch them after them, her eyes filled with anxiety.

Inside the den, Leafpool and Jaypaw were already awake. "This is the last of the tansy," Leafpool was mewing. "You'd better see if you can find more, and take it straight to the

Twoleg nest. Remember to put it on the flat stone outside the entrance."

"Okay." Jaypaw turned to go, then halted as he realized that Spiderleg and Lionblaze were there. "What now?" he asked.

Spiderleg answered with another fit of coughing.

"No!" For a heartbeat Lionblaze saw fear flicker in Leafpool's eyes. Then she was the quietly efficient medicine cat again. "Spiderleg, eat this tansy. It'll soothe your throat. Jaypaw, bring some more back here as well."

Jaypaw gave her a brief nod, whisked past the bramble screen, and vanished.

While Spiderleg was chewing up the tansy, grumbling under his breath, Daisy poked her head into the den. "Can I come in?" she asked Leafpool, her words muffled by the plump vole she was carrying.

Leafpool looked uncertain; the fewer cats around Spiderleg the better. Then she nodded. "Of course, Daisy. What is it?"

Daisy dropped the vole at Spiderleg's paws. "I brought you this. I thought you could do with a good meal before you go to the Twoleg nest."

"Well, you needn't have bothered," Spiderleg meowed ungraciously. "I'm not hungry."

Daisy took a step back, her neck fur bristling. "I chose it specially!"

Spiderleg didn't reply, just swiped his tongue round his jaws for the last of the tansy juices.

"Our kits are worried about you, too," Daisy went on. Her voice grew sharper. "It's a wonder they remember you, because you never come to visit them."

Spiderleg shrugged. "It's not that I'm not interested. . . . I just know that you'll do a great job of raising them without me."

"Why?" Daisy challenged him. "Because I've raised kits on my own before? But that wasn't my choice, Spiderleg, as you know very well."

Lionblaze exchanged an embarrassed glance with Leafpool; he wished he could leave the den, but the two quarreling cats were blocking the entrance. Leafpool was listening with a strange look in her eyes that Lionblaze couldn't interpret.

"Every kit is different," Daisy went on. "And every kit deserves to know its father. You're missing out, Spiderleg, and if you're not careful it will be too late, and your own kits won't know who you are!"

Not waiting for a reply, she spun around and stalked out of the den.

"She-cats!" Spiderleg exclaimed.

He turned to leave, but Leafpool slipped past him and blocked his way out. "Kits are a precious gift, Spiderleg," she mewed quietly. "You should take every chance you can to be a good father. It's even better than being a mentor."

"How would you know?" Spiderleg demanded.

Leafpool just gazed at him, her amber eyes clear and calm.

"Sorry," Spiderleg muttered after a heartbeat. "It's just . . . I never planned to have kits with Daisy. I feel useless and clumsy around them. And I feel every cat is judging me because I'm not closer to Daisy. It didn't work out, that's all."

"That's not the point," Leafpool replied. "Your kits still have a mother and a father, even if you and Daisy aren't mates anymore. You're punishing the kits by not being a better father. They won't judge you because they don't know any different. But in the end, they're the only things that matter."

"I don't know what to do!" Spiderleg protested. "I can't—" Another outbreak of coughing cut off what he was about to say.

"Then learn!" Leafpool's amber eyes blazed. "You've seen Brambleclaw and Graystripe and Dustpelt around their kits. I can't believe you don't see how important this is! You should cherish your kits with every breath you take."

As she spoke, Lionblaze felt a surge of warmth toward Brambleclaw. He was a great father, always ready to listen or to help if his kits had a problem. He'd spent a lot of time with the three kits, because Squirrelflight went back to being a warrior so quickly. Lionblaze trusted him completely; he couldn't imagine a better father. *If Spiderleg's not careful,* he thought, *he and the kits are going to end up like Crowfeather and Breezepelt.* They *don't even like each other!*

"Lionblaze." Leafpool had obviously realized that he was there, listening to every word she and Spiderleg were saying. "You can go now. Thanks for helping."

Lionblaze dipped his head, and slipped past Spiderleg into the clearing. As he left, he heard Leafpool meow, "Before you go to the Twoleg nest, you *will* eat that vole. You need to keep your strength up if you're going to get better."

As he left Leafpool's den, Lionblaze spotted Brambleclaw

choosing a squirrel from the fresh-kill pile. Squirrelflight padded up, and her mate dropped the fresh-kill at her paws.

"This is for you," he meowed. "I know how much you love young squirrel."

"So do you," Squirrelflight purred, touching her nose to his ear. "Let's share it."

Brambleclaw hesitated. "Okay, but you have as much as you want. The whole Clan wants you to get strong again."

The two cats settled down side by side to share the squirrel.

A surge of warmth spread through Lionblaze as he watched them. *Thank StarClan our parents are so close.*

"Hey, Lionblaze!" Brambleclaw lifted his head from the squirrel. "Now that you've dealt with Spiderleg, what about a hunting patrol? Ashfur is waiting for you. The mice aren't going to line up and come running into camp, you know."

"Sure!" Lionblaze waved his tail and bounded across the clearing toward Ashfur. Yes, he loved his father, even if he was a bossy old furball!

Lionblaze padded along the old Twoleg path with a squirrel and two mice dangling from his jaws. It was his turn to take fresh-kill to the tree trunk outside the Twoleg nest. A thin drizzle was falling, misting on his pelt and turning the path to mud.

Two sunrises before, when Spiderleg had started coughing, the hopes of every cat in the Clan had plummeted, afraid that Firestar's plan would come to nothing after all. But since then, no other cat had fallen ill. Lionblaze had begun to wonder if they had started to win the battle after all. He didn't know much about the sick cats in the Twoleg nest except that all of them, even Millie, were still alive.

Everything was quiet as the walls of the Twoleg nest appeared through the trees. Lionblaze brushed through the wet grass to leave his prey in the hollow trunk. The trunk wasn't empty as he had expected. A few pieces of fresh-kill, turning soggy from the rain, still lay at the bottom. The scent of cats around the tree stump was stale and faint.

Icy water, far colder than the rain, seemed to trickle down Lionblaze's spine. *Why aren't the sick cats eating? Are they all too weak to fetch the prey?*

With one paw he scraped the old prey—rapidly turning to crow-food—out of the tree trunk, and replaced it with the fresh, pushing his catch farther back into the hollow to keep it dry. Then he hesitated, looking around. He was meant to continue hunting, but he couldn't leave until he found out why the cats in the Twoleg nest hadn't collected all their fresh-kill.

Slowly he padded toward the entrance to the den. Leafpool and Firestar had both forbidden the hunters to go any closer than the tree trunk, but Lionblaze told himself that this was an emergency, and both would want him to break the rules. As he approached an eerie wailing rose from the Twoleg nest, the cry of a cat in deep distress.

Lionblaze stopped dead. "What's happening?" he called out, hating the way his voice shook. *Courage,* he told himself fiercely.

For a heartbeat there was no response. Then Lionblaze leaped back as Cloudtail's face loomed in front of him in the entrance, his white fur startling in the gloom.

"Firestar is dying," the warrior rasped.

Lionblaze clenched his teeth on a wail of despair. Forgetting to be wary of the sickness, he brushed past Cloudtail and entered the nest.

Firestar was lying in a den on the far side. Most of the sick cats were sitting around him in a ragged circle; Brightheart and Honeyfern were bending over him, holding scraps of soaked moss to his lips. Lionblaze pushed through the line of cats and looked down at his Clan leader. Firestar's breath was coming in hoarse gasps, his sides heaving with the effort of sucking in air. A stench of something more than sickness hung in the air.

As Lionblaze gazed at him, horrified, Brightheart looked up. "Firestar is losing a life," she mewed gently.

Taking a step back, Lionblaze stood alongside the other sick cats and watched in silence as their leader struggled to breathe. Gradually the heaving of Firestar's flanks slowed down; his breathing grew shallower, then stopped. His eyes closed and he lay still.

Lionblaze saw the faintest outline of a flame-colored cat rise from Firestar's body and pad away, to be lost in the shadows in one corner of the den.

Is that what it's like to lose a life? he wondered. *How many does Firestar have left? What if that was his last one?*

It seemed as if he stood beside his leader's body for countless moons, or perhaps it was no more than a heartbeat. Then he saw Firestar's sides give a convulsive heave. Bright green eyes blinked open, struggling to focus.

"Firestar." Brightheart's tone was soft as she bent over him again. "You're back with us."

Lionblaze felt his mouth drop open. Firestar really had died and come back!

Cloudtail padded up with a fresh bundle of soaked moss, which he gave to his mate. Brightheart held the moss to Firestar's lips. "Drink this," she murmured. "And then get some rest."

"Go and fetch him some fresh-kill," Cloudtail ordered Lionblaze. "He needs to keep his strength up."

Lionblaze ran outside again, and came back with one of the freshly killed mice. By the time he returned, Firestar was sitting up, a confused look in his eyes that gradually died away.

"Thanks," he murmured as Lionblaze dropped the mouse beside him. "But you shouldn't be in here. You could catch the sickness."

Lionblaze's pelt stood on end. Firestar had come back, but he needed to leave the nest right away. If he stayed, how long would it be before the dreadful sickness killed him again?

Firestar took a bite of the mouse, glancing around while he chewed and swallowed it. "It's okay," he meowed, meeting the worried gazes of his Clanmates. "Everything's fine now."

"No, it's not," Brightheart mewed sharply. "You're still weak, even if you haven't got greencough anymore. What if you lose another life? You should go back to the camp and let

Leafpool look after you."

Firestar shook his head. "There's nothing that Leafpool can do for me there that she can't do while I'm here. I'll stay with you all."

A murmur of respect rose from the cats around him. Rosekit padded forward to the edge of Firestar's nest. "Are you going to keep dying and coming back again?" she asked curiously.

"I hope not," Firestar replied, while Honeyfern shooed Rosekit back into the nursery area.

"I knew you'd insist on staying," Brightheart murmured, touching her nose to Firestar's ear.

Firestar blinked at her. "I am not the cat with the most to lose," he replied, his green gaze drifting toward the nest where Millie lay.

Lionblaze turned to look at the gray she-cat. She looked even thinner and more pitiful than when she had left the camp three sunrises before. She was lying sprawled on one side, her sides barely rising and falling with each faint breath.

Briarkit nuzzled into her belly, trying to feed and letting out pitiful mewling noises when she couldn't find any milk. Honeyfern bent over her, gently nudging her away with one paw. "Come on," she comforted the tiny kit. "I'll find you a mouse to eat. They're very tasty."

"Don't want mouse." Briarkit's voice was hoarse. "I want milk." Her voice rose to a feeble wail. "I want *my mother*!"

Lionblaze turned away, unable to watch. Around him, the sick cats were stumbling back to their own nests, heads and tails drooping in defeat.

How long before they're all dead like Firestar? And none of them have nine lives.

Guilt swamped him. He knew that he had the power to help his Clanmates—the power to do *anything*, he reminded himself—but he had refused to use it.

"I'm going," he told Cloudtail roughly, desperate to get out of the nest and as far from the sickness as possible. "I'll tell Brambleclaw about Firestar losing a life, and I'll be back soon with more fresh-kill."

"It's not fresh-kill we need," Cloudtail pointed out. "It's catmint."

"And the will of StarClan that we survive," Brightheart added.

Their words echoed in Lionblaze's ears as he ran back to the hollow, hardly feeling the stone path under his paws. StarClan did want the sick cats to survive. Otherwise they wouldn't have sent Jaypaw the dream where he found the catmint.

"Even if it wasn't StarClan who sent him the dream," Lionblaze argued with himself, "the three of us have been given our powers for a reason. Perhaps this is it. Perhaps this is the start of the prophecy."

When he pushed through the tunnel into the camp, he couldn't see Brambleclaw. Checking the warriors' den, he found it empty, but as he emerged he spotted the Clan deputy coming out of the tunnel with his jaws full of fresh-kill. Sandstorm and Berrynose followed him; Lionblaze met them by the fresh-kill pile where they dropped their prey.

"There's news," he meowed abruptly. "Firestar has lost a life."

"No!" Sandstorm's green eyes widened. She spun around as if she was going to dash out of the camp, but Brambleclaw laid his tail gently over her shoulders.

"You can't help him," he murmured.

Sandstorm sat down, her head bowed. "I know." Her voice was so low Lionblaze could scarcely hear it. "But it's hard."

"Did you see Firestar die?" Berrynose meowed, his eyes wide. "What was it like?"

Lionblaze glared at him, and didn't bother to answer. As he padded away, he heard Brambleclaw's voice raised scathingly. "I might expect a question like that from a kit, Berrynose, but not from a warrior, especially one that *I* mentored."

Forgetting the annoying cream-colored warrior, Lionblaze brushed past the brambles into the medicine cats' den. To his relief, Leafpool wasn't there, only Jaypaw, pawing through a pitiful collection of thin, shriveled herbs.

Jaypaw whipped around. "What do *you* want?"

Lionblaze bowed his head. "I'm sorry," he meowed. "I will go to WindClan."

Chapter 20

As soon as Lionblaze had caught more prey, he headed back toward the old Twoleg nest. Dropping the fresh-kill in the tree trunk, he noticed that the rest of the catch he had brought earlier had disappeared, and some cat had scratched earth over the soggy leavings. Slightly reassured that the sick cats were back to their normal routine, he doubled back and headed deeper into the forest toward the entrance to the tunnel.

Fear raised every hair on his pelt, but Lionblaze quickened his pace until he was racing through the trees. He felt sick at the thought of going through the tunnels in the dark. He wanted to do it while there was still some chance of daylight.

He halted a few fox-lengths away from the tunnel mouth, glancing around warily with his ears pricked and his mouth open to pick up any trace of his Clanmates. No cat must know what he was about to do. This was his and Jaypaw's secret, because the tunnels between the Clans represented nothing but invasion and bloodshed. To his relief, the only Thunder-Clan scent was stale; he guessed that the dawn patrol had passed this spot earlier in the day.

Flattening himself to the ground until his belly fur

brushed the grass, Lionblaze crept through the undergrowth and into the tunnel. A couple of tail-lengths down he encountered the thorn barrier he and his Clanmates had put there after the battle, to stop WindClan coming back that way. By the time he had scrabbled his way through the obstacle he had scratched shoulders and pricked pads, and left tufts of golden fur on the thorns behind him.

StarClan, please don't let any cat come here to check before I get back.

Darkness closed around Lionblaze as he walked along the passage. There was no sound except for his soft paw steps and rapid breathing, but his heart seemed to be thudding loudly enough to be heard in the WindClan camp. It wasn't the WindClan warriors he was afraid of, though. If he met any of them, he would fight and take the consequences afterward when Onestar complained to Firestar. The vision of his dream was what scared him, and he seemed to smell the reek of Heatherpaw's blood already.

At last Lionblaze realized that the darkness was giving way to a gray light. Ahead of him he could hear the sound of rushing water. Moments later he stepped out into the cave where the river flowed, its surface faintly reflecting the light from the gap in the roof. He glanced up at the ledge where Heatherpaw used to sit when she was Heatherstar, leader of DarkClan, but it was empty now.

Lionblaze felt a stabbing pain in his heart as if an enemy had sunk teeth into it. He *couldn't* wish for those days to come back again, when he was lying to his Clan and losing so much sleep that he couldn't train properly. He didn't want to remember them, either, not after Heatherpaw had betrayed him.

He shook himself vigorously as if he was scattering raindrops from his pelt, then headed for the tunnel that led up into WindClan territory. Soon he saw the crack ahead of him, a shaft of daylight breaking through it. Beyond he could see more rock and tough moorland grass.

Lionblaze paused, alert again, this time for the sound or scent of WindClan. But all he could hear was the faint whine of the wind as it brushed through the grass, and there was no scent of WindClan cats at all. Padding forward, he dared to poke his head out of the tunnel.

The place was just as Jaypaw had described it: a tumble of rough, lichen-covered rocks, with wiry moorland grass growing between them. *A spring of water welling up between two rocks . . .* Lionblaze's ears pricked, and he made out the sound of a tiny trickle.

Checking once again for scent, he picked up a new trace of WindClan, but couldn't see or hear any cats. Warily he emerged from the tunnel and crept toward the sound, pressing himself flat to the ground and taking advantage of all the cover the rocks offered him. Every hair on his pelt was bristling; he imagined his scent spreading all over WindClan territory, drawing every cat toward him, and the faint brush of his paws through the grass sounded as loud as an owl's screech.

Lionblaze felt as if several moons had passed, but it was only a few moments before he crawled around the base of a rock and spotted the stream that Jaypaw had told him about. It welled up from a crack into a tiny pool; huge clumps of catmint grew around it. He felt a pang of envy that another Clan had so much, when ThunderClan cats were dying for need of it.

Padding forward, Lionblaze buried his nose in one of the clumps, resisting the temptation to roll in the herb and soak his pelt in the clean, sharp scent. That wasn't why he had come. Working quickly, he bit off the stems until he had a massive bundle, as much as he could carry.

Gathering the herbs into his jaws, Lionblaze headed back to the tunnel. The catmint drowned any other scent, but he kept his ears pricked, and his gaze flickered all around him, alert for rival warriors.

He saw no cat. Slipping back through the crack into the tunnel, he relaxed, thankful to be away from the risk of the accusing gaze of WindClan cats.

Quickening his pace, Lionblaze bounded along as the tunnel grew wider, to halt abruptly when he burst into the cave. Standing in front of him, her light brown tabby pelt bristling and her blue eyes blazing, was Heatherpaw.

"Thief!"

Lionblaze's jaws dropped open, letting the catmint fall. "Heatherpaw!"

"Heather*tail*," the she-cat snarled. "You thought you'd got away with it," she went on, her voice scathing. "But I spotted you, creeping among the rocks. I guessed you would use the tunnels to get back to your own territory."

"Then . . . then why didn't you call for a patrol?" Lionblaze stammered.

Heathertail's eyes flashed and her lip curled. "You're not

worth it. You may think that you're the best fighter in all the Clans, but you don't scare me."

The red glare of blood surged through Lionblaze's mind, filling his eyes. "Traitor!" he yowled, leaping for Heathertail with his paws outstretched. He could feel his claws slicing through her throat, and the blood pouring out, soaking her fur and his own, pooling out on the cave floor. A rasping sound of horror came from his throat. The blood was hot and thick on his fur, the reek of it choking his nose.

Then as the red tide ebbed he saw Heathertail watching him, her fur unruffled and her gaze icy. Lionblaze shuddered. The vision had been so real, and yet he hadn't moved a paw.

Heathertail padded past him and paused in the mouth of the tunnel that led up into WindClan. "Go, and don't come back," she hissed. "You can take the catmint. I've no quarrel with ThunderClan; I don't want to see cats suffer, whatever you might think. Just be careful you don't end up a bully like your kin, Tigerstar."

Flicking her tail disdainfully, she vanished into the tunnel.

As he gathered up the scattered stems of catmint, her parting words echoed in Lionblaze's mind, and his belly churned with fear that they might be true. His dream had nearly come true—he had nearly killed her—and Heathertail had known. The difference between him and Tigerstar was fading, and Lionblaze was more scared than he had ever been in his life.

CHAPTER 21

Jaypaw delivered more tansy to the flat rock outside the Twoleg nest, then picked up Lionblaze's scent and followed it to the mouth of the tunnel. Not many heartbeats had passed before he heard scrabbling sounds from inside, where the ThunderClan cats had built the thorn barrier. Lionblaze's scent grew stronger, mingled with the smell of catmint.

"You found it!" Jaypaw exclaimed as his brother emerged into the open. "Did any WindClan cats spot you?"

Lionblaze hesitated; Jaypaw was aware of mingled fear and anger coming from him. "Would I be here if they had?" he demanded. "Can you smell any wounds on me?"

Jaypaw shrugged. He didn't have time to figure out why Lionblaze sounded as if he had ants in his fur. "You'd better fix that barrier," he mewed. "We don't want any cat guessing what we did."

Lionblaze retreated into the tunnel without a word, while Jaypaw picked up the bundle of catmint and headed for the Twoleg nest.

"Where did you get that?"

Jaypaw stiffened as he heard Leafpool's voice. He hadn't

decided what story to tell her, and he'd hoped for time to treat the sick cats before she found out.

"Catmint!" There was joy in Leafpool's voice as she padded up to him and buried her nose in the leafy stems. "And so fresh and well grown too! It can't come from the old Twoleg nest."

"No," Jaypaw mumbled around the stems. "It came from way up there." He waved his tail vaguely toward the deepest parts of the territory.

"Thank StarClan!" Leafpool whispered. "They must have shown you where to look."

"Er . . . yes, they did." It was true, Jaypaw realized. He would never have found the catmint if Brightspirit hadn't guided him to WindClan. "This is all there is," he added. "No point in looking for any more."

"This should be more than enough." Jaypaw could sense that Leafpool was too relieved to ask more searching questions. "Come on, let's give it to the sick cats right now."

As they crossed the scent markers around the Twoleg nest, she paused. "Tonight is the half-moon," she meowed. "I think both of us can go to the Moonpool this time."

Jaypaw nodded, his mouth too full of catmint to reply. He wondered if the StarClan cats would be waiting for him, to thank him for saving ShadowClan. He was tempted to walk in Littlecloud's dreams, to see what explanation he gave to his Clan's warrior ancestors for rejecting them in favor of Sol. But most of all, he wanted to walk in the paw prints on the path leading down to the Moonpool, and feel part of the ancient cats once more.

Though Jaypaw couldn't see the moon, he could imagine its silvery light washing over his fur as his paws slipped into the paw-shaped hollows on the spiral path. *Did I come here before, when I was Jay's Wing? Are any of these paw prints mine?*

He could feel deep satisfaction coming from all his fellow medicine cats, because Littlecloud had joined them again. Mothwing had made the journey with Willowshine this time, too. *Well, I suppose cats would start asking questions if she missed every time.*

He padded forward to the edge of the pool, and heard the other cats take their places around him. But as he was stretching forward to lap a few drops of the icy water, Leafpool meowed, "Wait."

Surprised, Jaypaw sat up, aware of his mentor's barely contained excitement.

"Before we share tongues with StarClan," Leafpool continued, her voice coming from the other side of the pool near the waterfall, "I have a task to do. StarClan has shown me that it is time I gave Jaypaw his full name."

Jaypaw couldn't hide his astonishment. Leafpool must be referring to the catmint that he had found. For a heartbeat he felt ashamed that he had used Kestrelpaw and Lionblaze to get the herbs, and then lied to Leafpool about where he had found them.

But ThunderClan will survive, he reminded himself. He didn't care what he had done to achieve that. Warmth spread through him from ears to tail-tip as he remembered the joy and relief of the sick cats when he and Leafpool had delivered the precious herbs. They were already sleeping more restfully, and there was plenty of catmint left to go on treating them.

"Well, Jaypaw?" Leafpool's voice was full of amused affection. "Badger got your tongue?"

"I . . . no . . . thank you!" he stammered.

"Then come here to me."

Jaypaw padded around the edge of the pool, setting his paws down carefully on the slippery surface. He didn't want to begin his naming ceremony by falling into the Moonpool.

As he passed Barkface, the old medicine cat grunted, "Well done," and Kestrelpaw rested his tail lightly on Jaypaw's shoulder.

At last Jaypaw stood in front of his mentor, startled by the depth of the love and pride that flooded out of her. It was even stronger than the emotion he had felt coming from Half Moon. Did he really mean so much to Leafpool?

"I, Leafpool, medicine cat of ThunderClan," she began, "call upon my warrior ancestors to look down on this apprentice. He has trained hard to understand the ways of a medicine cat, and with your help he will serve his Clan for many moons."

Every hair on Jaypaw's pelt pricked as he listened. He forgot about the watching cats; it was as if he stood in a high, remote place with no cat but Leafpool, and the endless voice of the falling water.

"Jaypaw," Leafpool continued, "do you promise to uphold

the ways of a medicine cat, to stand apart from rivalry between Clan and Clan, and to protect all cats equally, even at the cost of your life?"

"I do." Jaypaw spoke the words clearly and confidently. For a moment, he caught a trace of movement behind him, a lingering scent that wasn't quite Clan but carried hints of ThunderClan's territory. *Half Moon!* Had she come to watch him become a full medicine cat? Jaypaw hoped she understood what this meant, how he could never have belonged to her in the way she had wanted. In the way they might both have wanted, if things had been different . . .

"Then by the powers of StarClan I give you your true name as a medicine cat."

Jaypaw's belly lurched. *Don't call me Jaywing.* He could just about cope with the weight of knowledge his dream had brought him, but he didn't want to go through the rest of his life sharing the name of his ancient counterpart.

"Jaypaw, from this moment you will be known as Jayfeather." Leafpool's voice shook with feeling. "StarClan honors your skill and your thirst for knowledge. You have saved the lives of many cats."

In the midst of his pride and relief, Jayfeather wondered whether his mentor would ever explain exactly what he had done to deserve this ceremony. With so much uneasiness between the Clans, he guessed she would prefer to keep quiet about the outbreak of greencough. Otherwise, as he had told Lionblaze, she could simply have asked Barkface for some catmint.

He felt Leafpool's muzzle rest on his head, just as Clan leaders would do when they made a new warrior. In response, he rasped his tongue over his mentor's shoulder.

"Jayfeather! Jayfeather!" Littlecloud called out. All the other medicine cats joined in, even Willowshine.

She hasn't got anything to be snooty about now, Jayfeather thought.

"Now it's time for you to share tongues with StarClan as a full medicine cat," Leafpool told him.

"And may they send you a good dream," Barkface rumbled.

Jayfeather felt slightly nervous as he padded back around the pool. Would the cats of StarClan claw his fur for the dubious way he had earned his name? Yellowfang wouldn't be impressed, he was sure.

I don't care. I saved the Clan when no other cat could.

He settled himself on the edge of the pool and stretched forward to lap the water. Around him he could hear the other medicine cats doing the same, then making themselves comfortable to sleep and receive the dreams StarClan would send them. Jayfeather curled up, too, closing his eyes and wrapping his tail over his nose.

He woke, blinking in the unaccustomed light, half prepared to find himself on the bleak mountaintop where he encountered Rock. Instead, he found himself in the lush forest clearing where Brightspirit had come to speak to him. A warm breeze, full of the green scents of growing herbs, caressed his pelt; his anxieties melted away like ice in newleaf.

At first Jayfeather thought he was alone, but as the breeze

stirred the leaves he saw two cats crouched on a branch at the other side of the clearing; Shiningheart and Braveheart were looking down at him with gleaming eyes. At the same moment the bracken underneath their tree parted, and Brightspirit stepped into the open.

The beautiful silver tabby padded across the clearing until she could touch noses with him; her sweet scent mingled with the smell of herbs.

"Jayfeather," she greeted him, her eyes alight with happiness. "Now you are a true medicine cat."

"I owe it to you," Jayfeather admitted. "You saved my Clan by telling me where to find the catmint."

"I was glad to help." Brightspirit's green eyes shone with love and joy. "Once I thought to set my paws on the way of a medicine cat, but that was not the path StarClan laid down for me. Now I will do all I can to help those in need. Whichever Clan they belong to—or Tribe."

Jayfeather bowed his head in deep respect. "Thank you. Thank you for traveling so far to help us."

Once again Brightspirit touched her nose to his. "I think you have traveled even farther, my friend."

Jayfeather shivered. Hesitantly he asked, "Will I see you again?"

"That is in the paws of the stars," Brightspirit replied.

Her breath warmed his fur; Jayfeather was surrounded by a glittering cloud, as if the silver tabby was about to whirl him up into the sky to be a star alongside her. His paws tingled.

"Good-bye, Jayfeather," Brightspirit whispered.

Jayfeather's eyes snapped open on darkness. He was curled on the flat stones by the Moonpool, with the other medicine cats beginning to wake around him.

When he and Leafpool returned to the camp early the next morning, Jayfeather could hear his Clanmates talking loudly in the middle of the clearing. Brambleclaw's voice rose above the noise.

"Settle down, and I'll get everything sorted out, okay?"

Leafpool sighed. "Every cat is getting cranky and exhausted from all the hunting and border patrols. I'll go and fetch them some strengthening herbs." She padded toward her den.

"Jaypaw, can I have a word?" Brambleclaw called out as Jayfeather approached the cats, wondering what all the fuss was about.

"Sure, and it's Jay*feather* now," Jayfeather pointed out proudly. No cat took any notice. Stifling an irritated sigh, he asked, "What's the problem?"

"Brackenfur says the dawn patrol spotted a fox in Wind-Clan, not far from the border," Brambleclaw replied. "Did you and Leafpool see anything on your way back?"

"I didn't *see* anything," Jayfeather retorted. "I picked up a whiff of fox scent, but I'm pretty sure it didn't come from our territory."

"If it's near the WindClan border it could soon come over here." Daisy's worried voice spoke from nearby. "Our kits could be in danger."

"And the cats in the Twoleg nest." Jayfeather could sense

Graystripe's anxiety. "What if the fox gets in there?"

"Okay, Graystripe and Brackenfur, go and check it out," Brambleclaw ordered. "If you find any signs that the fox crossed the border, then follow the scent and see if you can find its den."

"Right, let's go." Graystripe sounded relieved to be doing something about the threat.

Jayfeather intercepted the two warriors before they could leave. "Leafpool has some strengthening herbs for you."

"Thanks, Jayfeather," Brackenfur meowed; Jayfeather heard him and Graystripe bounding over to the medicine cats' den.

"Right, hunting patrols," Brambleclaw went on. "Ashfur, can you lead one for the camp? Take Sorreltail and Birchfall with you. And—"

"What about my bedding?" Mousefur interrupted. "It hasn't been changed for days. Every cat is so busy that none of the regular jobs are being done."

Jayfeather heard Brambleclaw suppress a sigh. "Okay, Mousefur. The apprentices can get right on to that."

Mousefur snorted. "I should think so."

"I don't see why we should do that," Foxpaw murmured to his littermate. Jayfeather realized that Foxpaw and Icepaw were right beside him.

"Mousefur's as cranky as a badger with a sore paw," Foxpaw went on. "We never get any thanks."

"No, it's always, 'It's too damp,' or 'There are thorns in there,'" Icepaw whispered back.

Jayfeather turned until he was looming over the two apprentices. "You should be making yourself useful by fetching clean bedding for Mousefur," he snapped. "Show a bit of respect for your elders. How would you like to sleep in a dirty nest?"

"You're not our mentor," Foxpaw protested. "You can't tell us what to do."

Jayfeather bent his head until he was almost touching noses with Foxpaw. "Fetch Mousefur's bedding *now*. Otherwise I'll tell Daisy that you were planning to make Toadkit eat rabbit droppings by telling him they were a new kind of berry."

He felt a jolt of shock from Foxpaw. "How did you know that?"

"Never mind how I know," Jayfeather replied. "Just do it."

"You wouldn't really tell Daisy," Foxpaw blustered.

Jayfeather bared his teeth. "Try me."

"Okay, okay, we're going. Come on, Icepaw, why are you standing around like that?"

Jayfeather heard Foxpaw push his sister, and both young cats scurried off toward the barrier. Icepaw's bewildered voice drifted back. "Rabbit droppings? What's he talking about?"

"Never mind," Foxpaw meowed. "We have to fetch some moss *now*!"

Picking up the sharp tang of strengthening herbs, Jayfeather realized that Leafpool had reappeared from their den and was distributing the leaves to all the warriors.

"Thanks, Leafpool," Brambleclaw mewed. "Have you enough for the sick cats as well?"

"Yes, plenty," Leafpool replied. "I'll send Jayfeather to the Twoleg nest with them. There's something else," she added. "Can you ask the hunting patrols to look out for young prey? That's easier for the sick cats to eat, and now that we've got the catmint they'll start to feel hungry again."

"No problem," Brambleclaw replied. "You all heard that, right? Sandstorm, will you lead a patrol for the Twoleg nest? Take Spiderleg, Berrynose and . . . er . . . Ashfur. Now, we need a border patrol to go over to the ShadowClan border. I'll lead it, and—"

"You do realize," Berrynose broke in, "that you've just assigned Ashfur to both those hunting patrols? Is he supposed to split himself in two?"

"Oh, mouse dung!" Brambleclaw exclaimed. "Sorry, Ashfur. You can—"

"Ashfur, for StarClan's sake!" Squirrelflight broke in. Jayfeather winced at the fury spilling over from her. "Can't you speak up, instead of standing there like a tree stump?"

"Sorry, but—" Ashfur sounded startled.

"'Sorry' catches no prey," Squirrelflight snarled. "Why didn't you say anything? Can't you see how much pressure Brambleclaw is under? Does the Clan deputy have to sort everything out on his own?"

"Hey, Squirrelflight . . ." Brambleclaw sounded embarrassed by his mate's fierce defense.

Squirrelflight ignored him. Jayfeather realized that her anger was fueled by frustration that she still wasn't fit enough to hunt or patrol, as well as fear for her father and her Clanmates. "There's more than one cat that would like to be deputy if anything happened to Brambleclaw," she spat. "You're all quick enough to blame Brambleclaw for his mistakes, but would any of you like to be in his position now?"

"Squirrelflight, *be quiet,*" Brambleclaw interrupted again, more forcefully. "It's no big deal."

Squirrelflight let out a furious hiss, spun around, and stalked off toward the warriors' den. Jayfeather felt a glow of pride in her for speaking up. He was proud of his father, too, for taking on all the leadership responsibilities and holding ThunderClan together while Firestar was ill.

"Sorry about that, Ashfur," Brambleclaw went on. "You go on leading the camp patrol. Sandstorm, you can have Mousewhisker instead."

"Very well." Ashfur's voice was cold; he collected his patrol together and left.

For StarClan's sake, get over it! Jayfeather thought. *Brambleclaw made an honest mistake.*

Padding with Leafpool back to his den, he couldn't help wondering whether there was more to the quarrel than he realized. So much fury from Squirrelflight, Brambleclaw so quick to make amends, Ashfur clearly not forgiving him . . . Had Jayfeather missed something really obvious between these three cats?

He shook his head to clear it. Whatever the problem was, they could deal with it themselves. It had nothing to do with him, that was for sure.

CHAPTER 22

Gray-green clouds hung low over the forest and the air felt thick and clammy. Hollyleaf's pelt prickled with the warning of an approaching storm. As she padded through the forest at the rear of Ashfur's hunting patrol, the looming storm clouds seemed to echo the uneasiness inside her. However much she tried to push her worries away, she couldn't ignore the feeling that something was wrong.

Two nights before, Brambleclaw had chosen her to attend the Gathering. Blackstar had been there, but he had said nothing at all about Sol, or his decision to let ShadowClan live by the warrior code once more. Brambleclaw had taken Firestar's place with the three Clan leaders, telling them briefly that Firestar was sorry he couldn't come, but without explaining why.

What else are we hiding from one another? Hollyleaf wondered.

She was reminded of one secret as the patrol was passing the Twoleg nest. Lionblaze emerged from inside, along with Honeyfern and Rosekit. The tiny cream-colored kit bounced through the opening and hurled herself into a drift of dead leaves, squealing with excitement as they crackled around her, and batting them up into the air.

"Steady," Lionblaze mewed. "You don't want to wear yourself out before you get back to camp."

Rosekit sat up, a dead leaf clinging to the top of her head. "I'm fine!" she announced. "I want to catch some prey for my mother."

Purring, Honeyfern nudged her out of the pile of leaves and gave the tiny kit's pelt a quick grooming. Lionblaze padded up to his sister.

"More cats going home?" Hollyleaf asked.

"That's right," Lionblaze replied. "There's just Millie and Briarkit left now, and Firestar. He won't leave until every cat is back in camp."

"It was great that Jayfeather found that catmint," Hollyleaf remarked, her eyes narrowing as she watched her brother's reaction.

"Er . . . yeah." Lionblaze looked uncomfortable.

His behavior convinced Hollyleaf of what she had suspected already: that there was some secret about the catmint, and both her brothers were involved in it.

Why won't they tell me? We shouldn't have secrets from one another.

"Everything will be fine now," Lionblaze went on quickly as if he wanted to avoid any questions. "The catmint here is starting to sprout again, so there's enough for Millie and Briarkit. They're getting stronger every day."

"That's good. But what—"

"Hollyleaf!" Ashfur's impatient yowl cut off her question. The gray warrior had turned back, and was waiting for her a few tail-lengths along the old Twoleg path.

"I've got to go," she meowed to Lionblaze, certain that she spotted a flicker of relief in his eyes as she spoke.

"See you later," he replied, and headed back to camp beside Honeyfern, with Rosekit frisking ahead of them.

Hollyleaf watched them go, then padded along the path to join Ashfur.

"You're going to hunt today and not tomorrow?" he asked scathingly as she approached.

"Sorry," she muttered. "I just wanted a word with Lionblaze."

Not that it did me any good, she thought, as Ashfur snorted and led the way deeper into the forest, after the rest of the patrol. She was still no closer to finding out what Lionblaze and Jayfeather were hiding from her.

The air had grown heavier still by the time the patrol returned to camp. A hot breeze had sprung up, folding back the leaves that still remained on the trees. Hollyleaf's pelt was fluffed the wrong way and the scents of the prey she was carrying choked her as if she had a mouthful of crow-food.

Huge, tepid raindrops began to fall as Ashfur led his patrol through the tunnel. One of them splashed onto Hollyleaf's nose when she emerged into the camp; she twitched her whiskers irritably to shake it off. Thunder rumbled in the distance.

Good, Hollyleaf thought as she carried her prey to the fresh-kill pile. *The air will be fresh again after a storm.*

She glanced up, only to squeeze her eyes tight shut as a jagged bolt of lightning split the sky. Thunder crashed right overhead and suddenly rain started to pound down, splattering on the earth floor of the hollow and plastering Hollyleaf's pelt to her sides within a couple of heartbeats.

A wail went up from the warriors' den, and Cloudtail stuck his head out. "What's happening?"

Too terrified to run for shelter, Hollyleaf flattened herself to the ground. She caught a glimpse of Spiderleg streaking through the rain to the warriors' den with Mousewhisker hard on his paws.

Another bolt of lightning crackled across the sky. Hollyleaf stared in shock as a tree on the edge of the hollow burst into flames, red tongues of fire roaring upward. Even the torrents of rain couldn't quench it. Blackened leaves fell into the hollow; with a terrible groaning sound a blazing branch tore itself free and plummeted down to land with a crash a tail-length from Hollyleaf. Yowling in fright, she leaped to one side, cannoning into Thornclaw.

"The forest is on fire!" he screeched.

Yet another claw of lightning tore the sky apart. An earsplitting crack sounded above the roar of the thunder, and Hollyleaf saw a tree begin to topple, its roots ripped out of the earth as flames devoured its branches. Blazing leaves and twigs rained down into the clearing.

Panic-stricken caterwauling rose around Hollyleaf. She spotted Brambleclaw racing across to the nursery, and Sandstorm splashing water with her paws over a burning branch, trying to stop the flames from reaching the warriors' den.

Graystripe yowled, "Millie!" and shot into the tunnel on his way to the Twoleg nest.

The moment his thick gray tail vanished, Firestar appeared at the mouth of the tunnel and raced into the center of the clearing. His flame-colored pelt was darkened by the rain and streaked with mud, but he held his head high and let out a commanding yowl.

"Get out! All of you get out! You'll be trapped if you stay in here!"

Cats began to emerge from their dens. They splashed across the clearing, weaving or jumping aside to avoid the fiery debris that still rained down around them.

"Head for the Twoleg nest," Firestar ordered. "We can shelter there."

Brambleclaw emerged from the nursery, carrying Bumblekit; Daisy followed him with Blossomkit. Rosekit and Toadkit stumbled along beside their mother. Mousefur padded out of the elders' den with her tail over Longtail's shoulder to guide him. Icepaw and Foxpaw, their eyes wild with terror, were shoved toward the barrier of thorns by their mentors.

Hollyleaf looked around for Lionblaze and Jayfeather, but she couldn't see either of them among the fleeing cats. *Jayfeather would need help to get out,* she thought, trying to control her fear. *And what about Squirrelflight? Her wound was still hurting, and she hadn't regained her full strength yet.*

Struggling through the pelting rain, the glare of flame all around her, Hollyleaf splashed across to the medicine cats' den. She met Leafpool by the bramble screen, her jaws full of herbs; Jayfeather was just behind her.

"Go and help the others!" Hollyleaf gasped to the medicine cat. "I'll bring Jayfeather."

Leafpool gave her a nod of acknowledgement and raced for the tunnel.

"I can bring myself, thanks," Jayfeather muttered furiously.

"Don't be a mouse-brain!" Hollyleaf spat back at him. "There's fire out there. Now stop complaining and grab my tail."

Wincing as her brother's jaws closed around her tail-tip, Hollyleaf turned toward the tunnel. Suddenly Lionblaze loomed up out of the rain.

"You're here," he panted with relief. "Let's go."

Together the three cats headed for the tunnel. By now the clearing was empty; it looked as if the rest of the Clan, even Firestar, had already left. *Will they make it to the Twoleg nest?* Hollyleaf wondered. *Or will they scatter into the forest? Is ThunderClan going to break up after all?*

She and her brothers were halfway across the clearing when lightning clawed across the sky from top to bottom. The barrier across the entrance to the camp crackled and burst into flame. The tunnel vanished in a throat of fire.

Hollyleaf stopped, frozen in horror. "We're trapped!"

Staring around wildly, she tried to think what to do. The camp was littered with blazing branches, and more were cascading down from the lightning-struck trees around the hollow. The warriors' den was already smoldering; there was no shelter there.

"The apprentices' cave . . ." she gasped, even though she knew it was too shallow to give any real protection if the fire spread.

"No. Over here." Squirrelflight's voice spoke behind her; Hollyleaf whirled around to see her mother waving her tail urgently toward the rock wall. "There's another way out."

Hollyleaf was ashamed of the relief that swept over her, as if she was still a kit who needed her mother to look after her. Leading Jayfeather, she followed Squirrelflight around a clump of brambles that grew against the wall of the hollow. Lionblaze brought up the rear.

To Hollyleaf's surprise, the rock behind the brambles had crumbled away. Peering up through the rain, she saw straggling bushes and grass growing in cracks, all the way to the top.

"It's a secret way out of the camp!" she exclaimed. "And we never knew about it!"

"Thank StarClan," Squirrelflight retorted drily. "You were enough trouble as kits and apprentices, without this." Then her voice changed, growing tense again. "Jayfeather, you come first. Follow my voice. It's not a difficult climb."

"We'll come behind and catch you if you fall," Lionblaze assured his brother.

"I'm not a kit!" Jayfeather snapped, though Hollyleaf could see he was shaking with fear.

Squirrelflight scrambled up through the bramble thicket

and clung there, calling out to Jayfeather so he could follow. Jayfeather struggled up behind her, swinging out on a tendril of ivy when his hind paws lost their grip.

"Mouse dung!" he spat, scrabbling to get his balance again.

Squirrelflight went on guiding him upward, her voice calm now, even though she must have been terrified that one of them would fall as they climbed higher.

Hollyleaf and Lionblaze followed. Though Squirrelflight had said the climb was easy, Hollyleaf was convinced that the pounding rain was about to wash her off the rock face, or lightning would strike the thorns she clung to. Darkness, the glare of flame, and the crash of thunder surrounded her. She lost sight of her Clanmates, and thought she would never reach the top.

But at last she heard her mother's voice again. "Well done!" Teeth met in her scruff as Squirrelflight dragged her onto the top of the cliff. She lay there panting for a moment, watching her mother helping Lionblaze to scramble up beside her. Jayfeather was lying on his side, his eyes closed and his sides heaving.

"Come away from the edge," Squirrelflight warned. "The rock is crumbling." She turned, leading the way through the bushes.

Hollyleaf nudged Jayfeather to his paws. "Just a bit farther and then you can rest."

Her brother bared his teeth in a feeble snarl; she could see that he would never admit how hard he had found the climb.

"You can lean on my shoulder if you like," Lionblaze offered, coming to stand on Jayfeather's other side.

"Look, mouse-brain—"

Jayfeather's annoyed hiss broke off as the whole sky was lit up by a crackling bolt of lightning, stabbing down as if it was going to impale all three cats on its claws. Thunder rolled overhead as the bushes burst into flame.

Hollyleaf let out a yowl of terror. Greedy scarlet tongues licked toward her and her littermates, blocking their path away from the edge of the cliff. Smoke billowed up as rain fell on the bushes; Hollyleaf choked on it and began to cough, but the downpour was easing off, and the remaining flurries weren't enough to put the fire out.

A wave of heat rolled over Hollyleaf; instinctively she moved back, and felt the rock begin to crumble beneath her paws. Scrambling away, she glanced down, to see the clearing patched with flame and darkness. There was no escape that way, even if they could manage to climb down safely amid the fire and rain.

"What's happening?" Jayfeather was cowering down under the searing heat. "Which way should we go?"

"We can't go anywhere. We're trapped." Lionblaze's voice was calm. Flame reflected from his golden pelt and shone in his eyes. "Squirrelflight!" he called. "Are you there? Help us!"

As he spoke a branch edged with flames crashed down from one of the bushes; Hollyleaf dragged Jayfeather out of its path just in time. The littermates huddled together at the very edge of the cliff.

"I'm here!" Squirrelflight's voice was high-pitched with terror. "I'm going to push a branch through to you. You can run along it to escape before it catches fire."

"Right. We'll be ready," Lionblaze replied.

Hollyleaf felt a jolt of gratitude for her brother's courage. Without him, she was certain she would have panicked, trapped between the fire and the long drop into the camp. But they would stick together, the three of them, protected by the prophecy as they had always been.

Hollyleaf could hear the sound of something heavy being dragged through the undergrowth beyond the flames. Her burst of confidence blew away like ash.

"She'll never manage it," she muttered to Lionblaze. "What about her wound? She's not strong enough."

"Squirrelflight will always do what she has to," Lionblaze replied.

Small tongues of flame were creeping through the grass now; rain hissed down on them, leaving the ground blackened and smoking, but there were always more flames, and the acrid scent of burning filled the air. A blazing leaf floated down onto Jayfeather's pelt; Lionblaze knocked it off with one paw, adding the reek of scorched fur to the smoke-filled air.

Beyond the red-and-orange flames, Hollyleaf caught a glimpse of Squirrelflight, struggling to drag a branch up to the fire. Already she looked exhausted. Lionblaze's muscles tensed as if he was going to try leaping over the bush to help her.

"No!" Hollyleaf choked out. "It's too far."

Before Lionblaze could argue, another shape burst through the billowing smoke to stand beside Squirrelflight. His eyes glared; his gray fur was matted together and stuck with bits of burnt leaf and twig. Confused by the smoke and flames, Hollyleaf almost thought she was seeing one of her warrior ancestors, until she recognized Ashfur.

Squirrelflight dropped the branch. "Help me push it into the fire!" she yowled.

Grabbing the branch in strong jaws, Ashfur thrust it past the wall of flame and into the ever-narrowing patch of ground where Hollyleaf and her brothers huddled. But Hollyleaf didn't feel any sense of relief. There was a look in Ashfur's eyes that she didn't understand: the look of a cat who had just spotted an unexpected juicy bit of prey.

The branch made a bridge through the flames, but Ashfur stood at the other end of it, blocking the way to safety. Lionblaze nudged Jayfeather to his paws; Hollyleaf took a step toward the branch, then paused. She felt a cold weight in her belly when she looked into Ashfur's glittering blue eyes.

"Ashfur, get out of the way." Squirrelflight's voice was puzzled. "Let them get out!"

"Brambleclaw isn't here to look after them now," Ashfur sneered.

Hollyleaf felt her fur beginning to rise. What did Ashfur mean?

Lionblaze's golden pelt was bristling, too. "What have you done with my father?" he howled through the flame.

Ashfur looked at him pityingly; his eyes were twin points of fire amid the burning forest. "Why would I waste my time with Brambleclaw?"

The main branch was too solid to catch fire easily, but the leaves on it had shriveled and the twigs were beginning to smoke. Hollyleaf realized that they didn't have much time before their bridge to safety would be ablaze.

Squirrelflight staggered up to Ashfur. Hollyleaf had never seen her mother so angry. Her fur bristled with fury; she looked like a warrior of TigerClan. Yet it was obvious that the climb to the top of the cliff, followed by her struggle with the branch, had weakened her, and she was exhausted.

"Your quarrel with Brambleclaw has to stop," she hissed. "Too many moons have passed. You have to accept that I'm Brambleclaw's mate, not yours. You can't keep trying to punish Brambleclaw for something that was always meant to be."

Ashfur's ears flicked up in surprise. "I have no quarrel with Brambleclaw."

Hollyleaf exchanged a shocked glance with Lionblaze. "That's not how it looks to me," he muttered.

"I couldn't care less about Brambleclaw," Ashfur continued. "It's not his fault he fell for a faithless she-cat."

Faithless? A growl began to build in Hollyleaf's throat, but then she stopped and watched the cats on the other side of the blazing branches. Something ominous was taking place in front of her, and even with flame roaring around them she felt a sudden chill. She shrank closer to Lionblaze and Jayfeather, whose head was up, his sightless eyes intent, as if he could see the confrontation between his mother and Ashfur.

"I know you think I've never forgiven Brambleclaw for stealing you from me, but you're wrong, and so is every cat that thinks so. My quarrel is with *you*, Squirrelflight." Ashfur's voice shook with rage. "It always has been."

Horrified, Hollyleaf took a step back and felt her hind paws begin to slip on the edge of the cliff. Her head spun as lightning stabbed out and thunder drowned all other sounds, even the roaring fire. For a heartbeat she dangled over empty air, and she let out a strangled yowl.

Then she felt firm teeth meet in her scruff; blinking against the smoke, she realized that Lionblaze was hauling her back to safety. But there was no safety: only the hungry flames, and Ashfur blocking the end of the branch with fury in his eyes. Fiery sparks floated down on all three young cats, scorching their fur, and flames licked the underside of the branch; fear flooded afresh through Hollyleaf when she saw that it was already beginning to smolder.

Ashfur has to let us get out! But Hollyleaf couldn't find any words to plead with him. What was happening here didn't have anything to do with them, even if they died because of it.

"All this was moons ago." Squirrelflight sounded puzzled. "Ashfur, I had no idea you were still upset."

"Upset?" Ashfur echoed. "I'm not *upset*. You have no idea how much pain I'm in. It's like being cut open every day, bleeding onto the stones. I can't understand how any of you failed to see the blood. . . ."

His eyes clouded and his voice took on a wild, distant tone, as if he could see the blood spilling out of him now, sizzling on the burning ground. Terror burst through Hollyleaf and she pressed closer to her brothers. This cat was more dangerous than the storm or the fire, or the fall lurking perilously close to her hind paws.

Desperately she tried to step onto the end of the branch. At once Ashfur rounded on her, fully conscious again, his teeth bared in a snarl.

"Stay there!" Turning to face Squirrelflight but keeping one paw on the branch, he hissed, "I can't believe you didn't know how much you hurt me. You are the blind one, not Jayfeather. Who do you think sent Firestar the message to go down to the lake, where the fox trap was? I wanted him to die, to take your father away so you'd know the real meaning of pain."

Hollyleaf's shocked gaze met Lionblaze's. "He tried to kill *Firestar*?" she gasped. "He's mad!"

Determination glittered in Lionblaze's eyes, and he bunched his muscles for a giant leap. "I'm going to fight him."

"No!" Hollyleaf fastened her teeth in his shoulder fur. "You can't!" Her words were muffled now. "He'll just push you into the fire."

"Brambleclaw saved Firestar then," Ashfur went on to Squirrelflight. "But he's not here now. He's not here—but your kits are."

Squirrelflight's eyes blazed. For a heartbeat Hollyleaf thought she was going to pounce on the gray warrior, but she knew that exhausted and in pain, her mother would have no chance. Squirrelflight seemed to realize it, too. She drew herself up, head high; she was trembling, but her voice was clear and brave.

"Enough, Ashfur. Your quarrel is with me. These young

cats have done nothing to hurt you. Do what you like with me, but let them out of the fire."

"You don't understand." Ashfur looked at her as if he was seeing her for the first time; his voice was puzzled and petulant. "This is the only way to make you feel the same pain that you caused me. You tore my heart out when you chose Brambleclaw over me. Anything I did to you would never hurt as much. But your kits . . ." He looked through the flames at Hollyleaf and her brothers, his eyes narrowing to dark blue slits. "If you watch them die, then you'll know the pain I felt."

The flames crackled threateningly closer; Hollyleaf felt as if the heat was about to sear her pelt into ashes. She edged backward, only to feel the edge of the hollow give way under her hind paws. The three of them were pressed tightly together, so close that if one of them lost their balance, all three would be dragged off the cliff. Hollyleaf couldn't control the trembling that shook her whole body as her glance flickered between the cliff and the fire.

Jayfeather was crouched close to the ground, looking tinier than ever with his pelt slicked flat by the rain. Lionblaze's claws were unsheathed, glinting as the lightning flashed out again, but the tension in his haunches didn't come from preparing to leap at Ashfur; it came from the effort of keeping himself on the top of the cliff.

Squirrelflight raised her head, her gaze locked on Ashfur's crazed eyes. "Kill them, then," she meowed. "You won't hurt me that way."

Ashfur opened his jaws to reply, but said nothing. Hollyleaf and her brothers stared at their mother. What was Squirrelflight saying?

Squirrelflight took a step away from them, and glanced carelessly over her shoulder. Her green eyes were fiercer than Hollyleaf had ever seen them, with an expression she couldn't read.

"If you really want to hurt me, you'll have to find a better way than that," Squirrelflight snarled. "They are not my kits."

CHAPTER 23

The noise of the storm and the fire faded and the only sound Jayfeather could hear was the blood roaring in his ears. He shook his head, straining to hear what Squirrelflight and Ashfur said next, cursing the blindness that hid their expressions from him.

"You're lying." Ashfur's voice was choked with disbelief.

"No, I'm not." Squirrelflight spoke softly, but her intensity pierced through the crackle of the flames. "Did you see me give birth? Did I nurse them? Stay in the nursery until they were apprenticed? No."

"But—I" Ashfur began, then fell silent. Jayfeather could almost hear the paws of memory racing through his mind.

"I fooled all of you, even Brambleclaw," Squirrelflight went on scornfully. "*They are not mine.*"

"And no cat in the Clan knows?" Ashfur's disbelief was changing to uncertainty.

"No. They're all as blind as you are to the truth."

Jayfeather sensed a shift in Ashfur's thoughts, reaching out toward power once more. "What do you think will happen when I tell them?" he challenged. "Will your Clanmates let you stay in ThunderClan, knowing you have lied to them—to Firestar, to your sister, to Brambleclaw?"

"You'll tell them?" Squirrelflight's voice was sharp with pain.

"Do you really think I won't? I can still make you lose what you love most. Brambleclaw will want nothing to do with you. You were a fool to think I would keep your secret. But you have always been a fool, Squirrelflight. I'll let these cats—whomever they belong to—live. But your suffering has only just begun."

There was a rustling in the undergrowth, and Ashfur's scent faded as he stalked away.

"Jayfeather, here's the branch." Lionblaze's voice was tense. Jayfeather felt his brother's teeth sink into his scruff and lift him bodily until his paws felt the rough bark of the branch underneath them. Lionblaze kept hold of him until he had got his balance. "Straight ahead," he ordered. "Hurry."

Jayfeather forced his paws to move, trusting Lionblaze as he stumbled forward with the heat and roaring of the fire on either side. He let out a hiss as pain stabbed one of his pads, as if he had trodden on a burning twig. Then the worst of the heat died away behind him, and he half fell, half leaped off the branch. The ground beneath his paws was hot, but not burning. He was safe!

Heartbeats later he heard Hollyleaf and Lionblaze leap down beside him.

Thunder rumbled above them, but now it was farther off, as if the storm was moving away. Mercifully rain began to fall again, hissing onto the flames. The wind was dying down;

there would be no more danger from falling trees. Jayfeather heard yowls from down in the hollow, as if the cats were returning to the camp, and had spotted the cats on the top of the cliff. But he and his littermates ignored them.

"Squirrelflight?" Hollyleaf's voice quivered; Jayfeather could sense her disbelief warring with fear. "That's not true, is it? We are your kits, aren't we?"

There was a long pause, but Jayfeather already knew the answer. His mind was filled with Squirrelflight's desperate sorrow and regret—and overwhelming love, the love of a mother for her kits. That much had been a lie among what she had told Ashfur; Squirrelflight *did* love them. But she was not their mother.

"I'm so sorry," Squirrelflight whispered. "I should have told you the truth a long time ago."

"What do you mean?" Lionblaze demanded. Jayfeather reeled from the blast of his brother's growing outrage.

"We thought it was for the best," Squirrelflight pleaded. "I promise you, it was the hardest thing we've ever done."

"We? Who's *we*?" Lionblaze snapped.

Squirrelflight didn't reply, and her mind was such a chaos of love and regret that Jayfeather couldn't pick the answer out of it.

"Does Brambleclaw know?" Hollyleaf whimpered; Jayfeather heard her claws tearing at the ground.

"He has never lied to you," Squirrelflight meowed. "He . . . he doesn't know."

"You let him believe that we were his?" Hollyleaf's voice

rose to a shrill squeak. "So you lied to him as well. But . . . if you're not our mother and father, *who is*?"

Jayfeather reached out to Squirrelflight's mind again, searching for memories, but all he could sense was a blur of snow, a long journey, brambles clawing at her pelt and the guilt of her terrible secret already weighing her down. He was aware of another cat with her, but so shadowy that he couldn't make out who it was.

"I can't tell you." Squirrelflight's murmur was barely loud enough to hear.

"You can, but you won't!" Pain and anger filled Lionblaze's voice. Jayfeather sensed the same feelings in Hollyleaf, too, but something inside him stayed icily calm, as if he had always known this would happen. If they were the three, with the power of the stars in their paws, then it made sense that there would be something extraordinary about where they came from. This was just one more truth to be discovered, something done long ago that had cast a shadow over all the moons since.

"I'm sorry." Squirrelflight's voice had grown stronger. "I know it won't help, but I couldn't have loved you more if you had really been mine. I'm so proud of all three of you."

"Go away and leave us alone!" Hollyleaf hissed. "You have no right to be proud of us, no right to feel *anything* toward us! You let us believe you were our mother, and you're not!"

"Please . . ." Squirrelflight begged.

Lionblaze's voice was hard. "Just go."

Misery rolled off Squirrelflight like a choking cloud, almost carrying Jayfeather off his paws. He heard her turn and go blundering through the undergrowth as if she didn't care whether she burned her pads on still-smoldering leaves.

Left behind at the edge of the charred bushes, none of the three spoke. Jayfeather was numb with shock, and could sense that his littermates felt the same. They had almost died, and they had confronted Ashfur in his destructive madness, but most devastating of all was the secret that Squirrelflight had revealed.

"If they're not our mother and father, then who are our real parents?" Hollyleaf quavered at last.

"We can worry about that later." Cold anger still vibrated in Lionblaze's voice. "First we have to decide what we'll do when Ashfur tells the Clan."

"Do you really think he will?" Hollyleaf asked.

"Do you think he won't?" Lionblaze countered. "He doesn't care what he does so long as he can hurt Squirrelflight, and that will hurt her more than anything."

Jayfeather was strangely detached from his littermates' anxious questions. The secret was out, and no cat could stop the consequences. All he felt was a mild curiosity to see what would happen next.

"We mustn't say anything to our Clanmates," Hollyleaf mewed worriedly. "What if they punish us, too? They might think we knew all along. We'll have to go on just as usual. Maybe Ashfur won't say anything after all."

"And hedgehogs might fly," Lionblaze retorted. "But I agree we shouldn't tell any cat. Not until we find out the truth. If the Clan learns what happened, we need to be able to defend ourselves so they know we had nothing to do with this. Okay, Jayfeather?"

Jayfeather nodded. "Okay."

"Then let's get back to the camp," Hollyleaf meowed. "There'll be a lot to do there."

The stone hollow smelled charred and bitter when Jayfeather scrambled over the remains of the thorn barrier. He started at the sound of his father's—no, *Brambleclaw's*—voice. "Are you all right?"

"We're fine, thanks," Lionblaze replied tightly.

"Then can you help Brackenfur patch up the nursery? You too, Hollyleaf. You'll need to bring more brambles from the forest. And Jayfeather, I think Leafpool wants you. Spiderleg's paws are burned and Longtail had a nasty bang on the head from a falling branch. And there may be others I don't know about."

"Okay, fine," Jayfeather meowed. As he heard Brambleclaw bounding away, he turned to his littermates. "Don't forget, we say nothing."

But as he padded across to the medicine cats' den, limping a little from his scorched pad, Jayfeather was aware of Ashfur standing at the edge of the clearing. He knew that the gray warrior's eyes were fixed on him as clearly as if he could see the burning blue gaze.

Midnight said knowledge isn't always power, he recalled. *But sometimes it is. And Ashfur has the power to destroy us all.*

CHAPTER 24

On the morning after the storm, Lionblaze was chosen for the dawn patrol with Brackenfur, Sorreltail, and Cinderheart. Strengthening daylight shone down through the trees as they padded away from the stone hollow. There was scarcely a breeze to disturb the leaves that still remained on the trees. Lionblaze could almost pretend that he had dreamed the storm, if it wasn't for the litter of twigs and branches on the forest floor, and the blackened husks of the trees struck by lightning.

His pelt itched all the time he was away from the stone hollow, as he wondered what he would find when he returned, what accusations and gasps of shock would greet him. But the camp was peaceful, with Brambleclaw directing the repairs to the dens. Thornclaw and Mousewhisker were busy patching the last gaps in the brambles around the nursery; Foxpaw and Icepaw were carrying in huge bundles of fresh bedding. Cloudtail and Brightheart worked together, dragging burnt branches away from the warriors' den, while Whitewing, Birchfall, and Berrynose cleared debris from the floor of the clearing. Lionblaze overheard Berrynose grumbling that this wasn't a job for a warrior.

Nothing's changed! he thought. He couldn't spot Ashfur among the cats in the clearing, but obviously the gray warrior hadn't revealed the secret yet.

Lionblaze tried to believe that the storm of the discovery had passed away like the rain and thunder, leaving calm behind, but he knew in his heart that the damage from Squirrelflight's revelation would last for moons and moons.

"We need to talk about this," Hollyleaf muttered in his ear while they helped Dustpelt drag thorn branches into place to make a new barrier at the entrance to the camp. "Meet me in the forest. I'll fetch Jayfeather."

She bounded across to the medicine cats' den and emerged a moment later with Jayfeather following her. Lionblaze watched them go out at the edge of the barrier where the dirtplace tunnel used to be. He waited for a few moments, then padded over to Dustpelt.

"I think I'll go hunt," he meowed. "The fresh-kill pile needs restocking."

"There are hunting patrols out already," Dustpelt grumbled. "Is fetching branches a bit boring for you? Oh, go on then," he added, flicking his tail at Lionblaze. "But you'd better bring back something worth eating."

Lionblaze headed out at a fast trot, before the senior warrior could change his mind. He picked up his littermates' scent trail, and followed them into the forest.

Pausing at the edge of a clearing, he looked around, tasting the air. An urgent hiss sounded from under the trees. "Lionblaze! Over here!"

Lionblaze spotted Hollyleaf peering out from a clump of bracken. "What took you so long?" she demanded.

"I thought it best to wait a bit," Lionblaze explained as he padded over to her and slid in among the bracken stalks. "I didn't want any cat suspecting we were meeting in secret."

Behind the bracken, the ground fell away into a shallow scoop where Jayfeather was sitting; he raised his head as Lionblaze scrambled down to join him. "Okay," he meowed. "Now we're all here, we have to decide what we're going to do."

"There's only one thing we *can* do." Hollyleaf's claws worked furiously in the soft earth. "We have to find out who our real parents are. Squirrelflight won't tell us, but we need to know!"

"No, I don't agree," Lionblaze argued.

"What? But you said—"

Lionblaze raised his tail to silence her. "I want to know who our mother and father are, just as much as you do. But that's not the most important thing right now. Our biggest problem is what to do about Ashfur."

"I *hate* Ashfur!" Hollyleaf lashed her tail; she was working herself up into another storm of fear and frustration.

Lionblaze laid his tail across her shoulders. "He's madder than a fox in a fit, but that's not the point." Suddenly he remembered the fight he had once had with Ashfur when the gray warrior was his mentor. Ashfur's blue eyes had blazed with battle fury. *Was he trying to kill me then, to hurt Squirrelflight?* "Somehow we have to come up with a plan to keep him quiet. Squirrelflight will be in big trouble if this gets out."

Hollyleaf flicked her ears dismissively. "That's Squirrelflight's problem, not ours."

"It's a problem for all of us." Lionblaze couldn't help a pang of sympathy for Squirrelflight. True, she had lied to them, but she had always done her best for them, as if she really was their mother. "As long as Ashfur knows our secret, he has power over all of us." Every hair on his pelt tingled as he tried to imagine what that might mean.

"You don't get it, do you?" Hollyleaf snapped. Her gaze burned with green fire. "Don't you realize—*we might not be Clan cats*!"

Lionblaze opened his jaws to reply, but said nothing, too taken aback by what Hollyleaf was implying.

"We might have been born outside the Clan—outside the warrior code." She sounded as if she couldn't think of anything worse. "What if Squirrelflight took pity on a passing loner or a kittypet?"

"But—but we're the three," Lionblaze stammered. "The prophecy is about *us*. We have the power to be greater than the stars. How can we not be Clan cats?"

"I think you're both forgetting something," Jayfeather broke in, speaking for the first time; his voice was cool and detached. "The prophecy told Firestar that 'There will be three, kin of your kin . . .' If Squirrelflight isn't our mother, then we're not Firestar's kin, are we?"

Lionblaze and Hollyleaf stared at their brother. The small tabby was sitting calmly with his tail wrapped around his paws. "Well, are we?" he repeated.

"Cloudtail's Firestar's kin . . ." Lionblaze began confusedly, but Hollyleaf's shriek drowned his words.

"I knew it! There's *nothing* special about us! You're just really good at fighting, and as for Jayfeather—well, he's a medicine cat, of course he's going to have dreams!"

Lionblaze felt the blood chill and slow in his veins. Could it be true? *But what about the way I feel in battle?* I know *I can never be hurt.* I know *I could take on a whole Clan of enemies single-pawed!* He couldn't even consider the thought that he might not be part of the prophecy. *Because if I'm not, then I owe my fighting skills to Tigerstar, and he was right all along about my stupid dreams.*

Then another thought invaded his mind, even more worrying than the first. *If Brambleclaw isn't my father, then I'm no kin to Tigerstar. What will he do to me if he ever finds out?*

Days slipped by. The repairs to the camp were finished and at last Millie and Briarkit returned from the Twoleg nest, with Graystripe pacing proudly alongside them. Briarkit bounced ahead; Lionblaze could hardly believe she was the same kit who had been carried out of the camp, so limp that she looked as if she were dead. Millie was still thin and shaky on her paws, but her tail twined lovingly with Graystripe's and her eyes shone with returning health. Daisy welcomed her back into the nursery while the other kits leaped on Briarkit and wrestled with her joyfully.

Winds swept the forest, carrying the bite of approaching leaf-bare. The last of the leaves spiraled down from the trees. Prey became harder to catch, but the Clan was back to full strength again, able to keep the fresh-kill pile well-stocked. Squirrelflight returned to light warrior duties, and even the warriors who had been injured in the storm left the medicine cats' den.

Lionblaze noticed that Whitewing was growing plump, and Birchfall went around with a proud expression on his face. So there would be more kits for ThunderClan! Outwardly, everything was going well.

But Lionblaze no longer enjoyed patroling with his Clanmates. Ashfur's knowledge hung over him like a storm cloud. While Hollyleaf still fretted over who their true parents were, Lionblaze worried constantly about how they could persuade Ashfur not to reveal the secret. Often he caught Ashfur looking at him, a dark promise in his blue eyes. What was the gray warrior waiting for? Lionblaze couldn't believe that he had thought better of his threat to tell every cat what Squirrelflight had done.

On a morning of sun and brisk wind, Lionblaze pushed his way out of the warriors' den to see Ashfur and Firestar together by the fresh-kill pile. His belly lurched. Trying to look nonchalant, he padded over and chose a mouse for himself. Even though he didn't think he could choke down a single mouthful, he settled down to eat it with his back to his Clan leader and his ears pricked.

"There's a Gathering in a few sunrises," Ashfur meowed. "Is it okay if I go?"

Firestar sounded faintly surprised. "I don't usually choose warriors until the same day, but if you want to . . ."

"Thanks, Firestar."

Lionblaze dared to glance around, to see the gray warrior padding off toward the thorn tunnel. The scant mouthful of mouse felt heavy in his belly and every hair on his pelt tingled. *I know what Ashfur is going to do! He'll announce Squirrelflight's secret to every cat at the Gathering!*

Hollyleaf was slipping out of the warriors' den; Lionblaze padded over to her. "Usual place," he hissed. "I'll fetch Jayfeather."

When he peered around the brambles that hung in front of the medicine cats' den, Jayfeather was on his paws, arching his back in a long stretch. Leafpool was still curled up asleep in her nest.

"Lionblaze?" Jayfeather looked up. "What's the matter?"

"We've got to talk," Lionblaze told him.

He led the way to the gap behind the warriors' den, where Hollyleaf was waiting, her green eyes full of fear. "What's happened?" she demanded as soon as Lionblaze appeared.

"I've just overheard Ashfur asking Firestar if he can go to the next Gathering."

Hollyleaf's claws flexed in and out and her neck fur began to bristle. "No! He can't!" she wailed.

"Be quiet," Jayfeather snapped. "Do you want every cat to hear us?"

"We've got to stop him somehow." Hollyleaf lowered her voice, but it was still full of desperation. "Otherwise he'll tell all four Clans about us."

Lionblaze nodded. "Squirrelflight will be shamed in front

of every cat. And they might drive us away from the lake."

"Firestar wouldn't let them!" Hollyleaf sounded shocked.

"Firestar might not have a choice," Jayfeather pointed out. "You know how the other Clans are always blaming Firestar for taking in loners. Some of our Clanmates agree; they think it weakens ThunderClan. Firestar might have to send us away for the good of his Clan."

Firestar's Clan—not theirs. His brother's calm assessment of the risk chilled Lionblaze from ears to tail-tip. He couldn't trust anything anymore. He had tried to be the best warrior in the Clan, and now all that was threatened because of what Ashfur knew. "Maybe we should tell Squirrelflight," he suggested at last.

"Why?" Hollyleaf spat, her claws leaving deep scars in the earth. "What can she do? I don't want to talk to that lying cat ever again!"

"But it sounds as if she's the only cat who might have a chance of influencing Ashfur," Jayfeather pointed out.

"You talk to her, then!"

"We'll all talk to her." Lionblaze was trying to stay calm. "Show some sense, Hollyleaf. We have to do anything we can to stop Ashfur."

Without waiting for his sister's agreement he wriggled out of the narrow gap behind the den and scanned the clearing. His littermates followed, Hollyleaf's green eyes still sparkling with anger.

Lionblaze couldn't see Squirrelflight anywhere in the clearing. Thrusting his head through the branches of the warriors' den, he spotted her dozing in her mossy nest. "Squirrelflight!" he hissed.

The ginger she-cat's head snapped up, hope flooding into her eyes. Lionblaze felt a pang of sympathy. This was the first time any of the three had spoken to her since the storm; she must be hoping they were ready to forgive her.

"Can I have a word with you?" Lionblaze whispered, aware of the other sleeping cats inside the den.

"Yes." Squirrelflight leaped up eagerly and shook scraps of moss from her pelt. "Of course you can."

As she emerged from the den, the hope in her eyes changed to wariness when she saw all three cats waiting for her. "What's the matter?" she asked.

"I've just heard Ashfur asking Firestar for permission to go to the next Gathering," Lionblaze replied.

He didn't need to tell Squirrelflight what that meant. Her eyes stretched wide with dismay. "No . . ." she whispered.

"What are you going to do about it?" Hollyleaf challenged her. "Or are you fine with it? I don't suppose you'd care if Firestar drove us all out of the Clan."

The tip of Squirrelflight's tail twitched and anger flashed in her eyes, but she spoke calmly. "Firestar won't do that. Not to you."

"How do you know, if we're not Clan cats?" Jayfeather asked.

"You—" Squirrelflight broke off and began again. "I promise that you won't be punished. The lie was mine, and mine alone."

"Our real mother lied, too," Hollyleaf pointed out, a snarl creeping into her voice. "Whoever she was . . ."

Lionblaze looked expectantly at Squirrelflight, but her expression was closed and her jaws tight shut. Clearly she wasn't going to share all her secrets. "I'll talk to Ashfur," she meowed. "I'll make him understand that this won't just hurt me. It will damage the whole Clan. He's still a loyal warrior; he won't do anything to weaken ThunderClan." She dipped her head. "I'm sorry," she murmured.

No cat answered her. After a couple of heartbeats Squirrelflight turned away and slipped back into the den.

"She might trust Ashfur not to harm the Clan," Jayfeather mewed. "But I don't. We have to do something."

He turned and padded back toward the medicine cats' den. Lionblaze watched him go. That was easy enough to say, he thought, but harder to carry out. What could any cat do, to silence Ashfur?

That night, blood flowed through Lionblaze's dreams. His whole body quivered with power; he twisted and leaped against an unseen enemy until his claws were snagged with gray fur, and the reek of the sticky scarlet rivers clung to his pelt and filled the air around him.

He woke in the warriors' den with pale light filtering through the branches. Most of the nests were already empty. Scrambling up, Lionblaze felt his legs as stiff and his paws as heavy as if he had really spent the night battling his enemy. His jaws gaped in a yawn and he stretched out his forepaws, flexing his claws and working the muscles in his shoulders.

Feeling more awake, Lionblaze pushed his way into the clearing. He tensed when he saw Ashfur a couple of tail-lengths away, beckoning to Cloudtail and Brightheart, who were sharing tongues by the fresh-kill pile.

"Come on," he called. "Hunting patrol."

Lionblaze padded over to him. "Mind if I join you?"

For a moment Ashfur looked startled. Then his eyes narrowed. "Sure."

Cloudtail and Brightheart joined them, and the patrol headed out into the forest. Lionblaze brought up the rear. He knew that Ashfur must be suspicious; none of the three had spoken to him since the storm. But he wasn't afraid of Ashfur, and somehow he had to confront him where no other cats could overhear them.

Lionblaze had no idea how to separate Ashfur from Cloudtail and Brightheart, but he had no need to worry. As they padded along the old Twoleg path toward the abandoned nest, Cloudtail stopped and sniffed the air.

"I think I'm going to try in the Twoleg garden," he announced. "No cat has been there for a while."

Ashfur shrugged. "I think you're wasting your time, but go ahead if you want to. We'll catch up to you."

Cloudtail and Brightheart bounded off up the path. Ashfur watched them out of sight, then turned to Lionblaze. "Well? What do you want? I don't imagine you asked to come on this patrol for the pleasure of my company."

"No," Lionblaze replied steadily. He was finding it hard

to separate his respect for Ashfur, as his Clanmate and his former mentor, from his feelings about the raving cat who had threatened them on the night of the storm and now was threatening them again with his knowledge of Squirrelflight's lie. "I heard you ask Firestar to go to the next Gathering. I know what you're going to do there."

Ashfur's whiskers twitched. "So?"

"I'm asking you not to. Not for our sake," Lionblaze added, "but for the sake of ThunderClan. You hold its fate in your paws."

Ashfur heaved a deep sigh. "Spare me the appeal to my Clan loyalty," he sneered. "I've already had Squirrelflight mewling to me about that. I told her, and I'm telling you now—there's nothing that any cat can do to stop me."

Lionblaze felt his neck fur begin to rise. He slid his claws out of their sheaths. "I can beat you in a fight if I have to."

Instantly Ashfur's claws appeared, and his eyes narrowed, glittering with hostility. "You can try." Then he relaxed, drawing in his claws again. "The noble Lionblaze? Attacking a fellow warrior? No, you would never risk your place in ThunderClan by doing that."

With a snort of contempt, he began to walk away, then glanced back over one shoulder. "You're bound by the warrior code, just like all of us."

"And the warrior code lets you destroy our Clan?" Lionblaze challenged him as he stalked away.

Ashfur ignored him. Lionblaze watched him until he disappeared into the undergrowth. There was no way he was going to let this cat take away everything ThunderClan had fought for—everything *he* had fought for.

"Maybe I'm not as bound by the warrior code as you think..." he murmured.

CHAPTER 25

Jayfeather curled up in his nest in the medicine cats' den and waited for sleep to take him. Lionblaze had told him how he had confronted Ashfur in the forest, and how the gray warrior had refused his pleas and Squirrelflight's. *If that didn't do any good,* Jayfeather thought, *it's time to try another way.*

Yawning, he burrowed deeper into the soft moss. He pictured himself brushing past the bramble screen, out into the camp, and padding across the clearing to the warriors' den. Sliding through the branches, he picked his way carefully among the sleeping forms until he stood beside the mound of gray fur that was Ashfur.

In his mind, Jayfeather scraped at the moss until he had made a place for himself, then curled up beside Ashfur and matched his breathing to the sleeping warrior's.

Soon he felt a stiff breeze blowing across his fur, and woke to find himself in the forest, not far from the ShadowClan border. There was no sign of Ashfur, but the forest seemed subtly different. It wasn't just that he could see; there was something else. The scent of ShadowClan made his fur bristle as if he was anticipating a fight; he slid his claws out so he would be ready. He was more aware than usual of the scent of prey.

Wind flattened the grass, driving dead leaves ahead of it. Jayfeather pounced on one of them, enjoying the crackling sound beneath his paws; in the waking world he couldn't see blowing leaves to play with them.

"But you're not a kit anymore," he muttered.

In the same heartbeat he heard the sound of a cat pushing his way through the undergrowth. Fronds of bracken parted in front of Jayfeather, and Ashfur pushed his way into the open. He halted, startled.

"What are you doing here?"

Jayfeather shrugged. "I could ask you the same thing." He padded forward until he was close enough to flick a scrap of bracken off Ashfur's shoulder with the tip of his tail.

Ashfur's neck fur rose. "You can see!"

"Sure. You're dreaming, Ashfur. Don't you know that?"

The gray warrior took a pace back; his blue eyes looked troubled. "Why would I dream about you?"

"Because I want to talk to you where no cat can interrupt us. Where you have to listen to me."

Ashfur let out a snort. "I don't *have* to listen to any cat, let alone a scrawny excuse for a medicine cat. Besides, I already know what you're going to say. You're going to beg me not to say anything at the next Gathering. Well, you can save your breath. I'll say what I want. That lying she-cat will be driven out of ThunderClan for good, and no other Clan will want her, either."

Jayfeather narrowed his eyes. "You'll regret it, Ashfur."

The warrior loomed over him, anger smoldering in his

gaze. "Are you threatening me? I could break your neck with one swipe."

"Try," Jayfeather invited him. "This is a dream, remember?"

Ashfur looked briefly disconcerted; then he lashed his tail. "Yes, it's a dream. I'm imagining all of this. I still don't have to listen to you."

"Take warning, Ashfur." Jayfeather drew himself up and locked his gaze with his Clanmate's. "I'm a medicine cat, and I speak with the voice of StarClan. If you go ahead with what you plan to do, you will regret it."

Ashfur backed away again until his haunches brushed against the bracken. "My conscience is clear, and StarClan knows that," he blustered. "It's Squirrelflight who lied. She doesn't deserve the loyalty of any cat."

Whipping around, he plunged back into the undergrowth.

Jayfeather stood looking after him until the waving fronds of fern were still once more. Ashfur had heard his warning, but would it make any difference to him when he woke?

Jayfeather spent the next morning sorting herbs with Leafpool. His mentor seemed oddly distracted, as if her mind was on something else.

"We need more water mint," she murmured. "We used up so much when the cats were hurt after the storm."

"No, this is water mint." Jayfeather shoved a bunch of it under her nose. "We've plenty of it. It's yarrow we're out of."

"Oh yes . . . sorry."

Fed up of trying to work with her if she couldn't tell yarrow from water mint, Jayfeather headed out of the den. "I'll go fetch more," he tossed back over his shoulder.

At the entrance to the tunnel he heard the rustle of cats coming in, and stood back to wait for them. Cloudtail was the first to emerge into the clearing, followed by Ashfur.

"What do *you* want?" To Jayfeather's satisfaction, the gray warrior sounded thoroughly spooked. Feelings of anger and uncertainty crackled through his fur.

"I'm waiting to go out," Jayfeather replied calmly.

A snort came from Ashfur, followed by Whitewing's voice. "Ashfur, you're blocking the entrance." There was a hiss of annoyance from Ashfur and he bounded away.

Returning with the yarrow, Jayfeather picked up Ashfur's scent near the fresh-kill pile. Instead of going straight to the medicine cats' den, he headed toward the gray warrior. His sense of satisfaction returned as he heard Ashfur get to his paws and pad away, thrusting through the branches into the warriors' den.

I've got him worried, Jayfeather realized, veering off to his own den. *But will it be enough to keep him quiet?*

CHAPTER 26

It was the afternoon before the Gathering. Hollyleaf felt as if her whole world was crumbling around her. She had thought that once they got rid of Sol, life in the Clans would return to normal, but instead the terrible threat of Ashfur hung over them like a tree about to fall. *He's going to ruin everything!*

Her paws itching with restlessness, Hollyleaf slipped out of the camp and wandered into the forest. She felt completely powerless, now that she knew she wasn't one of the three: Her belief in the prophecy had made her feel that she could do anything, but Ashfur had torn that belief away from her. A cat with the power of the stars in her paws would have been able to stop one cat from speaking words that would tear his Clan apart. But plain Hollyleaf, no longer Firestar's kin, could do nothing.

A hot flood of fury swept through Hollyleaf and she paused, digging her claws into the sodden ground. More than anything, she *wanted* to be one of the three; she wanted to be special, to have a destiny beyond that of any other cat. *I deserve to!* Her need tore at her belly like sharp pangs of hunger. *I'd work harder than any cat to be a great leader, and leave my paw print on all the Clans. I* can't *let Ashfur destroy all my plans.*

Choking down her rage, Hollyleaf padded on. Since the storm, more rain had fallen, and she had to pick her way across boggy ground and leap over tiny new streams that scoured through the sodden earth. Bracken fronds released showers of raindrops onto her head and shoulders as she brushed by. Her fur became splashed and muddy, but she carried on, scarcely aware of where she was.

The strong scent of a ThunderClan cat brought her to a halt. She jumped as Ashfur appeared around the trunk of a gnarled oak tree. "Don't creep up on me like that!" she snapped.

"I'm not creeping," Ashfur retorted. "If you must know, I've been checking out the fox trail near the WindClan border. That fox Brackenfur scented is still around."

Hollyleaf didn't reply. She and Ashfur faced each other; Ashfur's blue eyes were wide and wary. "What do you want?" he demanded.

"How do you know I want anything?" Hollyleaf replied.

For a moment Ashfur looked disconcerted. "Aren't you going to try to make me change my mind, like Squirrelflight and your littermates?"

"No." Hollyleaf felt a stab of satisfaction at the startled look in the gray warrior's eyes. "I know there's nothing I can do. It's your decision to betray your own Clan."

"Betray?" Ashfur's neck fur bristled and his claws slid out. "I'm betraying no cat. Squirrelflight's the traitor, because she lied."

"And it's not betrayal when you weaken ThunderClan in

front of the other Clans, so soon after the Great Battle?" Hollyleaf spat in disgust.

Ashfur stretched his neck toward her, his lips drawn back in a snarl. "If you're trying to scare me, it's not working."

Hollyleaf stood her ground. "And you don't scare me, either," she declared. "Nothing scares me more than the thought that you're not afraid of what will happen after you've spoken out."

Ashfur's eyes narrowed. "I'll *purr* over what will happen after I've revealed the truth," he promised. Without waiting for a reply, he spun around and headed off through the forest.

The sun was sinking behind a ragged band of cloud as Firestar called his cats together to go to the Gathering. Shadows crept into the clearing, and the first warriors of StarClan were beginning to emerge into a sky stained with scarlet.

"Where's Ashfur?" Firestar asked, looking around.

Hollyleaf exchanged a glance with Lionblaze. The other cats chosen for the Gathering—Brambleclaw, Dustpelt, Ferncloud, Graystripe, Cloudtail, and Cinderheart—were already clustered around their leader, while Leafpool and Jayfeather were padding across the clearing to join them. But there was no sign of the gray warrior.

Firestar's tail twitched with annoyance. "He specifically asked to come tonight, and now he's not here. I asked Squirrelflight to come, too, and she's not here either."

"We'll be late if we wait for them," Dustpelt pointed out.

Tension churned in Hollyleaf's belly. She didn't want to *think* about Ashfur, much less stand around waiting for him. If he didn't turn up at the Gathering, so much the better for every cat. As for Squirrelflight . . . Hollyleaf didn't care if she never saw her again.

"Maybe Ashfur went on ahead," Graystripe suggested.

"Well, if he did, he should have told one of us," Firestar replied. "Let's go."

He led the way through the barrier of thorns. Hollyleaf brought up the rear with Lionblaze and Jayfeather. She knew that both her brothers would be desperate to know where Ashfur was. She could almost see their anxiety crackling off their fur like lightning. But none of them spoke his name.

The cats had barely left the tunnel when Squirrelflight came bounding breathlessly up to them. Her pelt was clumped and soaking, and splashed with mud. "Sorry," she panted. "I didn't mean to keep you waiting."

Brambleclaw gave her ear a quick lick. "What have you been doing?"

"Looking for herbs for Leafpool, near the ShadowClan border," Squirrelflight explained. "The bank of the stream was muddy, and I slipped in."

"Mouse-brain," Brambleclaw murmured affectionately. "You should be more careful. Are you okay? You don't have to come to the Gathering if you'd rather rest."

"I'm fine," Squirrelflight insisted. "And I'm not going to miss this Gathering. I haven't been to one in moons."

"Come on, we're wasting time," Firestar called from the front of the group.

He set off toward the lake; the forest floor was still sodden from the recent rain, and the cats had to scramble through muddy hollows or over branches that fell in the storm. Hollyleaf barely noticed the mud or the small streams her paws splashed through. She felt as though she was looking down a long tunnel into a future dark with fear and betrayal. She asked herself how far a cat should go to preserve the warrior code. And what happens if the code was broken no matter what you did?

The ThunderClan cats emerged from the trees and padded down to the edge of the lake, turning toward the WindClan border. A full moon already floated high in the sky, turning the surface of the water to silver. Looking up, Hollyleaf saw that clouds were drifting close to it, though none of them touched the shining silver disk yet. She swallowed. Were the spirits of their ancestors about to show their anger?

Firestar waved his tail. "Let's hurry. The other Clans will be waiting for us." Clear of the forest, he set a brisk pace, until his warriors were bounding along the edge of the lake.

Hollyleaf, still near the back of the group with Lionblaze and Jayfeather, saw Firestar halt suddenly on the bank of the stream that marked the border with WindClan. Graystripe, hard on his paws, let out a startled yowl.

Terrible foreboding filled Hollyleaf from ears to tail-tip. She put on a spurt until she was racing along, her belly fur brushing the pebbles and her tail streaming out behind her.

Lionblaze kept pace with her.

Reaching the bank, she pushed through the cats who were clustered there, staring down into the stream. Wedged behind a rock just below her paws, the lifeless body of a cat floated in the swollen water, his fur dark and sodden. His tail streamed out into the current, waving as if he were still alive.

Dustpelt was the first to speak. “It’s Ashfur.”

CHAPTER 27

Lionblaze dug his claws into the bank of the stream, only just managing to suppress a wail of dismay. Yet he couldn't feel any sense of grief for his dead Clanmate. Ashfur had been about to reveal something that would have destroyed them all; now those terrible words would never be spoken. Exchanging a glance with Hollyleaf, he could see that his sister felt the same. He hoped no other cat would ever know how relieved they felt at Ashfur's death.

"Get him out," Firestar ordered.

Dustpelt slid into the stream, with water washing around his belly fur. He gripped Ashfur's shoulder in his teeth and started tugging.

"Be careful," Ferncloud mewed anxiously.

Graystripe leaped into the water on Ashfur's other side, and together the two warriors freed him from the rock and hauled his body up the bank.

Leafpool crouched beside him, one paw on his chest as she gave him a rapid sniff. Jayfeather stood beside her, his whiskers quivering. Leafpool looked up. "He's dead."

"How did he die?" Cinderheart asked, her blue eyes wide.

"Did he fall in and drown?"

"I fell into the stream by ShadowClan," Squirrelflight reminded them; Lionblaze wondered if she too shared his relief. "It's easily done, when the water's running as high as this."

Cloudtail let out a snort. "Ashfur was a strong warrior. He wouldn't drown like a kit. If we want to know how he died, we should be looking at WindClan."

Firestar bent his head to sniff Ashfur's sodden body. "There's no WindClan scent."

"The water would wash it off," Cloudtail pointed out.

"We'll talk about this later." Firestar glanced around swiftly. "Dustpelt, Graystripe, can you take Ashfur's body back to camp? The rest of us must go on, or the other Clans will know something is wrong."

"I'll go, too," Lionblaze volunteered. "Ashfur was my mentor."

Firestar nodded. "Good. You others, follow me."

As Firestar and the rest of his warriors half waded, half swam across the stream, Lionblaze and his Clanmates picked up Ashfur's body. It hung between them, a dead weight, as they struggled back through the forest to the hollow.

Thornclaw was on guard at the entrance to the camp. "What . . . ?" His fur rose as they dragged Ashfur up to the tunnel. "What happened?"

Dustpelt explained, while Lionblaze and Graystripe carried the dead warrior into the middle of the clearing. The moonlight shone silver on his drenched gray fur; Lionblaze thought he looked strangely small in death. It was hard to imagine the power he had held in his paws, the power to drag down his Clan and bring shame on Squirrelflight and the kits who had believed they were hers.

Lionblaze flinched at the sound of a distraught wail behind him. Whitewing had emerged from the warriors' den, followed by Birchfall. "Did a fox get him?" she cried.

Lionblaze shook his head. "We found him in the stream on the WindClan border. It looks as if he drowned."

Whitewing shuddered. "That's dreadful."

Birchfall pressed his muzzle against hers. "You mustn't upset yourself," he murmured. "Think of the kits."

Whitewing nodded. Slowly she padded up to Ashfur's body and settled down beside it, her nose pushed into the cold, wet fur. Birchfall crouched protectively at her side, to keep vigil along with her. "He was a good mentor," he mewed sorrowfully. "I'll miss him."

By now other warriors were coming out of their den, forming a ragged circle around Ashfur and questioning one another in hushed, shocked voices.

"WindClan will be at the bottom of this, mark my words," Mousefur meowed as she padded up with Longtail.

"On the night of a Gathering, too." Honeyfern's voice shook. "StarClan will be angry."

"Firestar doesn't think any cat is to blame," Graystripe told them. "Ashfur was just very unlucky."

Mousefur snorted with disbelief as she bent her stiff joints to crouch beside Ashfur's body. Lionblaze lifted his head to gaze up at the moon as it floated above the treetops. The clouds had cleared away; perhaps Firestar was right, and there was no need for StarClan to show their anger.

Sighing, he crouched down in his turn and pushed his nose into his former mentor's fur. There was nothing to scent there but mud and water. Closing his eyes, he hoped that none of his Clanmates could sense that instead of grieving, his mind was numb with relief.

Lionblaze stayed beside Ashfur until the sky began to grow pale with the first hints of dawn. Other cats came and went around him, mewing in hushed voices.

At last Lionblaze heard the sound of movement in the thorn tunnel as Firestar and the rest of the Clan began to return from the Gathering. He stretched his cramped muscles and looked around to see Hollyleaf bounding toward him. Her eyes shone with a fierce light.

"You wouldn't believe what happened at the Gathering!" she hissed. "Firestar didn't say a single thing about Ashfur."

Lionblaze's pelt prickled with surprise. "He didn't?"

"Not a thing."

One or two cats gave Hollyleaf a curious glance as she passed; Lionblaze touched her mouth with his tail to warn her to be quiet, and drew her a pace or two away from Ashfur's body.

"He just passed on trivial bits of news about prey," Hollyleaf went on in a furious whisper. "And he thanked our warrior ancestors for watching over us. And that was all."

"Well . . . maybe he didn't want ThunderClan to sound weak," Lionblaze suggested.

"We're not weak because one cat dies!" Hollyleaf spat. Lionblaze couldn't work out why she was so angry. "Every Clan leader reports stuff like that. It's part of what Gatherings are for."

"And none of the other cats noticed that something was wrong?"

Hollyleaf shook her head. "Obviously Squirrelflight isn't the only cat who's good at lying."

"I don't think it's as bad as you're making out. Firestar must have had his reasons. And clouds didn't cover the moon, so StarClan can't have been angry with him."

Hollyleaf's only reply was a disgusted snort.

Lionblaze pressed his muzzle against hers. "Come on. Let's sit vigil with Ashfur for a bit."

His sister's eyes stretched wide. "Sit vigil for that mange-ridden excuse for a cat? I can't believe you want to do that! Ashfur would have destroyed the whole Clan if he'd lived for one more night."

Without waiting for a reply, she whirled around and stalked toward the warriors' den. Lionblaze watched her go, hoping she would sleep off whatever was troubling her so much, then padded back to Ashfur's body and settled down beside it.

Chapter 28

Jayfeather followed Leafpool back into the camp. A dawn breeze whispered across the clearing, and he could hear the beginnings of birdsong in the trees above the hollow. A hush lay over the camp; Jayfeather could detect mingled feelings of grief and bewilderment as the cats tried to adjust to the fact that Ashfur was dead.

He followed Leafpool as she padded into the center of the clearing where Ashfur's body lay. Jayfeather picked up the chill, watery scent that still clung to his fur, and the scents of Lionblaze, Birchfall, Whitewing, and Thornclaw, who still kept vigil beside him.

"He feels so cold and wet," Leafpool murmured, crouching beside Ashfur. "This isn't how we should send him to his warrior ancestors."

Jayfeather heard the rasp of her tongue as she began to lick the dead warrior's fur. Feelings of sorrow surged out of her in waves, almost like a mother grieving for her kit. *She wasn't in love with Ashfur, was she?* Jayfeather wondered. *She's a medicine cat!*

Gradually the cats around Ashfur's body began to withdraw and creep back to their den. Lionblaze was the last to go, touching Jayfeather's shoulder briefly with his tail before he left. Not knowing what else to do, Jayfeather settled down opposite Leafpool and began to help her lick the dead warrior's fur. Sleep began to drift over him as he lapped with long, rhythmic strokes.

A gasp from Leafpool jolted him awake. Horror swirled around her like a stream in flood. "What's the matter?" he meowed.

For a heartbeat he heard her tongue working busily. Then she hissed, "Come look at this."

Jayfeather bit back the sarcastic reply that he couldn't *look* at anything. He worked his way around Ashfur's body until he was crouching next to his mentor. All Leafpool's muscles were stiff and her neck fur was standing on end.

Jayfeather sniffed, picking up the scent of blood and raw flesh. Investigating with one paw, he felt the edges of a gash in Ashfur's throat, the kind of mark he would expect to see on a cleanly killed piece of prey.

The kind of mark a cat didn't get from falling into a stream and drowning, but was made deliberately. With a slash of claws.

"He didn't drown," Leafpool whispered hoarsely. "He was murdered!"

Jayfeather's mind whirled. If it wasn't for Leafpool's care over the dead warrior's body, no cat would ever have known how he had died. What would happen now?

"I'm going to tell Firestar," Leafpool meowed.

Jayfeather heard her racing across the clearing toward the

tumbled rocks. A few moments later two sets of paw steps returned and Firestar crouched beside him to examine the body.

"Who would do this?" Firestar sounded completely bewildered.

"WindClan?" Leafpool suggested, her voice sharp with suspicion. "We found him on the WindClan border."

"You know very well there was no WindClan scent on him," Firestar reminded her. Jayfeather could feel strong sensations of doubt coming from his Clan leader. "I know the water could have washed it away, but . . ." His voice grew softer, as if he was arguing with himself. "Why would WindClan kill just one warrior? Were they trying to warn us? But we're not a threat to WindClan."

"And Ashfur was Clanborn," Jayfeather put in. "WindClan has no reason to quarrel with him personally."

"True," Firestar murmured. Jayfeather could hear his claws scoring the earth. "But if it wasn't WindClan . . . then a ThunderClan cat must have killed Ashfur."

"No!" Leafpool's horrified whisper cut through Jayfeather like an eagle's talon. "No ThunderClan cat would do such a thing. It *must* have been WindClan." To Jayfeather it sounded as if she was trying to convince herself as much as Firestar. "What should we do?" she asked tensely.

The Clan leader hesitated. "This is no reason not to give honor to his body," he decided at last. "We'll let the elders go ahead and bury him. Then I'll speak to the Clan."

"I'll fetch Mousefur and Longtail," Leafpool meowed.

Jayfeather waited while the elders appeared from their den and the rest of the Clan gathered around to say farewell to Ashfur. Leafpool must have licked his fur back over the gash in his neck, because none of them seemed to notice it.

When Mousefur and Longtail had left the clearing with the gray warrior's body dragging between them, Brambleclaw padded up to Firestar. "I'll take the dawn patrol along the WindClan border," he announced. "There might be some traces there to tell us what happened."

"Good idea," Firestar replied. "But don't go just yet. There's something I need to say to the whole Clan."

Jayfeather picked up the deputy's puzzlement, then jumped when Lionblaze muttered into his ear: "What's going on?"

Part of Jayfeather wanted to tell Lionblaze exactly what he had found. But he couldn't find the words. The discovery was too huge, with too many consequences that he couldn't begin to imagine. "You'll know soon enough," he replied.

He stood beside his brother, his claws working in the earth, while he waited for the elders to return. Hollyleaf came to join them, anxiety boiling out of her like bees buzzing out of a tree. "Something terrible is going to happen," she whispered. "I can feel it."

Eventually Mousefur and Longtail pushed their way through the thorns, back into the clearing. Firestar climbed up to the Highledge; Jayfeather heard his voice raised to carry to every corner of the camp.

"Let all cats old enough to catch their own prey gather here beneath the Highledge for a Clan meeting."

Most of the Clan were already out in the open, though Jayfeather heard movement by the nursery as Daisy and Millie emerged with their kits. Foxpaw and Icepaw scampered into the middle of the clearing, excited rather than worried by the unexpected summons. Jayfeather caught the scent of Squirrelflight standing not far away.

"We've discovered more about Ashfur's death," Firestar began as soon as all the cats were assembled. "It wasn't an accident. There was a gash in his throat, and that means he was deliberately killed."

Yowls of dismay rose up from every part of the clearing. Jayfeather's belly churned when he heard the terrible truth put into words; he could feel Hollyleaf and Lionblaze stiffen, and picked up their sense of horror. Fear and distress swept over him from Squirrelflight.

"Did a fox do it?" Dustpelt demanded, raising his voice to be heard over the clamor.

"There was no fox scent." The noise died down as Firestar spoke again. "And a fox would have eaten him."

"Did he fall into the stream and cut his throat on a rock or a branch?" Squirrelflight asked; Jayfeather could tell how desperately she wanted that to be true.

"I doubt it," Firestar told her; there was regret in his voice as if he, too, would have been comforted by that explanation. "It was a clean wound, like a hunting warrior would make on their prey."

"You're saying that a *cat* killed him?" Cloudtail's voice rang out disbelievingly.

"WindClan!" Thornclaw yowled. "They must have found him by the border and killed him. We should attack them *now*!"

Caterwauls of agreement followed his words; it was several moments before Firestar could make himself heard again.

"We mustn't act too quickly," he warned his Clan. "There was no WindClan scent on Ashfur's body. In fact, there's no evidence at all that he was killed by a cat from another Clan."

Frozen silence filled the clearing. When Brackenfur broke it, his voice was shaking. "Are you saying that one of *us* killed Ashfur?"

Jayfeather's heart thudded as he waited for Firestar's reply. His littermates tensed beside him, and he could hear Squirrelflight trying not to gulp for air as if she were being smothered.

"Do any of you know a reason why anyone in ThunderClan might want Ashfur dead?" Firestar asked.

Beside him, Lionblaze and Hollyleaf quivered under the weight of what they knew. A little farther away, Squirrelflight held her breath altogether. Jayfeather knew they were all thinking of the scene on top of the cliff, when Squirrelflight's terrible secret had been shared in storm and fire. That, and that alone, had to be the reason for Ashfur's murder.

Now, for their own sakes and the sake of their Clan, they must all conspire to keep the truth hidden forever.

KEEP WATCH FOR

POWER OF THREE
WARRIORS

BOOK 6:
SUNRISE

Tigerstar spun to face him. "Better," he meowed, mockery still in his voice. "I mentored you well."

Before Lionblaze could reply, the huge tabby darted toward him, veering aside at the last moment and lashing out with one forepaw as he passed. Lionblaze felt Tigerstar's claws rake along his side, and blood begin trickling out of the scratches. Fear stabbed at him, sharp as his enemy's claws. *This is a dream, but what happens if he kills me? Will I really be dead?*

There was no time to worry about that. Tigerstar was already hurtling toward him again. Lionblaze leaped aside; he aimed a blow at his enemy, but only felt his claws pass harmlessly through the tabby's pelt.

"Too slow," Tigerstar growled. "You'd better work harder, now you can forget about that stupid prophecy."

Lionblaze knew that the tabby tom was trying to anger him. *I won't listen! All I need to do is fight!*

He sprang at Tigerstar again, twisting in the air as his enemy himself had taught him, and landing squarely on the massive tabby's broad shoulders. Digging in with his claws, he stretched forward and sank his teeth into Tigerstar's neck.

Tigerstar tried the same trick again of going limp and pulling Lionblaze down with him, but this time Lionblaze was ready. He wriggled from beneath the huge body, battering with his hindpaws at Tigerstar's exposed belly.

"I'm not falling for that one twice!" he gasped.

Tigerstar struggled to get up, but blood was pouring from a gash in his belly; he flopped down again. Lionblaze planted one forepaw on his chest and held the other, claws extended, against his neck.

His enemy glared up at him; for a heartbeat fear flashed in his blazing amber eyes. "You'll never do it," he growled.

"No." Lionblaze lowered his claws and stepped back. "You're already dead."

DON'T MISS:

SEEKERS
THE QUEST BEGINS

Lusa

"And over there you can see Lusa, our youngest black bear, who is five months old. She was born right here in the zoo. Black bears actually come in a lot of different colors like cinnamon or gray, but Lusa's name means 'black' in the Choctaw language, and if you look closely you won't find one speck of another color on her coat. That's her mother, Ashia, and her father, King.

"All North American bears are suffering from the changes in their environment. For the most part, black bears are doing better than white bears and grizzlies, but we have had to rescue some of them when they run into trouble. We found King, for instance, wandering at the edge of the forest. He would have starved to death if we hadn't brought him here. Lusa's never known any other place, and she feels safe around humans, so she is certainly better off living in the zoo with us."

Patches of snow covered the bare rocks and grassy ground inside the Bear Bowl, but the smell of leaftime was in the air, and a few purple crocuses were already nudging their way through the dirt. Lusa stood on her hind legs and twitched her ears at the group of flat-faces on the upper ridge of the

Bowl. Several flat-face cubs were leaning against the railing, pointing at her and chattering. They sounded like birds. She didn't understand most of what the zoo guide was saying, but she knew her name in the flat-face language. Her feeders called her Lusa when they brought her food, so she could tell when the guides were talking about her to the visiting flat-faces. The wind brought a whiff of their strange scent to her—a warm, milky smell covered over by sharp, almost flowery scents. Their high-pitched voices made her ears hurt, but she liked the sound of their laughter.

Dropping back down to her paws, she scrambled into the part of the Bowl where three tall trees grew next to a log that never rotted. Lusa called this the Forest. Raising herself onto her hind legs again, she batted her paws in the air, as if she were fighting a butterfly, to catch the attention of the flat-faces. When she was sure they were watching her, she jumped onto the log and ran along it, jumping down on all fours at the other end.

As she'd hoped, the flat-faces made the quick huffing sound that meant they were pleased, and the guide leaned over the rail to give her some fruit. Lusa had to stand on her back legs and stretch as high as she could to reach the pear.

"What you see Lusa doing here is similar to what bears like her would do in the wild—stretching up into the trees to reach food like fruit, nuts, berries, and honey," the guide chattered.

Lusa wrapped her paws around the piece of fruit and nibbled at it. Suddenly she felt a paw cuff her shoulder. She knew from its size that it wasn't one of the bigger bears, so she had a good chance of defending her pear. With a snort, she tucked her paw around the fruit and turned to face Yogi, the other cub in the Bowl.

Yogi was one season-circle old, but he hadn't been born here. He talked sometimes about another zoo, where his mother lived, but he didn't remember it very well. He was almost as black as Lusa, but he had a pale splash of white fur on his chest.

With a huffing sound, he lifted himself onto his hind legs so he towered over her. "Lusa, share!" he demanded. "Give me some!"

"No!" she said. "It's mine!" She stuffed the fruit in her mouth and ran away across the enclosure. The flat-faces up above chattered and giggled as Yogi chased her.

Lusa scrambled up onto the Mountains near the back of the Bowl. She was better than Yogi was at balancing on the four large boulders. He huffed and grunted as he climbed after her. With a playful snort, Lusa leaped off the last boulder and tumbled straight into her father, King, who was dozing in the sun.

"*Hrr*—what?" her father mumbled. Then Yogi came bounding off the rocks after Lusa and crashed into King as well. This brought the giant black bear to his paws with a roar.

"Get off!" he bellowed, swatting at them. "Go away!"

Yogi fled to the Fence at the far end of the Bowl. On the other side of the Fence, Lusa could see the old grizzly rolling on his back, muttering to himself. Chuffing with laughter, Lusa followed Yogi.

"How can you find that funny?" Yogi asked, his fur standing on end. "Your father is so scary!"

"Oh, he's a big furball," Lusa said. "His bluster is worse than his bite."

"You don't know that," Yogi pointed out. "He's never bitten you—yet!"

"He wouldn't!" Lusa protested. "He was just startled, that's all. You know he's a bit deaf. He probably didn't hear us coming." She was pleased to see that Yogi had forgotten about the fruit. She sat down and finished eating it, licking the juice off her paws with her long tongue.

"Well, I'm not going to bother him again," Yogi said. "I'm going to stay over here and watch the white bears through the Fence." Lusa was glad that the bears in the Bowl were kept apart from one another by the cold gray webs of the Fences. She liked being with other black bears, but she was a little bit afraid of the big brown grizzly and the massive white bears. They were much, much bigger than she was, and their deafening roars sometimes kept her awake at night.

"That sounds like a good idea to me." Lusa turned and saw her mother, Ashia, lumbering toward them. "You two should learn not to disturb King, especially when he's resting."

"We weren't *disturbing* him," Lusa objected.

"Just stay out of his way and don't cause trouble," Ashia scolded.

"I don't want to watch the white bears," Lusa said to Yogi. "They're boring. Let's go hide in the Caves."

They scampered off to the back corner of the Bowl, where

a ledge of white stone hung over a rocky patch of ground hidden in shadow. Lusa and Yogi crowded into the shadows, each trying to keep their paws out of the sun. They crouched as low as they could get and held very still.

"Shhh," Lusa whispered. "There's a grizzly crashing through the forest."

"It's coming after us," Yogi whispered. "It's going to chase us with its giant hooked claws."

"But if we stay very still, it won't know we're here," Lusa breathed.

"Whoever moves first loses," Yogi challenged.

"All right," Lusa said, pressing her muzzle to her paws. "I'm going to win."

They fell silent. Lusa willed every muscle in her body to stay perfectly still. She felt the wind tickling around her ears and nose. She could smell every other bear in her section of the Bowl: King dozing in the sun, Ashia snuffling around the bottom of the wall for anything the flat-faces had dropped, Stella scratching her side against one of the trees.

In the next enclosure, one of the giant white bears was swimming around and around in a circle, from one lump of stone to the next. Lusa had seen it do this for hours. The white bears were even less friendly than the grizzly, who lived on his own and didn't say much. Lusa didn't know their names. The white bears stayed on their island of gray stone or in the chilly water and ignored the bears on either side of them. Lusa was fine with that; they were nearly three times her mother's size, and she sometimes got the feeling that they'd be perfectly happy to have her for dinner instead of the slabs of meat the flat-faces threw over the wall.

Her nose was beginning to itch. Lost in thought about the white bears, she forgot about the competition and reached up to scratch it.

"Ha!" Yogi yelped, jumping to his paws. "You moved! I win!"

"Oh," Lusa said, feeling foolish. "Well, it doesn't matter anyway. If a grizzly spotted me, I would just run up a tree. I can climb much better than any old brown bear!"

ERIN HUNTER

is inspired by a love of cats and a fascination with the ferocity of the natural world. As well as having great respect for nature in all its forms, Erin enjoys creating rich mythical explanations for animal behavior. She is also the author of the bestselling Seekers series.

Visit Warriors online at www.warriorcats.com.